BREAK ON THROUGH

A MAFIA KINGDOM NOVEL

JESSICA RUBEN

Visit my website at www.jessicarubenauthor.com

Cover Designer: Sarah Hansen, Okay Creations
Cover Photographer: Michelle Lancaster, www.MichelleLancaster.com
Editor: Jovana Shirley, Unforeseen Editing, www.unforeseenediting.com
Editor: Nicole Bailey, Proof Before You Publish
Publicity: Autumn Gantz, Wordsmith Publicity

This book is a work of fiction. Names, characters, places, and incidents either are products of the author's imagination or are used fictitiously. Any resemblance to actual persons, living or dead, events, or locales is entirely coincidental.

Paperback ISBN: 978-1-7334751-9-8
E-book ISBN: 978-1-7334751-8-1

❀ Created with Vellum

For my Husband

BLURB

From international best-selling author Jessica Ruben comes a new enemies-to-lovers, arranged-marriage, stand-alone romance—with a dark Mafia twist.

Talia:
My only goal in life is to play the cello in a world-famous orchestra. Unfortunately, education, lessons, and connections don't come cheap.
So, when the most notorious Mafia boss in New York City offers me millions to marry one of his men, I have two choices: take the money and follow my dreams, or risk death.
I choose to take the money.
But if I had known who my husband would be, I would have picked death.
Leo might be gorgeous and lethal, but he has never met a woman who refuses to bow.

Leo:
After being pushed out of my country, I lost my woman, my business, and my life.

The streets of New York City are dangerous but nothing compared to the wrath growing within me.

Joining the Mafia is a natural progression, especially when they help quench my thirst for revenge.

When the boss offers me a marriage that will help me reach vengeance, I jump at the chance.

I figure she'll be a sweet, quiet girl ...

Not the stuck-up musician from the club.

She thinks she can always get the last word, but I'm on a warpath that she can't derail.

She can either fall in line or fall into pieces.

1

Leo

WE SMILE AT EACH OTHER. The silver moonlight shines through Daisy's bedroom window, illuminating her pale skin and shining black hair. She turns to her side, so we're facing one another. Her creamy breasts are bared to me, the soft white sheet draping across the left side of her hip. She's a model in an Italian painting.

"You should go soon." Her delicate hand moves to my forehead, long nails scraping against my scalp as she brushes my hair back. "My father will be coming in an hour."

Dark eyes twinkling, she dares me to leave her. Or maybe she dares me to stay.

My gaze moves down to her breasts and back up again. "Father? What's a father?"

I kiss her deeply, the back of her neck in my grip, and swallow her laugh with my lips. My free hand wraps around the small of her back, bringing her closer to me. When we are chest to chest, warmth radiates between us.

"You know"—she lifts her lips from mine to speak, and mine move to her neck—"my father, also known as the man who already wants to kill you?" she reminds me, giggling quietly.

I kiss her down lower, pausing on an area of soft skin above her belly button. I grumble, "Oh, that one."

"Leo, listen," her voice whispers in a slow and sultry drawl. "I want more. You know I want everything with you. But if you're going to ask his permission to marry me, it would be better if he changed his mind about you. Him catching us would be catastrophic."

"Just a minute more—"

"But he really is on his way." Kiss. "Only"—kiss—"one more hour." Kiss.

She has to push against my chest to force my mouth off her skin. This woman makes me feel drugged. I can't wait to spend my life with her.

"I love you."

She looks deeply into my eyes, and I swear, I feel the vibrations of her feelings. She's all I see.

"I love you t—"

The door opens.

There is a moment of absolute pause on all of our parts. No one moves. Hell, no one takes a breath.

Daisy's father is an enormous, hardened man. He spent years fighting in the Kosovo Liberation Army before settling down and joining the police. He's a good man. But right now, he wants to kill me. And I know this like I know my own name.

"You." His voice is so low and dark. With his feet planted on the floor, he points at me. "Get the fuck out of my house. I've warned you once before. You shame my daughter, you shame my entire family!"

I jump out of the bed, head bowed, thankful that I'm wearing my boxers.

"Daddy, no." Daisy stands up, dragging the white bedsheets with her body. I cringe at her obvious nudity. "It's okay, Papa. You know we're in love. Nothing we do is without my consent. It's been three years. We want to get married. If he gets into college in America, he'll save money and bring me there with him."

Her father is so mad that he can't even reply. Just angry breaths, like a bull. I won't look at him to find out what he'll say. I'm getting dressed like my feet are on fire. There's a madman in my midst, plotting my death, and there's nothing but his nude daughter between us.

I do my best to slide my pants on as Daisy, clearly out of her mind, walks in front of her father and begs him to stay calm. It's all a blur in my haste, but her hands are at his barrel-sized chest, the sheet tucked beneath her thin arms. I probably have just a few more seconds before he wakes up from this anger-induced trance and grabs his gun to shoot me in the head. My entire body shakes as I drop my shirt on and slide into my sneakers, forgetting the socks. I pull up on her bedroom window. Daisy on her knees before her father, begging, is the last thing I see. Her sobbing is the last things I hear.

Walking home on the tree-lined street, I can hear him railing. He might hate my guts, but he loves his daughter. He's never raised his hand to her, and he never would. I remind myself not to be worried. I'll get back to my room and call her. She'll be okay. We'll convince him to let us marry, and even if he refuses to allow it, we will do it anyway. We are old enough now to make our own choices. No, her father never caught us in bed before. And, yes, he hates me, even before this moment. He's been telling her that I'm too tough and we wouldn't make a good match. But he doesn't know the real us. But it's all going to be different now.

"You're not the right match," her father explained as calmly as he could after we first asked him to allow us to date each other. "I've seen you with your friends, and I know your type. Sporty, physical, and tough. You will not make each other happy in the long-term. Daisy should have a man who is gentle. Not you. And if people knew she was with a man like you?" His heavy hand cut through the air. "They would imagine terrible things happening between the two of you. The answer is no."

She turned to me, worried, her lips pressed together.
Although I wanted nothing more than to put up my fists, I simply nodded
at Daisy before turning back to him. "I understand, sir. I will try to change
people's perception."
"I do not believe that will be possible." He stood up to leave, waiting for his
daughter to join him.
That night, Daisy and I spoke on the phone for hours, planning the best
way to change his mind. Nothing could stop us.

I AM MY OWN MAN, and I make my own choices. Once Daisy's father agrees to let us marry, I'll tell my mother. And if he never agrees, we will tell them both after the marriage is official.

My brother, Albi's, face comes into my head, darkening my mood more than I thought possible. He's the only one who knows that we continue to see each other without anyone knowing, and he holds it over my head as though the secret were a set of knives that he could use to maim me. But I love her. And I would do anything for her. Unfortunately, Albi knows this.

I kick a rock across the dark dirt road, cursing. Still, I have to believe our love will prevail. I imagine meeting her in history class and her small smiles to me when she thought no one was looking. Keeping our relationship secret, so as not to upset her parents, was a strange thing. Particularly for a man like me, who's had plenty of conquests in the past. But Daisy is different from other girls, and I respect her enough to not tarnish her reputation. A girl like her must stay pure to get married. It hasn't been easy, living without proclaiming to the world that she is mine and I am hers, but in some way, it's beautiful to have our love private, without prying eyes or gossip.

My friends figure I am busy, focusing on my studies and football; my dream of studying in America is something they all know. They would never imagine a girl had been taking up my time. No one would ever assume that the kind, beautiful, and religious Daisy would have a boyfriend. Particularly not one with a reputation for fighting.

I finally make it to the lower end of town, where my house sits. It is a good house. My father built it with his own hands. I have already planned the house for Daisy and me, and of course, I will build it. Large and white with blue shutters. A mansion for my queen.

Pulling the key from my front pocket, I open the door.

The lights are on, and my mother and brother stare at me. I look at my watch—10:07 p.m. Mother has tears in her large green eyes but not unhappy-looking ones. My brother though? He looks ecstatic.

"You're leaving for America!" He jumps off the couch and embraces me.

My body goes rigid, as I'm confused by his affection. My brother and I have a twisted relationship, if you could call it that. He was born seconds after me, and as my mother likes to tell the story, in the last moment before our birth, I apparently pushed myself ahead of him. Even though we are twins, we are completely different from one another. And while we have the same parents, have gone to the same schools, and have both been given the same course of studies, we simply have contrasting personalities and abilities.

My father loved me best, as I am the most like him. We both loved challenging the forces of nature and using physical skill to overcome obstacles. He was tall. Strong in both spirit and physicality. A fighter in the Kosovo Liberation Army. When he walked in the street, others would part. I grew up hearing countless stories about how he'd killed enemies and saved the lives of his friends. He taught me how to handle weapons and how to protect myself. How to stand tall when I needed to, and how to lower my head when necessary to show deference and respect. When the war was over, he opened a construction company to rebuild the city.

My father's death was painful for me, but it only served to push me harder to succeed. Everything I am today; I owe to him.

Our mother, on the other hand, has always loved Albi the most.

Albi has patience to sit and read. He prefers staying home, writing in his journal. He likes to review numbers and comb out details, whereas I see the bigger picture of things. Most of all, he despises anything physical.

My father used to laugh, telling me that when I tried to walk, Mama would knock me down, insisting that I was not allowed to stand until Albi could too. Suffice it to say, I spent an extra six months on the ground when I wanted to run.

But at a certain point, there was no stopping my growth. I'm close to two meters in height, and Albi is a head below me. It's true that studies come more naturally to him, but I put in the work and succeed in my own way. The girls have always flocked to me while he has barely kindled a relationship with a woman. Why should I pay for his lack of skills?

Our father always wanted more for me than what Albania could offer, and over his lifetime, he encouraged me to go to America to study and learn American building techniques so that I could return to Kosovo with not just money in my pocket—the likes of which would be impossible to make here—but also with what I'd learned to help our company.

As I'm the firstborn son in my family, the business became mine after Father's death. Originally, I tried to tell Albi that if we both worked hard enough, we could leave for America together. But in typical Albi fashion, he couldn't handle trying for something if there was a chance he could lose.

"America?" I tilt my head to the side, stomach dropping with excitement. My immediate reaction is a smile, but I snap it back. I feel much emotion, but showing it to my brother would be beneath me.

"Yes, Leo." Mother nods, holding up a large white envelope. "You got this from New York University. They accepted you to their school for Arts and Sciences. You can study architecture!" Her eye twitches, and her breaths are labored. Sweat beads at her dark hairline. "I knew you could do it!"

Albi visibly bristles but keeps a smile on his face.

I take the letter from her hands and pull out the paper from the envelope. I read the first word—*Congratulations!*—over and over again, and the world around me blurs. Taking a seat on the couch, I review the letter. Normally, I would do this in my room. But I just can't wait.

"There is so much I must do," I mumble to myself, looking upward. I glance through the envelope again, surprised there isn't more paperwork. Still, I did not ever think they would accept me. My grades are solid but not excellent. "Was there anything else they sent over? About housing or the food hall? Scholarship?"

"That was all." My mother smiles encouragingly.

My brother looks happy. Too happy. "I'm sure once you get there, they will greet you and figure it out. We will make calls in the morning."

"Sure. Still, I'll need to secure my visa. And this is dated from last month! I need to act quickly."

Daisy comes straight into my mind. I'll need to find a good job to be able to bring her over with me. Of course I'll return, but I can't be away from her.

"I'll let you boys figure out the rest. I am so glad for you. Tomorrow will be a big day. The next few weeks even." With a last kiss on my forehead, she leaves the room.

My mother has never been affectionate with me. I guess she really must be proud.

I am alone now with my brother, but can't shake the feeling of Daisy. *I hope she's okay.*

"Oh no." Albi shakes his head. "Do not tell me that Daisy is giving you doubts. That look on your face is distraught when you should be over the moon. She's beautiful, but nothing more than dead weight. Leave her and move on."

"No." I put the paper down. "She and I will get married. I know her father doesn't approve of the Jetch, but we believe that in time—"

"In time?" He laughs out loud. "You are leaving for America. You can't take the girl with you. For years, Papa worked extra hours and put money aside so that *you* could get this chance."

"You could have tried," I spit out. "But as always, you never stepped up to the plate."

"Oh yeah?" He tilts his head. Before I can get another word out, he says, "Let's put all the nonsense of Daisy behind us. What if Mother hears us? How it would break her poor, poor heart."

He is full of guile, and my stomach turns.

"Nonsense of Daisy behind?" I repeat his words, clenching my teeth. "I will go to America, and once I am there, I will find a way for Daisy to join me. We'll come back to Albania together, eventually."

"Join you?" He shakes his head. "Her father will never allow it. If you ask me, she'll be married in a month. Before anyone finds out that you took her virtue, of course. If anyone were to hear, she'd be shunned. Imagine what would happen to her if people knew how I'd found you guys, wrapped up together, in the field ..." He shudders, overexaggerated.

I grit my teeth. "She won't be shunned because she and I will be husband and wife."

My brother shrugs casually before chuckling. "When you leave, she'll be here alone, without a husband and without her virtue. If she's smart enough, she has likely already planned to place another man in the picture ..."

One, two, moments pass, and my fist collides with his face. He falls to the floor, hands covering his jaw.

"Don't you ever talk like that about my woman."

He slowly sits up, his cheek already smarting. "Just go and be grateful. Let the rest of us live in peace."

I stand up to my full height, pointing at him on the ground. "I'm not letting her go. But I will live my dream. Papa's dream. And in time, I will bring Daisy with me. After I finish school and work to make money, I will come back here and grow my business."

"Your business?" He rubs his jaw.

"Yes. It was Papa's, and now that he's gone, it's mine."

He shakes his head, glaring. "I've been the one there after school, overseeing the books. I've been the one making sure Mama gets her stipend each week to pay for groceries. You've been screwing around with Daisy and playing football." He grits his teeth, angrier than I've ever seen him.

"While you've been sitting in the back office, I have been watching the construction on the new project Papa was building!" I point to his face. "I will return from America. And when I do, I will take what is rightfully mine. As the firstborn son, this is my birthright."

I point to my own chest before taking a step closer to him. He shrinks back, afraid of my shadow. Turning away, I walk into my bedroom and shut the door, the hinges rattling.

Hearing the freezer opening and closing, my mother chirps, "What did you say to him? Why do you anger him when you know his temper? Just like Papa. He can't help himself! How many noses has he broken in his life? Five?"

I take out my phone and call Daisy. After the tenth attempt at reaching her, getting nothing but her voice mail, I put my phone on vibrate and leave it on the corner of my desk.

I review the paper from New York University, confused by the fact that they barely gave me any inforJetion at all. *Maybe there is a second letter coming?* There must be. The mail took too long to get here. School starts in three weeks, and I don't have enough inforJetion. *What if they already gave my spot away?* I open my desk drawer, gathering all the forms that I filled out, just in case the opportunity arose. I even made a friend at the consulate, so that if the time came, everything for me could be expedited.

I fall asleep with my phone beside my face and clothes all over my floor.

~

Two Weeks Later

"She's gone." Albi leans against the side of my bedroom door, the morning sun high in the sky.

I take a look at my bedside clock, ten in the morning.

"What?" I sit up, scratching the back of my neck, and I stare at my brother in confusion.

"Her father sent her away. To an aunt in Montenegro. I heard at the fruit store this morning. The whole thing was very rushed, apparently, but word is, she had a job offer."

I pull out my phone from beneath my pillow, relieved that it isn't dead. I need to reach her. The last weeks have been awful. I've barely been able to sleep, worried about Daisy. Between trying to find her in town, calling and e-mailing her, running to and from the consulate for my student visa documents and interviews, and working at my uncle's pizza shop to make some extra cash before leaving, I've been moving nonstop. The separation from Daisy sucks, but we love each other. We will find a way.

He clears his throat. "There is no way she has her old phone. Come on, Leo. Use that brain of yours. She's been sent away, and her father will make sure she has no contact with you."

"I've got to find a way to reach her." I stand up, full of resolve. "An aunt, you said?"

"Sure." He smiles as I get out of bed, heading to the bathroom to brush my teeth. Facing the mirror, I see him pull out an envelope from his back pocket. "Five hundred US dollars."

"What?" My jaw drops, and I quickly spit and rinse out my mouth with water.

Albi laughs out loud. "You're leaving. Once you are in America, you'll figure it out. You're smart and resourceful. I have no doubt. This will help you get started before life *really begins*."

His smirk reaches under my skin, but I ignore it. Looking at my brother now and seeing how happy he is for me, I feel badly about the poor standing of our relationship. We're family after all. And giving me what is probably two months' worth of his wages is nice. Maybe nicer than anything he has ever done. I guess it took me leaving for us to finally connect.

He even called New York University on my behalf, and they told him not to worry that I missed the acceptance deadline. When I arrive, I should go to the admissions office, and they will set every-thing up for me, including lodging.

"It's all set," Albi said.

"Albi ..." I clear my throat, feeling guilty at the lasting bruise on his jaw. "I know it hasn't always been easy between us. But maybe when you're ready and I've set up an apartment, you can come too. For a visit."

"Sure." He looks at me then, and a flicker of something like anger flashes in his eyes. Before I can make sense of what I saw, it's gone. He covers the glare with an easy laugh. "Yeah. That's right. One big, happy family. Get your stuff together. I'll find a way to learn more about Daisy. *Trust me.*"

I WAKE up and run to the bathroom, vomiting in the toilet. When my stomach is empty, I lift my sweaty head and smile. I leave in a few hours to America! I'm excited but nervous. More nervous than getting on the field for the football championship. I won then, and I'll win now.

I get myself up off the floor and shower before getting dressed. When everything is organized and my backpack is filled with my passport, my mobile, and my wallet, I head into the kitchen. My mother has prepared an enormous breakfast. She serves me what will likely be my last breakfast at home.

Her hand moves to my back, rubbing in circles. "Life isn't always easy, but I believe you will make America your home."

I tilt my head, confused by her comment. "America will be where I live, but Kosovo is my home."

"Hmm," she replies, noncommittal.

Albi asks for more eggs. She stands up and plates more for him from the stove.

After we finish eating, she rinses the dishes quietly. The air in the house is somber.

The drive isn't much better. The music is on, but I can barely hear it.

My mother pulls up to the terminal at curbside on the departure's level. I take out my suitcases from the trunk and find my mother beside me. She hugs me, longer than maybe she ever has. I can smell her flowery perfume that she has worn all of my life.

I let go, and pound fists with Albi.

Finally, I turn around to enter the airport. My new life awaits me.

2

Leo

LaGuardia Airport in New York City is busier than the movies show. There is no way to accurately describe the manic hustle as I walk across the airport through seas of people, following signs to the baggage claim. I'm glad I always watched television and movies in English. Without them, I would be handicapped.

Finding my black suitcase is easy; Mother tied a thick red ribbon to the handles, so I could spot it among others that looked just the same. I smile. The trick worked.

After pulling it off the carousel, I make a stop in the restroom. It's gray and old-looking but not too dirty. I open my backpack and take out my toothbrush and toothpaste. After brushing my teeth, I wash my hands and face in the sink and retie my shoelaces.

Walking out of the terminal, I feel a hell of a lot better about myself. Finding the bus to downtown New York City is like a puzzle. Numbers, letters, Uptown, West Side, East Side ... it never seems to end. It's a Tuesday morning, not the weekend, and my bus needs to take me downtown.

According to Albi, the admissions office at New York University is awaiting my arrival. Once I get there, they will take me to the dorms and set me up with access to the food hall. I look around and follow the signs to the taxi and bus lines.

I exit the airport and am suddenly bombarded with men hassling me, asking to give me a ride.

One seems decent and clean, in dark jeans and a white button-down, a cigarette hanging from his mouth and a gold chain dangling around his neck. "Need a ride?"

I look at him closely before looking back down at my phone. My trip to New York University will likely take close to two hours by bus and subway, but with a car, it could be less than thirty minutes. I quickly open the Uber app I was told is necessary for life in New York City and type in my address. For the right price, maybe I'll go with this guy.

I slide my phone back into my front pocket. "How much to Lafayette Street?"

In an accent I can't place, he tells me, "Oh, that's very, very far. A hundred."

I roll my eyes and keep walking. The Uber would cost fifty dollars. I might be new in this town, but I'm not one to get swindled.

"Wait!" he cries, catching up to me. "How much do you want to pay?"

"Thirty bucks."

He throws his smoke onto the floor, not bothering to put it out. "I'm only doing this because it's off-peak. Cash only. Follow me."

Together, we walk along the terminals until we finally reach an enormous parking area. I try not to gape. I've only just gotten here, and already, I'm in shock over the size of the cars. I know gas is cheaper here, but still! We pause at a black car that's small in comparison to the others. A compact Toyota.

He opens the trunk, and I pause before giving him my suitcase.

"Let's go." He claps. "Time is money."

"Yeah, sure."

As we finally drive off, my leg bounces up and down. My heart is beating so fast that it feels like it might jump out from my ribs.

His eyes move to the rearview mirror. "Can you settle?"

I want to be polite, but I don't have it in me to relax. I give him a hard look. "No."

"New in town, I see. Where are you from?"

"Kosovo."

"Oh, wow. Albania. Long flight?"

"Yes." I pull out a toothpick from the pocket of my backpack and bite on it.

"Going to school?" He brings down his window, lighting up another cigarette. "NYU?"

I don't feel like responding. I'm exhausted. But then again, he's driving me for a good deal. I should be nice enough.

I sit up taller. "Yes, NYU." The moment I say the words, pride builds in my chest.

"Planning to get a job? I'm a real estate broker. There are always people coming in and out of the city, wanting to rent an apartment. Not great money yet, but one day, I'm going to own my own company. Life will be good then."

I shift in my seat. "Where are you from?"

He exhales smoke out the window. "Israel. My name is Yosi. And you?"

"Leo."

I look out the window, and we're finally off the bridge. The city is enormous. Bigger than my dreams. With towering buildings and people packed on the sidewalks, I'm not sure how I'll ever navigate. My gaze holds as I scan the street signs.

I find myself praying. I'm so far from home. Far from my love, Daisy, who I still can't find. I swallow hard, an emptiness settling in my chest. Mother. I miss her too. When will I see her next? Even Albi. I have never been without him in all my life. The whole move happened so quickly that I was barely able to process what was unfolding. It was as though my brother and Mama had put skates on my feet and pushed me forward.

I put my hand into the zipper pocket of my backpack, glad my money is still there. Mama wanted me to sew it into my clothes, but I told her that was ridiculous. I sort of wish I'd listened now. What if I lose this cash?

The driver stops, and I see the sign. *New York University. I finally made it!*

"Admissions."

I discreetly open my zipper pocket and undo the band around my cash. I remove three ten-dollar bills and hand them to him. "Thank you, my friend."

He takes off his belt and turns his body in the seat. Taking the money from my hand, he gives me a card. "If you ever need a ride somewhere or a job, I know people who know people. Or if you need an apartment, I can find you a good one for no fee." He winks.

I give him my hand, and we shake. "Thanks."

I hear the trunk pop before opening the door and stepping out. The weather is nice and mild. Warm even. I take out my suitcase and make my way into the building. This area feels more like home than the industrial streets we came down. Opening the door, I see the sign for the office and make my way in.

"Hello. Can I help you?"

"Yes." I put my suitcase beside me. "I have been accepted to your undergraduate Arts and Sciences program."

"Mmhmm. And?" She stares with a blank face.

"And I was told to come here first and you would set me up with housing."

"Here? Housing?" She tilts her head to the side, as though I were speaking Albanian.

I clear my throat, suddenly getting hot.

"What's your name?"

"Leonard Nikqi."

"Leonard, do you have any paperwork with you?"

I drop to the floor and open my backpack, taking out the admissions letter. Standing up, I hand it to her.

She studies it closely. "Anything else? After accepting your admission, you should have received all of the paperwork."

"No, nothing else. I just received this letter two weeks ago. It must have been delayed. I'm from Kosovo, you see—"

She puts her hand up, the universal sign for quiet as she types on her computer. Finally, she raises her head. "I'm sorry, but you are not a current student here. I see you were mailed an acceptance, but we did not hear from you. Actually ..." She pauses, clicking on her keyboard again. "It says here in the notes that you were called as well, and you said no to admission."

"Impossible! My brother just gave me the letter two weeks ago. He called here on my behalf, and you told him that I should come in and you would handle the rest." I don't mean to raise my voice, but it's unstoppable. Heat crawls through my body until I can feel sweat bead upon my skin.

She swallows hard, pity lining her face. "We have no record of that in our system."

"There must be an error ..."

"On May 24, you denied admission."

I shake my head. "I have nowhere to go. I was told to come here and you would find housing ..."

"Why don't you call home? Maybe there is something else your brother forgot to tell you?"

"I need to speak with someone else, please."

She opens and closes her mouth, wanting to argue, but suddenly, she changes her mind. She lifts up the phone and says something into the receiver. "You can take a seat. I'll call you when he's ready."

I sit down in a state of utter shock. I swallow hard. The truth is too painful to bear. Reality knocks, but I'm not able to answer. No. Not yet.

People walk in and out of the cold office, but all of them seem to work here.

Finally, the secretary tells me to come in. "Leave the suitcase by your seat. I'll keep an eye on it for you."

I nod and wordlessly grab my backpack, walking into the meeting.

The conversation moves in a blur.

Application received ...

Failed to reply to all letters sent, requesting paperwork ...

No acceptance ...

Send over your transcript and possibly ...

Reapply now for spring ...

He hands me a fresh application. It's identical to the one that I filled out a year ago. Paperwork for scholarships, also copies to the one I filled out a year ago. My hands are full with paper, none of which can help me.

I stand up and shake his hand like the man I was raised to be. "Thank you, sir."

"I hope this works out for you."

I leave in a trance. Take my suitcase. Mumble a thank-you to the secretary's bent head and walk outside. Sit on the steps. Head in my hands.

Not enough money. *Where will I sleep?*

I pull out the cash I put aside, including the five hundred Albi handed me. I thought housing and food would be handled. I figured I'd get a part-time job to cover smaller expenses. This will not last me long.

And then it comes to me. *Albi.*

My hands shake as I pull out my phone. I call him again and again but no response. Nothing.

He set me up. He hid the admissions letter and made me wait. He told them I did not accept. He sent me here to get rid of me.

I stand up, hauling my suitcase as I walk, the red ribbon flowing from the wind. Moving has always helped me think. Daisy comes back into the forefront of my mind. Her father wasn't supposed to be home for another hour. When I got home from her house, how did my brother know I would be walking through the door? He was the one who told me he'd spoken with NYU. I was so busy with my visa and tracking Daisy that I trusted him. The frequent flashes I saw in his eyes. Guilt? Jealousy?

Finally, I stop at a park, finding a bench.

He set me up. My brother set me up. He took my love. He stole my business. He took my life!

A group of kids walk by me, smiling and laughing. Heavy backpacks are slung over their shoulders.

I lift the phone again.

"Hi, brother," he answers.

"Albi." I inhale and exhale. "What did you do?"

"You're lucky I answered—"

"Tell me everything, Albi."

"I guess no reason not to at this point. You now know that you're in America with no job, no home, and no school." He chuckles.

I fume, so angry and in so much pain that the words stick to my insides.

"Well, the truth is, Daisy called me. She wanted me to give you information on how to find her, but I didn't. Told her you were leaving and you were done with her."

Dots block my vision, and I blink to clear my sight.

"Wasn't too hard to hide the acceptance letter either. Frankly, I am shocked at how easy it was to fool you." He laughs, and my stomach drops.

"Why?"

"Why?" He laughs out loud. "Firstborn son you are no more."

"Firstborn ... what is this for, the business?"

After my father left the earth, all of his business dealings and money were under my control. His construction company. Now that I am gone, Albi thinks he can have it.

"You thought you could take my life from me? Papa's business belongs to me. And when I return—"

"When you return, nothing!" he screams. "You already signed the business over to me."

"I did no such—"

"Yes." He chuckles. "I gave you paperwork to sign, and you

signed it."

I blink, remembering signing numerous papers for my visa. "What? Did you sneak it in?"

"You signed it. That's all there is."

"And Daisy?" I keep my mouth shut, panting loudly through my nose.

"I sent her father there that night, earlier than expected, and he shipped her off rather quickly. But don't worry about her. I have plans, and she'll be taken care of."

"You lie!" I scream.

"Unfortunately not." He laughs. "Come on, Leo. Wake up. She's a good girl. A beautiful girl. You think her father would let her sit alone when the man who defiled her left for America?"

Moments of silence pass, and there are no more words. I hang up. I want to call my mother. Need to. My heart pumps as I dial her number. My veins feel as though they were filling with tar.

She clears her throat. "Hello?"

"Hi, Mama."

"So, I assume you got there safely?"

"Mama, what do you know about my acceptance here?"

"I do feel badly. But the truth is, Albi is the one who should be taking over the business. He is the intelligent one. He is the kind one. You are the muscle and brawn. He deserves it, and you were in his way. And why? Because you were born first? It's ridiculous. Go to America and make your own life there."

"But I'm here now. In America. With no school, no job, and no home. Why did you take the school away from me then? Why not let me come here and be a student? I still would have been out of your way."

"After everything you put Albi through, you deserve a little hardship."

My own breaths turn to pants. "How could you?"

"You will figure it out. I have no doubt. Be well, my son."

I scream at the top of my lungs, yelling so loud that the sound bounces off the skyscrapers. I don't stop until my voice is raw.

3

Leo

THE PARK BENCH I'm sitting on has a view of buildings. Which park? I don't have a damn clue.

I replay everything in my head, retracing my steps from the moment Daisy's father walked in through her bedroom door until I landed in America. How did I manage to get caught up in this mess? And how did I not realize the extent of Albi's hatred for me?

I see people walking by, laughing maybe, but I barely focus.

Could I have done something differently? I should have.

Somehow, the sun begins to set. The weather isn't too bad, and where else am I going to go? I need some kind of plan, but I'm practically comatose. Luckily, I have enough sense to realize my suitcase is beside me. If I stay here for the night, someone might come and steal it. I have nothing on me for protection either. I make a fist and recognize that I might feel broken, but I'm not. I'm still strong.

I want to rise, but I can't seem to move. Where would I go anyway?

Night turns into day.

Another night, another day.

I'm hiding in plain sight, just a kid hanging on the bench. But I'm also sleeping on the bench.

No food, but I do manage to pick up a few bottles of water from the bodega on the corner. The owner asks me if I want something else, but I don't feel like eating.

Mid-morning a few days later, I know that I can't go on like this. I'm starving, and I have to figure my shit out. Slowly, I walk back to NYU—at least, I think that's where I am headed. The sidewalk is narrow, lined with buildings of all sizes. The ground is paved in stone.

I look up and notice the sky has turned a cloudy gray. A man is behind a small counter in the middle of the sidewalk, selling snacks and cigarettes.

"Marlboros, please."

"That will be twenty dollars."

"Twenty dollars?" I think my jaw must drop because the man laughs out loud.

"Welcome to New York City."

I scratch the back of my neck. Honestly, I need these right now. Hopefully, it'll pull me back into the real world. I pull out a twenty from my meager stash and take the pack. Luckily, he hands me some matches with it.

"Thanks."

I light up, leaning against a white stucco building. The smoke helps to calm my nerves and settle my empty stomach. The smell reminds me of home. A light wind moves past me, and I realize darkness is on its way again.

A group of students holding bags walks by me, and on instinct alone, I follow them. We climb some stairs into a glass, modern-looking building. I walk along, as though I were part of their group, and keep my suitcase to my side so as not to draw attention to myself. They all flash IDs to the front desk, and I mimic like I'm doing the same. The security guard waves to the group, and without a word, I'm inside.

I look up, seeing the words *NYU Steinhardt* written in large black letters against a marble wall. I keep walking down an expansive foyer and follow them straight into a silver elevator.

We get out together on the fifth floor. They're all talking animatedly, and that's when I realize they aren't holding bags but instruments. They walk into an auditorium and head toward the stage. It's filled with identical wooden chairs. I take a seat in one of the back rows, where it's dark, keeping my suitcase glued to me. I pull up the hood of my sweatshirt, hoping I can blend into the shadows.

It doesn't take long for the entire stage to fill up with people, all sitting with instruments in hand. They must all be tuning up because it sounds more like noise than music. That's when who I assume is the conductor says a few words, and suddenly, they play. It's soft and classical. Somewhat soothing to my frayed nerves. And while I've always liked music, I've never been one to listen to anything like this. They stop and go, playing and replaying. It's amazing, is what it is. It's slow but loud and then fast but quiet.

And for the first time since I arrived, I find myself unwinding. God only knows what will become of me, but for now, I'm here. Listening to music.

The conductor shouts something else, and everyone stops playing. That's when I hear a single instrument play alone. It's slow and deep, heavy like the mountains surrounding my home. It makes me think about hiking with my father up into the hills. Watching the sunset with him. One time, we were climbing, and I mentioned that my bag felt like it was filled with rocks. He laughed, telling me that he had in fact put rocks in my bag.

"It will make you stronger," he said, chuckling.

We always used to pull pranks on each other like that.

I blink a few times, wanting to cry like a baby. *How could they do this to me?*

I scan the stage. It's a cello playing. My eyes pause on the musician. Her brown hair is curly and long. Gathered over one shoulder, it drapes over her enormous brown instrument like a shroud. I can't tell if her eyes are closed, but she sways with her bow like she's using more than just a hand to play. I let myself focus on her and enjoy the sound. It's astounding.

She's astounding.

A few minutes later, all of the cellos in the section play. And finally, everyone joins back in.

When the practice is over, I try to stay still and hide in the shadows, lowering myself into my seat. No one expects me to be here, so they don't seem to notice my presence.

When the auditorium is empty, I exhale. I might as well stay here and get comfortable. Maybe now is a good moment to use the bathroom actually. I used a McDonald's, and I hated it. I'm sure this will be better.

I stand up, leave the auditorium, and walk through the hall as though I were just another student. Some people are walking through, but I guess I'm young, just like them. Why should anyone find my presence strange?

I spot a men's restroom and push through the door. After taking care of business, I wash my face and hands with soap. I hold the side of the sink, staring at my reflection. Water pours down my face, and my eyes are bloodshot. I look thinner.

My life ... what will become of me? I think about my aunts and uncles who immigrated to Switzerland years ago. Do I know anyone here, in America? No, I don't. Maybe I should check out my Facebook to see if anyone else has friends or family here who I can connect with, but that seems wrong.

I don't want to admit what has come to me. It's embarrassing. My friends think I'm here to study, and I don't want people thinking otherwise. I might have nothing of value, but my pride is still intact.

And Daisy. If I were to find her now, I might make a mess of her life. And even if I wanted to find her, she's no longer on any social media platforms. I asked some of her friends before I left, but no one had any idea where she was. Either that or they had been told not to tell me. Who knows what fucked up games have been played by my brother? Regardless, it seems utterly impossible to find her now.

I shut my eyes, squeezing them tightly.

I finally pick up my head, determined to stay strong. I leave the restroom and walk back into the auditorium, my small steps from earlier turning into heavy strides. I find my seat. Pull up my hood. My sadness, disappointment and pain turn into anger. And once I tap into that feeling, it fills me.

I swear on my father's grave that I will get my revenge. I will go back to Kosovo and take my business back—by force if I have to. And I will kill my brother. With my bare hands, I will end his life.

I open and close my fists, imagining him screaming and crying. I grind my teeth together. He thinks he won. But he has no idea what I'm capable of.

I WAKE up with a crick in my neck, but I'm relieved that I slept somewhere safe. I touch, feeling my suitcase still by my side. I check my watch, noticing it's six o'clock in the morning. I have no idea when the building opens its doors, but I definitely don't want to get caught. Still, I could use the restroom and brush my teeth. My stomach is also grumbling, on top of feeling raw.

I make my way out of the auditorium with my suitcase and backpack.

A janitor sees me. I want to run, but I play it cool. I wave my hand to him.

"Getting your early morning practice in, I see?"

"Yes, sir," I reply in my best American accent.

And then he's gone.

I go back into the restroom, brushing my teeth and washing my face and hands. I quickly open my suitcase and take out some fresh clothes and underwear. After changing in a stall, I actually feel a lot better.

I have hands. I have a brain. I will find work and a place to stay. And if I don't figure it out, which I probably won't, I'll come back here for the night.

Before walking out, I instinctively put my hand in my back pocket.

When I feel the card, my jaw drops. Pulling it out, I pray it's what I think it is.

Yosi Peretz

Licensed Real Estate Broker

917-504-7672

The driver! And he did tell me to call if I needed anything. What do I have to lose?

I check my watch again, seeing that it might be too early still to call him.

I should finally eat.

I head downstairs, deciding that I'll simply play along with the *early practice* story. On my way out of the building, I pause at the security guard in the lobby, waving to him like we know each other.

"Hey, man. Do you think you can hold on to my suitcase for me? I'll be back in about an hour."

"No problem." He takes it, rolling it behind the desk.

"Thank you." And I walk away, feeling slightly lighter.

I take my time as I go, being sure to check my surroundings. I find a café with a pink awning a few blocks from the building. It's called Le Chalet. I walk in, and a silver bell chimes from above the doorway. It smells like fresh desserts and bread.

"The quiche just came out from the oven. Filled with eggs." The girl at the front smiles at me, almost shyly.

"Okay. I'll take two. Do you have Turkish coffee?"

She blushes, looking down at her feet before bringing her eyes back at me. "Yes, sure."

She packs me the food and hands me the coffee and a paper bag, her hand holding on to it for a moment too long. I smile, finally pulling the bag out of her grip. I leave the café and sit outside at a round table, lighting up my cigarette. I didn't smoke too much because Daisy didn't like it, but right now, it's keeping me afloat. When I'm finished smoking, I enjoy the food. It's delicious.

Almost no one is out on the street. Little by little, I see a few people walk by. They're moving quickly with coffees in their hands. At home, everyone would be at cafés in the mornings, sitting and smoking. Coffee is meant to be savored. Not something to drink on the go.

My leg starts to shake. It might be early, but I can't wait any longer. I pick up my phone and dial Yosi.

He answers on the third ring. "Hello?"

"Hey, Yosi. This is Leo. Remember you drove me from the airport to NYU?"

He coughs. "Yeah, sure. What's happening?"

"Well, I had a few plans, but they all fell through. Any chance you know of someone hiring?"

"It must have gone really bad, eh?"

"You have no idea." I look at a red car, suddenly feeling the urge to smash its windows.

"Are you enrolled at least?" He laughs, like this whole thing is a joke.

"No." I grit my teeth.

"No?" He sounds a bit more surprised.

"No," I reply a little more forcefully.

"Shit."

"Yeah."

"Listen, there's a chain of pizza stores. Famiglia. It's owned by my cousin, but he has Albanian guys working for him. I'm sure he can fit you in the schedule. I've got about an hour now before I'm showing an apartment Uptown. I'll pick you up and take you there."

"That would be great." I find my heart moving more quickly. "I helped my uncle at his pizza shop in Kosovo." I swallow hard, imagining Uncle Besart behind the cash register, flour over his forearms.

"I'm sure the pizza is different there than here, but that's good enough. I'll get you from the corner of Houston and Wooster in ten minutes." He hangs up the phone.

I quickly pull up my Maps on my phone and figure out how to get there. Once I do, I start running.

The moment I see his black Toyota, I walk toward the car. This time, I sit in the front seat, beside him.

Could it be that I just saw him so recently? It feels like a lifetime ago.

"You're quiet." He smiles, turning up the music. I don't recognize the language, but I assume it must be Hebrew.

"Not usually. But my life is fucked right now."

We drive Uptown. I know this because the street numbers keep rising. The buildings grow too. I'm still in somewhat of a daze, but this time, I know I have to wake up and get a grip. I must make sure I secure this job and then figure out where I will live. Maybe the pizza shop owner will be able to set me up. Or the guys who work there.

When we get to 84th Street and Lexington Avenue, he finds a parking spot and pulls in.

Before leaving the car, he shuts off the music and turns to me. "Your people helped my people once. My grandparents fled Germany after Hitler's rise in power and went to Albania. Their neighbors refused to comply with German and Italian orders to turn over lists of the Jewish people living there. Even your government came to their rescue, giving them fake documents so they could continue living with the Albanians in peace. I promised my grandparents to never forget the kindness your people had bestowed on us. The only European country with a Muslim majority took care of us. So, yeah, man, I'm going to help you. If there is something you need, you can always call me."

I blink a few times, floored. "Wow, man, thank you."

Who knew that a good deed from my country's past would be repaid in this way?

I put out my hand, and we shake. Maybe I'm not alone after all.

"The guy who owns the pizza shop is called Itai." Yosi tells me as we walk inside.

"Hey, Yosi!" A short guy with dark hair greets us from the register.

They make small talk when finally, Yosi introduces me. "This is Leo. Smart guy. He just moved from Albania and needs to make some money."

After they chat some more in Hebrew, Itai pats me on the back.

"Perfect. Start today. *Yalla!*" He grabs a red T-shirt from a desk drawer and throws it at my chest, telling me to change in the restroom. "When you're ready, meet Veton by the cash register."

"Veton?" Hearing an Albanian name makes me happier than I thought possible.

"Yeah. Good kid."

I switch my shirt and head to the front. "*Hej, njeri. Un jam Veton,*" he greets me in Albanian, and I let out a breath I didn't even realize I had been holding. He's in the same red t-shirt as I am. He has dark hair, tan skin, and bright blue eyes that remind me of my own.

"*Hej. Un jam Leonard.*"

We shake, and I give him my first real smile since coming to America.

It turns out, everyone who works here is Albanian. It doesn't take long for me and the other guys to connect the dots, and as luck would have it, I know some of their aunts and uncles and even parents who still live in Kosovo. Most of them came to America to study, just like I was supposed to do. But while they're doing work and school, I'm no longer planning to study. I'm not sure yet of my plan, but school isn't going to happen. Not now. When they ask me questions, I keep my answers simple. Came to work construction and learn and make money. Company back home. Will return.

People rush in and out of the store, ordering quickly. They all seem to know what they want before they even walk inside. And just as they order quick, they want their food even quicker. No small talk. No *how are your parents?* It's all business here.

America is interesting. So many people of all kinds, in one city. Black, white, brown. Mixtures. When a man of Asian descent walks in, I almost can't speak! The only time I saw anyone Asian was in the movies. After he leaves, the guys laugh at me, telling me that they were shocked, too, at first. So many kinds of people. My history teacher once described America as a melting pot. She wasn't kidding!

The place quiets down for a few minutes until the bell chimes again. In walk two men. They're big and almost larger than life, both wearing dark sunglasses. One has jet-black hair, but the other has lighter hair, pulled back in a bun. They lift their hands to us before taking seats in the back.

I turn to Veton. "Who is that?"

"Them?" He shakes his head, motioning me to the back kitchen as the other guys hustle to make food.

The men haven't ordered, but it seems everyone knows what they want. And it isn't pizza. From the large refrigerators, they take out fresh vegetables and cheese.

"Only the two most notorious men in New York City. Nico and Darius, who run the Mafia Shqiptare. They're scary as fuck, but make sure you always hold your own when they're near. They hate weakness."

I whisper, "The shqipe? Here?" My mouth drops open.

Of course I've heard of them. Everyone has. The Albanian Mafia is serious and worldwide, known for their black-market dealings ... among other things.

"You're in New York City, brother. If not here, where?"

"Shit." I have no reason to be afraid, but there is no denying the fact that the shqipe are known as the most powerful men in the world.

"When they come, they always want the same thing—kackavall salad."

"At a pizza shop?"

He laughs. "I keep forgetting that you only just arrived. The Albanian immigrants work in pizza shops. A lot of us are building supers, too—you know, the guys who fix things in people's apartments. We maintain and manage. But anyway, the shqipe knows they can come here to eat our food."

I exhale. "Do they know you?"

"They know all of us. Likely, they'll want to meet you too. Make sure you're cool. Just don't ask too many questions. Stay quiet and keep your head down. I will introduce you."

We both walk back around the counter when Veton takes a basket of hot bread from the counter. He shuffles over to Nico and Darius. I watch as he sets the food in front of the men.

I hear one of them say, "Bring the new kid over here."

I stand up tall and walk to the table myself. I'm not a pussy. And while I've never met any members of the shqipe before, I don't fear them.

"This is Leo. He just arrived." Veton's posture is completely erect. He looks like a kid in the army, ready to obey.

The men look me up and down. I lean on my left side, refusing to act like a monkey. I'm not one of their soldiers.

"This is Darius." Veton gestures to the lighter-haired guy. He has a nasty-looking scar down the side of his face and a strong jaw.

I don't blink. I maintain eye contact like I would with anyone else. We shake hands. His grip is crazy hard, but I give it back just as strong.

"Nice to meet you." His accent is strange. Close to perfect Albanian—from Tirana maybe—but there is something else melted in there.

"This is Nico." Veton rushes out his name, like he wants to get the conversation over with as quickly as possible.

"*Hej,*" he greets. A thick gold watch is unmissable on his wrist.

"Good to meet you." I smile, recognizing his accent immediately. "You're from Kosovo?"

He smirks, like he thinks it's funny I'm making small talk. "Yes."

"Me too." My reply is a little too enthusiastic, but I can't help but feel relief that he's from home.

"And when did you arrive here?" He tilts his head to the side.

"Just recently."

He and Darius lock eyes, and something wordlessly passes between them.

Nico shifts in his seat. "You have a place to stay?"

I consider lying, but what would be the point? "No. I was

supposed to study at New York University, but my plans fell through. As luck would have it, I got a job here today. Hopefully, I can crash with one of the guys until I can afford a place."

"*Luck*. Interesting word." He looks me up and down. "Sometimes, you're discussing a problem with a friend of yours, and the answer just shows up."

"Maybe *luck* is the wrong word then." The anger in my voice can't be concealed. "What brought me here was the opposite of lucky circumstances."

Nico leans back, a smile spreading across his face.

I look between the two men, knowing that, for some reason, I have made it onto their radar.

Darius pulls a card from his pocket. "Call me when you're done for the day. I will pick you up and bring you to one of our apartments. You'll be comfortable there."

I open and close my mouth, unsure of what to say. I look to Veton, but he seems frozen to the spot.

"Yeah, sure." I nod. "That's real good of you guys."

"Yeah." Nico laughs to Darius. "That's us. We're the good guys."

"The nicest." Darius chuckles darkly.

"Let me know if I can bring anything else," Veton spouts out quickly.

We walk away, going back behind the counter.

Under his breath, Veton tells me, "Listen, Leo. You have to be careful with those guys."

"Why? What would they care about me for?"

"Who knows why they might want you? Who knows what they know about you and your history? I know you've got something hot on your mind—you look like there is a fire burning inside you. But, Leo, please remember, it's blood for blood in that world. Once you ask something of them, you'll never be able to rid yourself of the crew. I'm telling you as a friend, whatever they ask, say no nicely. And walk away. Stay with me at my place. I've got a good couch. Don't use their apartment."

"To get involved with the Mafia? Me?" My heart pounds.

Somehow, things clear in my head. *Who else is as connected as they are? Who else has the power to destroy my brother and mother or find Daisy? And what do I have to lose anyway?* I'm alone in this world.

Before I can think on it more, I face him fully. "I'm staying in the apartment they offered."

"Listen—"

"No. I'm not a green kid who just arrived, dazed and confused. And I'm not a typical American kid who doesn't know shit either. I'm a man. I know who they are and what they do. I've heard about them, like we all have. And I have my reasons for getting involved."

He shakes his head, almost sadly. "All right, Leo. All right."

4

Leo

THREE YEARS Later

DREN PICKES me up from my apartment downtown, honking from the street until I exit the building, eliciting a few *fuck you*s from passersby.

I laugh as I jog down the steps, yelling, "I'm here. Shut up, man!"

The windows of the car are pulled down as we speed into the night.

I wish I could say that after three years of being banished from my home that my anger had ebbed and that I was now a carefree guy who went out with friends and laughed and chilled. That I no longer thought about Daisy and my business that had been stolen from me. Or that I had forgiven my brother and mother and that I prayed for them each night.

But that's not the case.

My anger has grown.

Puno Construction, which is officially owned and run by Albi, has become one of the largest construction companies in Kosovo. Daisy has two young sons with Albi, and my sources tell me she is happy, shopping and throwing parties in her home. It riles my blood, but I've seen the photos, and it's all true. She's moved on—and it didn't take her long. If I could go back and tell my younger self a few things about love, I would never have gotten into this mess. I was naive. Stupid. Her father might have been devout, but as I've since learned, she was just after money. She knew that when I came of age, I was going to inherit a big business. And with me gone, it was Albi who would inherit.

And as far as my brother and my mother are concerned? *Revenge* is too casual a word. Killing them wouldn't even be enough. At first, I want them to stay alive and to watch everything they built disappear. I need them to have their eyes working, so they can see their lives being torn to shreds by my hands. Once they know it's all gone, I'll end their lives happily. Albi stole Daisy from me? They can have each other for all I care. But the fact that he thinks he won? That he got away with taking what was mine? I refuse to allow that.

The disintegration of my good, young self happened quickly. I'm still a decent man to my friends, as I've always been, but I've stopped being friendly to anyone outside of who I care to know. People are liars and cheaters. The only person I can count on is myself and, of course, the men in the shqipe. Once they saw my value, they brought me into their fold. I guess Nico and Darius saw something in me that they liked.

That first time I met them at the pizza shop, they set me up in an apartment, fully furnished and rent-free. In return, I did some small-time business for them. I got to know the guys in the crew and helped different people out. Realized that even though I was far from my own country, there was a community here that felt a lot like it.

One night over drinks at The Mark Hotel, I explained to them about my business in Kosovo and all the dirty shit my brother and mother had done to steal it from me.

Nico looked at me in all seriousness. "It's time to join the fold, brother. And then, together, we'll get your revenge."

We shook hands, and within a month, I was sworn in.

Nico knew all the details about my business and life back in Kosovo, so it came as no surprise when he decided that it was time for the shqipe to diversify into the construction business. Nico is nothing, if not sharp.

"Why don't you go to the Hamptons, Leo? See if there is anything you can accomplish there."

Well, I had never heard of the Hamptons before Nico mentioned it to me. The name rang no bell. I wasn't even sure it was in New York. But Nico had spoken, and that was all I needed to hear.

Everything from land acquisition to the build is now under my command. I recently bought a ten-acre plot in Water Mill, a gorgeous area in Southampton, and plan to build five spec homes on it. Nico always has to okay my ideas for investment, but once he does, I'm free to work as I please. Dren, who used to be strictly muscle for the crew, has since become my building super. He visits construction sites or sometimes sits full-time on bigger builds that need constant supervision.

Of course, I have to bury people or weapons from time to time beneath the concrete, but other than that, it's all pretty clean. And we're making a killing. I am making more money than I ever thought possible, to be honest. Just like my father hoped I would. The power doesn't hurt either.

Two of Dren's cousins are here from Kosovo tonight, fired up and ready to party. The clubs in the city are the best in the world, and I try to enjoy them when I can. I don't have much time these days, as I'm studying part-time at Baruch College for construction management.

I went back to school because of Darius's encouragement. It might not be NYU, but I am still fulfilling that dream I had long ago.

Unlike my fucking bullshit twin, I'm not afraid to work and get my hands dirty.

Dren tells the guys in the backseat, "The Meatpacking District is where the party is always at. The girls are super hot too. American girls really know how to have fun, eh?"

I smirk, remembering when he told me those same exact lines when I first came. He finds a parking spot and expertly pulls in between two trucks, easily maneuvering his Mercedes-Benz C-Class.

We leave the car together, walking in our nearly identical black button-down shirts and jeans. I tuck my shirt in my pants, making sure I'm neat-looking. I'm not a man who cares too much about fashion, but I still hate sloppy dressing.

The line for the club wraps around the block. Girls in short skirts and dresses, guys in suits or jeans. I look up, the sign for Little West 12th Street in front of me. To the south, skyscrapers are silhouetted in orange by a low fading sunset. Atop a hotel on the avenue, in green neon letters, stands the name of the club—Wild Orchid.

To the front of the line we go as I light up a Marlboro, exhaling calmly. A few words pass between myself and the bouncer as I let him know who we are. We shake hands, and the red rope parts.

Dren tells his cousins, "In New York, everyone is part of a community. Some groups intermingle, and others stay apart. But if you keep yourself involved socially, you'll see the space where we intersect. And in that space is where you can make connections. And money."

The kids hang on to his words like he is a New York City survival guide and follow on his heels like baby kittens. He pushes through the front doors, and I keep myself beside him.

"You don't have to be so fucking rough, eh?" He looks at me like I've got a set of horns on my head.

"To who?"

"To my cousins! Every time I think you couldn't get meaner, you do. Smile, for fuck's sake. Say hello. It wasn't long ago that you were green, worried one of these buildings might fall on your head."

I ignore him even though he's right. I prefer to forget that time of my life.

We shuffle through a dim corridor and open another door. I feel like I've been blasted by candy-scented sweat and a punishing techno sound. We hustle through what feels like hundreds of bodies, dancing in a massive cluster. The bar is like a lighthouse, calling us over to safety. It's a good thing I'm as tall as I am, or I would be drowning.

I was never a big drinker, but I have had some decent experience with alcohol since I've been in New York. In other words, I've drunk so much that I've puked. Drunk so much that I've passed out. Drunk so much that I've woken up with random women in my bed. But I've learned that drinking alters my reality to the point that I can't focus. I lose the clarity I need to remember my pain. And to forget my pain would be death to me. I need it like I need fuel. The revenge I plan to exact will be more satisfying than any drug, any party, and any woman. That's what really gets me going.

The DJ sits up in a high booth to our right, a stage between us. We all lean against the bar, ready to start the night.

"Four tequila shots!" Dren shouts to the bartender.

"Hey, look!" Dren points upward, a smirk lining his face.

His cousins raise their faces before their jaws drop.

Women are dancing in silver birdcages, dressed in nothing but skimpy lingerie—if you can even call it that. Stringy, lacy, leathery. That's how I'd describe what's on their lithe bodies. The cages are suspended from the ceiling, close enough to the mob that you can almost touch it but still just a hair out of reach.

"Are we in heaven or hell?" He winks and takes back another shot. "You must be glad you came."

I am practically frozen to my spot, watching a woman with long red hair turn upside down, wrapping her legs around the bars and undulating to the music.

Christ!

"Only in America!" I pick up my drink, taking it back.

5

Talia

I TAKE out my electric cello, excited to get onstage. We've been playing here at Wild Orchid on Saturday nights for the last three months. The club is basically alcohol-tinged ruins, a black box of nothingness. But after ten o'clock, it's full of good-looking people with four bars lit in electric colors, women dancing in cages from above, and of course, the DJ with its accompaniment—two violins and a cello.

And while each of us takes our music studies incredibly seriously, it's awesome to occasionally break free from classical binds. Plus, we get paid a decent amount—in cash. It's the only money I make from legitimate means, and nothing feels better than taking my share at the end of the evening. Well, that's not necessarily true. I do love playing my cello. Electric, regular, whatever. Playing music is definitely better than money.

Leora and Ronna tune their violins, looking so similar in their short black dresses. Golden skin, light-blonde hair, and green eyes, they're typical Israeli model fare. I'm the oddball in our friendship. My dark hair is long, to my waist, and curly, and my eyes are large and brown. I know who I am and what I am, and therefore, I know what I need. And right now, that's money.

Jonny yells at someone backstage before stepping over to us. "Hey, ladies," he croons. The man can go from hard-ass boss to sweet-talker in seconds. "Tell me, why are you Israeli women so damn beautiful? I swear, someone pinch me!" He looks up at the sky, as though God would give him some answers.

What a loser.

"We are an immigrant-based society." Ronna glares at him, but he doesn't seem to get the hint. "It's in the mix, Jonny. The mix."

"Oh!" He laughs. "Of course. Makes sense. Anyway, ladies, you've got two minutes." He claps a few times, as though we were dogs, and struts off.

I look at my friends, shaking my head. I wouldn't mind kicking his ass, and I know they would love to join me. But I take a deep breath and keep myself in check. Being rational is something I've been trying to do lately despite the shitshow of my life. Finally making it into New York University's Steinhardt School for music has been incredible, and my dream of playing for the New York Philharmonic is closer than ever. But I've been rejected twice now for financial aid, and knowing that I have no choice but to continue on this path I'm on so I can keep studying makes me cringe.

I'm living the life of a woman I never thought I'd be. When I started up with Jet, I swore it wasn't me but just something I had to do *for now*. But seriously, how long can I lie to myself?

I don't fuck Jet for tuition, but it's what I do.

I'm not the kind of girl who stays in an apartment fully paid for by a married man, but it's where I sleep.

It's not really me or who I am, but for how long can I tell myself these things when it's literally how I live?

I feel like a fraud. But how else can I manage this or follow my dreams?

My parents kick ass, but they only have enough money for themselves. And while I could crash with them, I wouldn't feel right. They have a one-bedroom in Forest Hills, Queens, and they supported me as best they could for as long as they could.

After school, I took cello lessons at Diller-Quaile—the best music school in New York City, if not the country. It wasn't cheap, but they insisted I follow my dreams of music and found ways to get me there, on time, twice a week. They pushed me academically, so I could graduate at the top of my class in high school, helping me to study and focus. Kept me straight when other girls my age were partying. But most of all, they loved me.

I don't want them to think they failed me. And God forbid they knew how I pay for my life. I would die if they found out. They didn't immigrate to this country for me to be a loser. They came, so I could win.

And come hell or high water, I will find a way to play for the New York Philharmonic and make my dreams come true. And if that means I've got to be with a man to do it, so be it.

I look up to see my friends standing at the entrance of the stage. It's time.

We run on, the entire crowd wild and dancing. Drugs and alcohol fuel this party, and frankly, I love playing for people like this. They have no idea if I get the notes right or wrong. They aren't sitting in suits and gowns, waiting for a performance. They just want to feel the beat, and that's something the three of us can deliver. Playing classical is in my blood, but this is something freeing.

Those first electric notes have people screaming, and we play it loud. But while my friends run around the stage, dancing with their violins, I take my seat in the center of the stage with my cello. With my long hair loose at my side, I drag my bow back and forth, letting it play me like the beast it is. I don't need to sit when I play electric, but I prefer it.

With my eyes closed, it's nothing but adrenaline playing this instrument. I hear the violins and the DJ and move with them, rocking out. When we get in sync like this, it reminds me of all the reasons why I love music as much as I do. The heat rushes through my veins, and I swear I feel like one of Pavlov's dogs, salivating to the music before it's even had a chance to filter through the audience because I *know* what's to come.

Still, every time we play, it's a different adventure. Be it clubs downtown or posh weddings at The Plaza Hotel. Last summer, the three of us were flown to the desert in Israel to play for an uber-wealthy kid's bat mitzvah.

Playing cello is something I simply have to do. It's not technically a compulsion, but it's become so much a part of the fabric of who I am that without it, I feel like I would die. Unfortunately though, it's not free.

But I found a way to pay.

On your back, my conscience reminds me.

Sweat pours down my face, but I force my mind to settle back into the music.

Suddenly, I feel something—eyes on my body. I'm used to the gawking of the crowd, but somehow, this feels more intense. I open my eyes and continue playing, searching for the stare that I would bet is somewhere in the crowd. My bow is on automatic now, my shoulder and elbow pulling and pushing with the beat.

A few fans focus on our playing. A boy with hoops through his nose. Two girls completely tatted up from their wrists to their shoulders, glasses of alcohol filled to the brim. A clusters of well-dressed men, laughing. But the stare isn't coming from them.

There is a man leaning against the bar, his stare trained on me. I swallow hard, playing, but somehow, it's as though the music is now in the background. Our gazes lock, and recognition passes between us, like I've seen him before. But of course, I haven't. He's unbelievably handsome. Chiseled jaw and cheekbones. Jet-black hair. And even in the bright lights, I can tell his eyes are a lighter color. He's also tall—really, really tall. A head above most of the others. Wide shoulders.

I want to hear his voice. *Is it as sexy as he is? I wonder if he's single.*

Someone bumps into him, and they seem to have words. The other guy scurries away, and I try not to laugh.

He looks back up at me, smiling, and I smile back.

Hi, he mouths.

My blush reaches the roots of my hair as sweat beads at my temples. I should ignore him, like I do all of the random guys who party here, but I don't want to. I've never met a man who electrified me like this with just one look.

God, he's hot.

A bit of laughter from the DJ.

My heart leaps as the buzz from my instrument centers in my core.

The guy standing next to him taps his shoulder, and he turns his head. They talk, and he is focused. My man nods his head, like he understands something. Thinking maybe. He takes out his phone, reading. In a blink, they walk away.

As I play, I twist my chair around to see where he's going. This is totally out of character for me, but frankly, who even cares? I've got the music going, and I'm not stopping. But I also want to see him for as long as I can. I drop my bow onto the ground, plucking my strings to the beat to give me more room to move.

The men push through the crowd, and I turn stage left, following his form with my eyes.

When I see Jet greet them in the VIP section, my fingers falter.

He's Albanian, and from the looks of it, he runs with the Mafia Shqiptare.

Dread fills my stomach, but I play on.

6

Leo

THE SONG CHANGES to a new techno beat. And the woman playing the cello has me mesmerized. Her instrument isn't delicate, like the violins. It's large, and it sits between her legs like a piece of bark. And while the violinists are sexy in their short black skirts, flirting with the crowd and dancing with their instruments, she barely smiles.

The instrument forces an outline of her voluptuous body in the gold lamé dress. Heavy breasts and deep curves carve into her hips. She's demanding with her bow, taking it seriously despite the upbeat party music. No flirtation with the audience but focused on playing. In contrast to the toughness of her vibe, her fingers are so delicate. Flying over the strings, up and down they go. She looks tiny, sitting there in that seat, with a head full of curly, dark hair draping the cello. So sexy that it almost hurts.

"They're talented, right?" Dren asks.

"The girls are good. Very, very good."

"They play here often, I think. I've always wanted to meet them, but they jet offstage so quickly."

"How hard could they be to track? Maybe the bouncer knows them?"

We fall back into a friendly quiet, taking in the amazing performance.

The cellist's eyes finally open as she skims the crowed. But then, she spots me. Eyes widening, as though she likes what she sees. Fuck, she's gorgeous. And crazy talented, too.

Almost everyone else is too fucked up to notice, but she is a real deal musician.

Someone knocks into me. I turn around, annoyed. The kid who hit me goes slack-jawed, knowing he bumped into the wrong guy. His white shirt is soaked with sweat.

"I, uh, I'm, uh, sorry." He tries to walk backward, tripping over someone else.

Dren laughs out loud. "That kid almost shit himself. Dude, you need another drink to relax. Damn."

I roll up my sleeves, the tats on my forearms reminding me of who I am and what I stand for. The red Albanian eagle represents bravery, strength, valor, and of course, bloodshed. On my shoulder is a special piece done by a famous tattoo artist who came to New York City from Hungary. Getting an appointment with him was impossible, but Nico made it happen. It's a square of deep and dark water with a hand pushing out, holding up five fingers. It's meant to show that I'm unsinkable. A moon looms above because even in the darkest night, I refuse to fall. He also did another piece for me on my forearm—of an eye.

The song changes, shaking me out of my reverie. The cellist catches my eye again, and we lock.

Before I can think, my mouth opens. *Hi.*

Her eyes are like large honey-brown almonds, too big for her face. But so expressive. So beautiful.

She smiles at me, full lips widening to show gorgeous straight white teeth. Her eyes? They twinkle. Maybe it's the lights shining down on her, but it's also *her*. Her skin is tan and looks like it's covered in diamonds from the light. She's boring a hole into my chest with her smile. I've seen her before, but I couldn't have.

Dren yells in my ear, "You know, the crew is here tonight also. Do you think we should introduce my cousins to them?"

"Yeah, whatever. Sure."

Dren hits my back, as if to wake me up. "The cello player, huh?"

I look at him from the corner of my eye. "Maybe."

"Well, I'm going to bring the guys to meet Nico. I have a feeling they could be of use to us; plus, they're cool. Very trustworthy."

My phone buzzes from my back pocket, and I take a look.

Nico: Got some news for you. Come to VIP now.

As we walk away from the bar, I see the cellist from the side of my eye. I can tell that her darkly lit doe eyes are still trained on me, like she's ready to chase me down. I walk away quickly, wanting her out of my sight.

I can't get involved in anyone so intense. Fun with women is one thing, but this woman is much more than that—I can just feel it. I'm not interested in meeting any woman outside of the bedroom. Not until I ruin my brother's and my mother's lives. Until I accomplish these things, I will not move forward.

We push through the crowd again, but this time, we walk into the VIP section. Jet immediately greets us. We hug, and I spot Darius standing alone in the corner with a menacing face, wearing a dark suit. When he raises his hand to me, I walk to him. A glass of tequila sits in his hand, but I doubt he's actually drinking it. As Nico's guard, he barely leaves his side. He grew up in the Mumbai slums and ran a world-famous brothel, so it's hard to imagine how he wound up protecting Nico. But as I've since learned, the Albanian Mafia is an enterprise whose business knows no borders.

"Nico is waiting for you, brother." Darius nods toward where Nico sits. "Everything cool?"

"Yeah, man. It's all good."

Nico is relaxed in the corner, flanked by two men. When he sees me walking to him, they all stand to greet me.

"Leo, I've got some big news," he tells me in Albanian, shaking my hand.

"Yes?" I reply in our mother tongue.

"The time has finally come for you to go back to Kosovo. Some business for the shqipe, some personal work for you. Are you still game?" He smirks, knowing the answer.

I want to reply, but I can't. That's how caught off guard I am. I've been waiting for this moment for so long. My twin flashes in front of my face, and the fire in my heart rages. I want to crush him.

He chuckles darkly, scruff lining his jaw. He taps my back with a heavy hand. "Don't worry. I know you've been dreaming of this day for a while. But you've shown your loyalty and your strength. You've been a great asset to the crew, and I'm glad to help you with your revenge."

A compliment from Nico is so rare.

I lift my face to his and nod. "Thank you."

"There is just one thing. You still have no citizenship, and so traveling out of the country will be difficult."

"That's right," I agree.

"I have a connection in the immigration department. I will maneuver a few things for the sake of fixing the timing, backdating documents, but we have to prove that you've been married to an American."

"Wait. Married?" I exclaim.

"Yes. It's in name only, although you'll have to live with her for a few months and take photos to prove your marriage. I'll make sure to get you an interview within a few months. Once you get your US passport, you can get back to Kosovo."

I nod, exhaling. I can manage this. "Okay. I'll do whatever it takes."

"You'll meet her next week. I'm going to throw an anniversary party for the two of you. Let's begin the paper trail. Try to get out with her as much as possible and don't forget to take photos. The officer conducting your interview will want to see proof of your relationship."

"Do you know her?" I pull out a pack of cigarettes from my pocket and light one up.

"Well enough. She's beautiful and smart. It won't be difficult, trust me." He taps my back and moves away as his wife, Elira, struts toward him. They embrace, kissing so deeply.

I swallow hard. *Fuck love.*

I walk away, feeling angrier than I should. The cigarette drops from my lips onto the carpet below. I don't bother picking it up. I should be relieved that my revenge is so close, but I hate the fact that my mother and brother even put me into this mess in the first place. I resent them for fucking me over and forcing me out of my life.

My blood? It boils. The fact that they sit at home, smiling and laughing, happy, thinking that they got rid of me, makes me sick. I plan on getting them back. Limb by fucking limb.

I could hang out here and get drunk with the guys, but I don't feel like talking.

I'm not even sure where to go, but I keep on moving forward, one foot in front of the other. I put another cigarette in my mouth, needing the nicotine, until I find myself in what looks like the back of the club or maybe behind the stage. It's quiet with some waitstaff hanging out, probably on their break. An exit door is illuminated, and I walk through it. The world around me is dim.

I picture Daisy with Albi, laughing together. They're in my bed. Sweat dripping from her naked body onto the white sheets. Her mouth opened wide, moaning.

I find myself in a seedy, dark alley. My stomach rolls.

"No loitering!"

I lift my face, searching for the sharp sound. It's dark all around me.

"Did you hear me, dickwad? Get the fuck out of here. It's for employees only out here."

"What?" I step away from the wall, throwing the cigarette from my mouth onto the floor. *Who the fuck is trying to give me shit right now?*

Suddenly, light filters through. I recognize her right away with her curly, long hair and huge brown eyes. Her cell phone is raised, flashlight on. It's the cellist. And she seems to recognize me too. We're both quiet.

"Oh, uh, yeah." She flips her hair to the side, laughing awkwardly. "Well, we can't have patrons hanging out here. People sometimes come to fuck or do drugs, and then the cops come and give the owner a ticket. It's also bad for me because I use this exit to go home, and if there are shady characters here, it can be dangerous for me."

I blink, listening to her jabber. Her voice is strong and slightly husky. A light accent, although I have no idea where it could be from.

She looks me up and down, my silence obviously confusing her. "Are you high? And did you follow me out here?"

"Follow you?"

"Yeah, follow me. That isn't cool."

I don't reply, but I pull out the pack of cigarettes from my back pocket and slide another one between my lips. My arteries are short-circuiting. I need something to soften the blood flow. As I light up, she watches me intently.

I exhale, wanting to tell her that I am dangerous. That I'm close to getting my revenge and I need to consider a plan. That all of my anger is bubbling to the surface now that I'm near the finish line. I take deep inhales, trying to calm down.

This girl has nothing to do with me. A beautiful woman. A cello player.

And suddenly, it dawns on me: *Why does she get to live such a fucking carefree life while I'm stuck in this bullshit?*

I eye her enormous instrument. "Is it fun to play?"

"Yeah. It's amazing actually. I've been playing since I was seven."

"Do you study?"

"Of course I do." She haughtily raises her chin. "I play at NYU."

I repeat, "You play at NYU?"

Holy shit, but my anger just ratcheted up a notch. I look at her shoes. They look expensive. Her dress doesn't look cheap either. The shine in her hair. Her clear eyes. She's living the great life—a life I could have been living had my family not sabotaged me.

I shake my head, pointing my finger at her. "You know what? You're a stuck-up bitch."

She squints her eyes, like she can't believe my words. "What?"

"What?" I mimic in a high-pitched voice. "Get the fuck out of my face. NYU must be nice, huh? I'm sure you've got a perfect family paying for your lessons and classes. They must be so proud. Their lovely daughter following her dreams." Sarcasm drips from my mouth, and frankly, it feels good. "Well, fuck your dreams."

"Who do you think you are?"

She stomps a proud foot, and I realize how tiny she must actually be. I would guess she is slightly over a meter and a half. I could crush her if I wanted to. And, God, do I want to.

"Who am I?" I laugh darkly, stepping closer to her. "I'm a man with nothing left to fucking lose!" I scream into the night, opening my arms. A light rain decides to fall from the sky. I look down at her, more menacing than I ever thought to be capable of. "I'm a man who might kill you if you don't get the fuck away."

She laughs up in my face, like I'm nothing more than a loser in her wake. "Kill me? Yeah, right. Well, I won't disagree with the fact that you look like you've got nothing left to lose." She looks me up and down, licking her sexy-as-fuck lips as she dismisses me.

She swings her cello, which is almost as large as she is, over her back and walks away into the summer night like she's stronger than Hercules and more beautiful than any goddess. And maybe she is.

7

Talia

THE CAR JOLTS to fifty miles per hour as the Aston Martin hits a bump, the bottom of the car scraping against the street like nails on a chalkboard.

"Fuck!" Jet screams, pressing on the gas harder and with more purpose.

I adjust my white suede hat, crossing and then uncrossing my bare legs. Another day, another temper tantrum. Last week, it was the waiter at a hot new restaurant, Cathédrale, who didn't bring our dinner fast enough. The week before that, it was the kid on the street who told him to stop smoking.

"All these fucking taxes we pay in New York City, and they can't fix the damn road? We need to relocate to Florida. Or Texas maybe."

"It was a speed bump."

"Yeah, and?"

"That's not a broken road. It's meant to slow you down."

"You know, you've got an answer for everything."

"True."

He shakes his head. "Sometimes, it's hot. Other times, it's annoying as fuck. You're a know-it-all."

"Yeah, I've heard that before."

He pulls over abruptly on 95th Street and Fifth Avenue, angrily putting the car in park. "Why can't I have the last word?"

"Okay, have it then."

He mutters to Allah, looking up at the cloudless blue sky. I smile. Inwardly. I love pissing him off like this. But at the same time, I don't have a death wish. Dating a man in the Albanian Mafia—or the Mafia Shqiptare, as they call it—has its benefits. On the other hand, they do some really bad shit. I have to remind myself often that the guy I'm with has a dark side. A really, really dark side. Under normal circumstances, with a normal person, it isn't easy for me to remember when to shut up. But with him, I have to try. Well, sometimes.

He twists his body to the side, putting his finger in my face. "I'm going to speak, and you are not going to reply."

I widen my eyes sweetly. "Should I verbally accept, or do you want me silent?"

Smacking the wheel, he yells, "Why do I put up with you?"

I gently lick the corner of my lips and raise a brow. We both know why he puts up with me, but the question is whether or not he wants me to spell it out. I click my tongue, and he stays quiet, seemingly waiting for a reply. I smile, feeling my heart rate pick up. I never thought of myself as an actress, but I'd be lying if I said it didn't come naturally to me. I tilt my head to the side, exuding sex from the way I angle my body toward his and graze his thigh with my nails.

"Your wife is too dutiful in her black hijab. Too obsessed with your kids. And you married her too young and for the sake of your families' wishes. You're with me for fun. For sex. To converse. To open your heart as an equal and not to a wife who is essentially your servant. Plus, I turn a blind eye to all the crazy shit you do for work."

His eyes positively boil.

I unbuckle my belt, straddling him in the front seat. I can feel the outline of his cock, slightly hard. "You put up with me because we talk and fight and fuck. And I play music, which you love. And in return, you take care of me, so I can follow my dreams. Not a bad bargain for either of us, huh, Jetmir?"

He grunts. "We're going by full names now?"

I lick the side of his neck, tasting a light sheen of salty sweat. "Jet, Jetmir—what's the difference?"

"Talia Mizrahi, let's get to East Hampton. I want to hear you play that cello. Preferably naked."

I sit back in my seat, pressing my lips together as I re-buckle my belt. Much more calmly now, he pulls out and gets onto the highway.

"So tough. Tougher than half the men I know. You sure you don't want to join the shqipe?" He laughs. "On my life, Nico and Darius would make an exception for you. They basically said as much a few weeks ago."

This time, I don't reply. Because he's right. I was born and raised tough. It's in my blood—or maybe even deeper than that. My DNA. I work and live and demand respect because if I don't demand it, I will never get it. Sometimes, people say I'm stuck up, but that isn't true. I simply know my worth and refuse to settle for less. I also lack the fear gene. Times when others would be scared to death, I don't cower.

My grandmother is the same way. She lived through the Holocaust and was transported to four concentration camps, and she managed to escape death over nine times. She always tells me that you have to have a strong mind and heart to survive life. It's not about the strongest body, but the strongest will to live. She is now 101 years old, and still yells at the butcher if the meat isn't fresh. How's that for strength?

My great-uncle Meyer, who lives in the apartment above my parents, managed to come to America before World War II, but he fought on the Bronx streets for petty cash and ran with the Jewish underworld, bootlegging booze, selling slot machines, and running gambling rings.

You see? I'm made from tough stuff.

A few hours later, we make it from New York City to the Hamptons. My ass feels broken from sitting for so long in such a low car, but the beautiful weather and quiet, tree-lined house make it worth it.

Jet's home is a five-bedroom Hampton shingle style on Meadow Lane. I'm not even sure his actual family knows about this place. I have no idea where he tells his kids and wife he is every weekend, but frankly, it's not my problem. At least, I tell myself that.

Nico and Darius stay together at Nico's house down the street on the beach, and a few of the other guys rent in the area too. It's not just nice here. It's *insanely* nice. I've met Nico and Darius more than a few times, but I've never met anyone else in the crew. Jet has never requested it of me, and I prefer it.

Nico's house is easily worth fifty million dollars with full glass paneling facing the ocean and a backyard to rival the best hotels in the world. I'm talking infinity pool with a built-in hot tub and a magnificent waterfall on the edge of the pool that reaches a lower level, featuring a firepit. And get this: the entire house faces the beach. True, at first, I was scared of this life. But for the record, it's also true that anyone can get used to anything.

Jet opens the front door of his house, and everything is crisp, clean, and ready. The shqipe has a personal assistant who sets up all of their homes prior to their arrival. The Sub-Zero fridge is stocked, the wine is already chilled in the cooler, and reservations have been made for lunches and dinners all weekend long. I know that Jet's wife would faint if she knew he drank alcohol, as it's not allowed in Islam. But like I said before, he's with me to live free.

The housekeeper sets our suitcases in his bedroom, and I place my cello in the corner along with my new white Balenciaga bag. I don't like him spoiling me too much, but as he always says, he likes me to look taken care of. If I don't look hooked up, it would make him feel like he was being cheap with me. Members of the shqipe are known to keep their women well—all of them, from wives to girl-friends to casual hookers. For the record, I'm a girlfriend and not a casual hooker.

I touch my cello case, itching to play. But as usual, we have to eat first. Jet becomes an asshole when he's hungry, and I don't feel like dealing with that.

Albanian food is not so different from what I'm used to, and I'm thankful for that. Lots of fruits and vegetables. Cheese. Crispy, warm bread. His housekeeper pours us ice water with lemon in one glass and cold white wine in the other. I thank her graciously. Like I said, I'm not a bitch.

He taps my thigh, and I lift my foot and place it over his legs. When we're together, he loves to touch me. It's relatively annoying, but either way, I've got to pay. We spend the next hour eating and drinking and laughing, our conversation sprinkled with a little debate about women in the workforce. He gets annoyed with my big mouth, but sometimes, like now, he loves how much I know. And I like to believe that I'm making a dent in his *man strong, woman weak* mentality he was born with.

A FEW HOURS LATER, he's sated and sleeping. It's not that Jet is bad to me, but he and I have nothing more than an understanding. Does he care for me? Sure. And I guess I care enough about him to make this arrangement work. But holding my cello, I remind myself why I'm really here and what it's for. I block him out, imagine an audience, and focus on my breaths.

Closing my eyes, I play. It doesn't take long for the blurry audience to turn into a man of one. The man from the club. His dark hair. Those light eyes. The angles of his face. He was the best-looking asshole I'd ever met, even hotter than Nico and Darius, which is saying something.

My grandma reminding me that I should find a nice doctor barges into my head. I smile, but I am who I am. And I've never been partial to nice guys.

Finally, I lose myself to Bach's music and play for hours.

The next morning, Jet wakes up and gets to his usual Hampton weekend routine of a hot coffee with two sugars and then a four-mile jog. I don't mind it for two reasons. One, it keeps him in decent shape. I wouldn't say he's hot by any means, but he's handsome in a *successful fifty-something who still has his hair and exercises regularly* kind of way. The other reason is, I get to have a peaceful morning to myself.

When he gets back, he always showers and then wants to read a paper over breakfast, cooked by the chef. I'm sitting at the outdoor dining table, enjoying the view of the infinity pool and the Long Island Sound while I drink my latte. I smile, taking a bite of my shak-shuka and dipping the crust of the crispy ciabatta bread inside, gathering the cooked toJetoes. It's an Israeli egg dish that's off-the-charts good. Jet must have requested the chef make it for me.

You see? He isn't so bad.

I'm off from school this summer. I could have found a job for the next three months, but the same exact thought I had about the last few summers enters my head. Technically, this is a job. Being Jet's girlfriend in the summer cannot coexist with an actual nine-to-five because he needs me in the Hamptons every single weekend. What kind of work could I get that's so flexible that I could take off Fridays and return late on Mondays? Not least, Jet covers my entire tuition, books, room and board. And extras for food and clothes. Spending cash for whatever else I want. There is literally no other job on earth that could take care of me like this.

I stand up, stretching from side to side. I adjust my white bikini and run inside to bring out my notebook and cello. I've been composing a lot in the last year, and my new song has been evolving very nicely.

Before I can take out my sharpened pencil from its case, Jet comes running outside. He's sweating but not in a good *I just worked out* way. To the contrary, he looks freaked out.

Worriedly, I ask, "What's wrong?"

He's silent, looking at me, sweat dripping off his forehead and soaking his white shirt. Under normal circumstances, his face would make anyone nervous. But since he's part of the dirtiest Mafia of this century, bad can take on a whole new meaning.

"Talia ..." His voice trails off, eyes pleading.

"Come, sit down." I put my arm on his back, bringing him to my chair. "Min-Sun!" I call out to Jet's housekeeper. "Bring Mr. Prifti a glass of ice water. Now."

I rub his back, trying to settle him. A full-body shake takes over him.

"Tal"—he clears his throat—"I have something to tell you. And I have to first say, I am sorry we are having this conversation. You were my solace. I have my family, who I care for deeply but have limited in common with. And I have the shqipe, to whom my life is eternally bound. I know I don't do good things. But with you, I had normal. You are beautiful. Hard but kind. Sexy but very strong. But unfortunately for you, your good qualities have gotten you noticed ... and I know it must be my fault. I bragged about you. I joked about your toughness. I brought you around to meet Nico and Darius, and they saw your virtues with their own eyes."

"Just spit it out, Jet. What is it?"

"There is a man in the shqipe. He's my brother in this world, and I would kill for him, but I would be lying if I told you he was gentle. He came here from Kosovo with a student visa, but through no fault of his own, he became unable to study. Regardless, he has months left before he will technically be illegal. Nico needs him to leave America for a job. But like I said, citizenship."

"I'm not following."

Min-Sun brings the ice water and asks if he'd like breakfast served.

"Not yet," I reply. "I'll call you when he's ready."

"Yes, ma'am." She walks away with her head bowed.

"Talia, they want you to marry him."

"What?"

"Yes. You heard me."

"Why me?"

"Since you've been with me, you've been quasi part of the life. An inside outsider, so to speak. You don't know anyone in the crew, but you've met the boss and Darius. You are also strong. Competent.

Smart. The shqipe knows you're capable, Talia. They know you can keep secrets. And they think you'd be a good fit as a wife. For the family, you're a win."

"I'm not even Albanian! I didn't start this up with you to become a mobster's wife!"

"But you're American. And in this case, that is much, much better than being Albanian. And I understand you never intended on marriage, and frankly, that's one of the reasons I knew you'd be good for me. Because you'd never ask me to choose. But Allah has plans for you that are greater than this relationship."

I clench my teeth, wanting to turn the table upside down. "And what if I refuse?"

He looks at me pointedly. "Refuse? Refuse the shqipe?" He shakes his head, laughing. "They could kill you, you know. They could ask me to do it. And I would."

We're quiet for a few minutes, my mind racing. *How am I going to get myself out of this?*

"There's more," he adds. "Nico fixed the paperwork so that you have technically been married for three years."

"Three years?" I shout. "How could he do that? I didn't sign any marriage certificate."

He laughs, like my comment is naïve. "Nico handled it. Next comes the interview, where you must prove your marriage. If you pass it, he'll get his citizenship."

"Well, I want more than just my life spared for doing this." I blink, shocking even myself at my insinuation. I cross my arms, everything both clear and unclear. Clear is the fact that I have to marry this man. Unclear is what will happen after the fact and what I can get in the meantime.

"You want money?"

"Maybe. No. Yes. Yes, I want money. If I'm becoming business, then tell Nico to put cash on the deal, so I can finish my education. I have a dream to play music, and no part-time job is going to cover my tuition. I-I can't just flush it down the toilet and become a wife. I need security for my future."

"Nico already offered a sum. Five million. And he'll pay you on the books, if you want. He plans to say he commissioned you to do a piece of music for him. Priceless, eh? But if you prefer cash, we can find a way to make that happen. Nico is honorable, and if he says he will pay you, he will pay you. You can finish school. Join the New York Philharmonic. Whatever you want."

"I have to think about this." I turn my face away, half of me wanting to cry, the other half wanting to scream.

Who the hell did I think I was, gallivanting with a member of the Mafia and thinking there would be no repercussions? Of course I'd get burned. But pulled into their fold? On my life, I never thought this was a possibility. And the few times I hung out with Nico and Darius, I figured it was just casual. I didn't realize they were sizing me up.

"I want nothing to do with anything outright illegal. I refuse. I have a life to live. And I'm divorcing this guy the moment I can."

He shakes his head again. "Divorce? From a member? Don't even say that out loud, Talia. The only way out is a body bag. Likely, you'll know too much."

"Is that what they said?"

"No. But it's what I know."

"So, this is my entire life? How about children? How about love?"

He stands up. "Consider our relationship terminated, Talia. You're a smart girl. If you think hard enough, you'll realize that you already know all of the answers. Regardless, Nico wants to have a party for the two of you tonight. An anniversary party. I hope you brought something nice to wear. Otherwise, treat yourself to a morning of shopping. Call the masseuse and get a massage. I'll have a driver here at four o'clock to take you to the Bronx. Oh, and wear white. Black is for funerals."

He walks away, and I'm left in a fog.

8

Leo

JOINING the shqipe was a natural progression. I realize they're bad, but they aren't bad in their day-to-day lives. Wives, girlfriends, and kids surround them. Well, most of them. Others of us live to kill.

Lots of football, too, which I didn't remember how much I'd missed it until I started playing again.

We have some legitimate businesses and some black market. And while our hands are in all underground trades, Nico runs everything like a Fortune 500 CEO. It all feels strangely decent with a seven-floor office on Park Avenue and at least two secretaries on each floor.

I welcomed this life with open arms. Because there is nothing on this earth I want more than to burn down my brother's business and to kill him too.

As far as the American girl is concerned, I'm not worried. I tried love once before, and I'll never do that to myself again. A real marriage will never be in my cards. Marrying her for citizenship is nothing short of a technicality.

She'll have to deal with the fact that I'm still going to sleep with whatever woman I choose. They mean nothing to me, but I'm a man with needs.

When I first arrived in America, I was tormented over Daisy and refused to spare any woman here in New York City a second glance. But once I gave in and opened up my body and a little bit of my time, they all flocked, wanting more and more of me.

I met Anna, and she was good in bed. Unfortunately, she moaned too loud and woke the neighbors. Dark haired Cindy came to my apartment four or maybe five times, and we had fun until she wanted to stay over. I hated the way her perfume smelled on my pillow. Karina was sexy, but she barely said a word during sex, and it made me feel like I was fucking a Barbie doll. Allison had a gorgeous face but asked me to meet her parents after the second night we spent together.

My weekends are now parades of nameless, faceless women. Models and aspiring actresses. Bartenders. I need them and want them all, but I can't stand them for more than a few nights. And somehow—and for reasons I can't understand—they all want me.

Each and every woman I meet, I find myself looking for Daisy in them. Or at least, what I thought was within Daisy. Her innocence, which none of them have.

I put on my tie as well as I can without a mirror. As fucked up as this might be for the American girl, arranged marriages are not uncommon in Kosovo. If it's good for the shqipe, it's good enough for me.

Veton comes into the back of the restaurant, clapping my shoulder. "Ready to meet your wife?"

"Sure I am."

Veton has nothing to do with the shqipe, but I told him to come tonight. It's my anniversary party after all, and he was my first real friend here in America.

We're in the back of an Albanian restaurant in the Bronx—Teuta Qebaptore—which everyone loves. It's casual, and the owner bends over backward for anything the shqipe needs. They shut down the restaurant tonight for us and put long buffet tables around the perimeter. I hope they're serving meat.

He raises his brows and shakes his head, pointing to my eye. "What the fuck happened to you?"

"I like the fights. Always have. I thought you'd be used to seeing me like this by now."

And that might be the truest thing about me. I smile fondly at the memories of all the scuffs I got into—on and off the football field.

My father taught me how to fight at a young age, and I like using my skills. Here in New York, I play around at some fight clubs. Some of the guys in the shqipe used to try to fight me, but it became clear early on that I always won.

He frowns. "And this is how your woman is going to see you? For the first time?"

"She'd better get used to it."

"You think you'll like her?" he presses, looking at me intently.

"Why not? I'm sure she's fine."

"Well, why the fuck do you think she's doing this?" He takes a seat on the couch as I struggle with my tie.

I shrug. "Nico told me he found her. She's trustworthy and smart. She's also a musician, and he claims she's beautiful. He didn't seem to be too worried."

"What if she's hideous—to you?"

"Nah. I'm sure she's pretty enough. Have you seen Elira? Nico has good taste."

"And you're just going to go along with this marriage? Without at least knowing her for a minute first?"

"Why not? I'm sure it'll be easy, as we both know the score. People get married for citizenship all the time. And she's getting paid for this. She'll be fine. I'll be fine. Nico fixed the papers, so it looks like we've already been married for three years. Now, all we have to do is pass the interview, and I'm done."

He looks at me like I'm crazy.

"Once I get my revenge, I'll leave her."

He shakes his head. "Your funeral."

"My nothing. She's just a woman I have to marry to become an American. People do it all the damn time. We'll be roommates. And the only person's funeral that's coming from this is my brother's and mother's. I would marry a dog if it brought me back to Kosovo to kill them."

I clench my fists, wishing I could press fast-forward. I need this girl to help me pass the interview, and I hope it's easy. The quicker I can get back to Kosovo, the quicker I can ruin my brother's life by ending it. The girl is nothing but a simple pawn.

"Well, I came in to tell you that your wife—I mean, roommate— has arrived." He stands up and adjusts my tie. "Try to smile when you meet her. Don't want to look too scary."

"Like this?" I give him a goofy grin, and he laughs, trying to hit the back of my head. I duck so his hand hits my hair before we walk out together.

9

Talia

THE WEATHER IS TOO BEAUTIFUL, considering the shitstorm coming my way.

I thought about calling my parents earlier, but thankfully, I stopped myself. I will meet him first, and then, depending on how he is, I'll work out a story. Even the truth might do. I can tell them that I married an Albanian guy as a favor to a friend because he needs citizenship and my schooling will be paid for in return. Not too bad of a half-lie, right?

I spent the afternoon playing my cello on the outdoor porch. I didn't shop, I didn't get a massage, and I didn't swim either. I played song after song, and I dug deep inside myself. It came to me quickly, but there is simply nothing to be done but to marry this guy. Maybe I can convince Nico to let me divorce him when he gets his citizenship. I'll even forgo the money if it means I can gain my freedom. I'll work a regular job at night. I'll push for the scholarship. Five million dollars is a lot, and maybe if Nico trusts me enough to keep my mouth shut, he'll let me go, so he can keep that money.

I step out of the black Escalade and politely thank the driver that Jet hired to bring me here. I hear the trunk open, and I walk around the car to the back, taking out my things. A wrong wind whines, but I continue my way forward.

Walking into the restaurant all alone, I wear a casual, long white LoveShackFancy dress that I thought I'd be wearing to a beach party at The Surf Lodge tonight. It isn't the fanciest, but I guess it'll do. I have my cello and my bag, glad that I have these items to hold.

The restaurant is full of people, but I barely notice a thing as my thoughts pick up their pace.

What if I can't ever get out of this marriage?

I spot Jet in the corner, wearing a stiff white button-down shirt and slacks. I smile and wave at him, expecting him to say hello. But he doesn't. He looks through me. It's like he has no clue who I am.

I look around the rest of the crowd, none of whom I know, and resist the urge to bail. All the time Jet and I were together, I was never introduced to his friends outside of Nico and Darius. I'm tough, but I do have a heart. I find my way to the coat check in the corner and ask them to hold my things. They take it graciously and hand me a ticket.

I find Jet again, willing him to look at me. I have never wanted his attention more than I do now. No, it's not love. But at least I know him.

What if this new guy is psycho? What if he recently left an insane asylum and the shqipe needs him to do their dirty work? My heart feels like it's going to explode. *What the hell have I gotten myself into?*

I notice a shift in the vibe of the room. A very tall guy in a navy suit has just walked in. His head is turned as he says hello to everyone, but his hair is dark, and his back is wide. The men and the women stand up, congratulating him and clapping his back. Someone makes a joke, and he seems to be laughing. Two girls cling to either side of him, both with long black hair. He seemingly ignores them, continuing his hellos, but they don't get the obvious hint.

Could it be him? I have to assume it is. I stare, frozen to the spot. I wish I had someone with me. I would have called my best friend, Rachel, but everything happened too fast. I would have even brought the violinists, Ronna and Leora. Anyone to anchor me.

A tear threatens to fall down my face. And that's the moment he turns to me.

I gasp, and his jaw drops.

It's him.

Dark hair slicked back but shaved close on the sides. Blue eyes, almost electric. That cut jaw. Those defined cheekbones. He has a bit of a tan, better than the ghost look he was sporting the last time I saw him in the alley. Something else he has now that he didn't have before? A bruise around his eye, like he was recently in a fight. Even his lips are puffy. It makes him look like a thug.

I shiver. God, he is so unbelievably hot. Too bad that behind that perfect exterior is a fucking asshole.

A man stands next to him, looking nervous. He doesn't belong, but he's here. But whatever. Who cares about that idiot? My husband is the dickhead from the alley! If my big mouth ever got me in trouble before, it's nothing compared to the grave I've just dug myself into now. I yelled at him. I called him a loser. He threatened to kill me. And now, I'm his wife!

My stomach twists as something that feels a lot like shame settles in my bloodstream. *Does he know about my relationship with Jet? Do all of them know?* I swallow hard, unable to move my legs even though I want to run. I realize I dated him for money, but I'm not a whore. *Does he intend to treat me like one?*

I finally build the strength to look up again. His eyes positively burn. He looks me up and down like I'm the devil in a white dress, and it infuriates me. *How dare he!* I'm doing him a fucking favor. He should be thanking me. Maybe getting on his knees and apologizing. Sure, I was with his "brother." But I didn't have to do this. I could have picked death, right?

Nico claps a few times, and everyone turns to face him. The room goes silent. Who would have the balls to speak over Nico, the boss of the Albanian Mafia, and the most powerful man in Manhattan? Not me.

A cameraman runs up out of nowhere, taking photos from so many angles. I shut my eyes, breathing deeply. I'm sure we'll need these photos to prove our marriage. Nothing here has been done by accident.

Nico's wife, Elira, is by his side. She has never given me much thought before when I was with Jet, but now, she's smiling at me like I'm her newfound best friend. She's tall with long black hair and green eyes, and she's wearing a silver slip dress.

Nico, as usual, is a wolf in sheep's clothing. He's incredibly good-looking, but I know better than anyone that beneath that Armani suit is a killer. He'd snap my neck if he needed to. Any of the men here would. I grew up with some rough sorts, but the shqipe is a beast of its own.

"I want to welcome everyone to the three-year anniversary party of Leo and Talia."

My gaze darts around the room to find a cameraman trained on Nico.

"May their happiness continue to be a blessing to all of us." He raises a champagne glass just as the waiter hands me one of my own.

"To Talia and Leo!" the group replies, all smiles.

A few more flashes go off, and Leo moves next to me, draping a heavy arm around my back. His touch is searing, and my entire body tightens like a bowstring. My smile is so forced that it hurts. I remind myself over and over again that this is an act. It's all just documentation for his citizenship. My words prove to be true because when the camera guy moves away, Leo walks away from me. Not even a hello. Not even a *nice to meet you*—again.

When he gets to the other side of the room, I stare at him, and his eyes lock on mine. I raise my chin and straighten my back. He thinks he can scare me with that handsome but cruel snarl? He has no idea who he is dealing with.

Someone whispers something in his ear, and he clenches his jaw.

Slowly, like a panther going for the kill, he walks back over to me.

The room seems to watch with bated breath. I swallow hard as we stand toe to toe, his shiny loafers to my open-toe platform sandals. He is easily twice my size. I try to hold my breath, not wanting to take him in. He smells so good; it's disgusting.

His lip twitches. "So, you're the one, eh?"

"Yes. I'm the stuck-up bitch who plays the cello. Isn't that what you called me?" I smile widely, and his eyes turn a deep midnight blue.

Under his breath, he tells me, "They must have really threatened you good to get you here today. I pegged you for many things when we met, and it seems I was right on all accounts." He looks me up and down like I'm scum.

I finish the champagne, needing all the strength I can get. "The threat of death *and* money. That's what it took to get me here. But if I had known it was you, no money in the world would have brought me here." I'm being mean, and I know I am. But this whole thing is just too fucked up.

A guy struts over to us, wrapping his arm around Leo's shoulder. "You got a good one, Talia. Welcome to the family." He puts his thick hand out to me. "I'm Dren."

I take in the man before me, who looks more like beef than human. "Nice to meet you." My voice is measured, and I refuse to take his hand. I don't want to give any of these assholes even one iota of my energy.

I can tell I've pissed the man off, but what the fuck does he expect me to do? Hug him?

Darius walks over. He's silent, but I've always been able to tell that he's deadly. It's just in the way he moves. His entire demeanor is threatening. He mostly ignored me while I was with Jet because I was nothing but a side piece. And now, suddenly, here he is, welcoming me. I bristle.

What has he told everyone? Was there some kind of large round table meeting about me with every man here? Was there a vote?

"Congratulations, Talia." He smiles. "I know this is a funny way to start your life, but Nico and the family do believe this is an excellent match."

I swallow hard, wanting to reply. I want to tell him that he has no clue about me and what an excellent match would be for me. I want to tell him that Leo is a fucking asshole and that I am no one's whore. Then again, I also want to drop to my knees and beg him to let me out of this. I don't want to be welcomed into this fucked up family. I have my own crazy brood, and they're enough for this lifetime. I press my lips together, and an awkward silence fills the air.

"Thank you for your kind words, Darius." Leo and he shake hands, and I'm glad he was the one to reply. "We look forward to the future."

He smiles, and I turn, finding a videographer behind us.

"Let's get to the bar. A drink is in order." He pulls Leo away, and I feel relief.

When he's near, I feel like my entire body is on freeze.

Elira and another woman walk over to me, smiling widely.

Elira hugs me close to her chest. "Hi, Talia! I want to introduce you to Gini. She is Darius's wife and in medical school right now."

"Oh, wow. That's great."

I casually give her a once over. She has skin the color of light sand, and her eyes are clear grayish-blue. Wearing a long, flowy pink dress, she reminds me of Nick Jonas's wife, Priyanka Chopra.

She turns her head, and I follow her gaze to Darius, who is staring right at her. She waves before smiling at us.

"He's protective." She shrugs, trying to explain his intense stare.

"How do you manage your studies with a man who is so ... territorial?"

She shakes her head from side to side, like an actress in a Bollywood film. "Oh, he loves that I'm following my dreams! He's the one who taught me English and pushed me to pursue medicine."

"Uh-huh." I smile tightly, feeling sorry for her.

She seems so sweet but also really naive. To have a man be so protective must be suffocating. I know that I shouldn't judge anyone because who knows about her history? But frankly, I'm not down with that dynamic. A woman should have her independence and her pride. Not be watched like an infant.

"He usually has one of the guys picking me up or dropping me off at the hospital," she continues. "He'll come in and check on me often. But I like knowing he's close." She smiles, like it's the most normal thing in the world and she's the luckiest girl on earth.

I wonder if Leo thinks he can be that way with me. "Oh, uh, Leo isn't that possessive, is he? Because I'm not used to that kind of thing." I pause, realizing that maybe these girls can give me more information about him.

Gini smiles. "No, he isn't. Darius is probably the worst of them."

Elira shrugs. "Nico doesn't bother me much. Not when I'm at work."

"Where are you from?" I ask Gini, curious about her accent.

"Darius and I are from India, but he is ethnically Albanian."

A waiter walks around with skewers of grilled meat, and Gini and Elira each take one off the tray.

"I love these!" Elira gushes.

I turn to the waiter. "Is this pork?"

"It's beef. We don't serve pork here. It's all halal." He smiles, like he's proud of me for asking.

I take a skewer and thank him.

Elira takes a big bite of meat. "Do you follow Islam?"

"No. But I don't eat pork."

I don't offer them any more information about my religion. I'm proud to be Jewish, but I'm not an idiot. I know how much anti-Semitism exists around the world, and the last thing I need is a target on my head. Jet never cared, obviously, but maybe the girls do. It's not even that I'm religious or follow Jewish dietary restrictions—also known as kashruth. But I don't touch pork out of respect for my family and my history.

The guys all laugh out loud and then shout, "*Gëzuar!*" They clink their drinks together.

"So, what do you do?" Gini asks sweetly, tucking a lock of dark hair behind her ear.

"I'm a musician. I play the cello. I'm studying now at NYU, but I hope to get a seat in an orchestra after I graduate."

"Oh, wow. That's amazing. I hope we can hear you play sometime." Elira is nice, but I can tell she isn't one to be pushed around. She's measuring me, and I can feel it. "So, Leo is a really good guy. Everyone loves him."

"Is that right?"

"He's super tough—that's for sure." Gini nods. "But he also doesn't speak just to hear himself talk. He's a gentleman too. Darius has had him pick me up from the hospital many times, and he is always quiet and decent."

"Quiet and decent? Something tells me that might not be the case." My eyes focus on him.

He's smiling with his friends, but he is also reserved. Like he isn't letting himself have fun.

Elira lowers her voice, getting closer to me. "He's also hot. Like, ridiculously hot. When I first met him, I was in a state of shock. Like, you think men like that can't actually exist. And then poof!"

"Poof is right." Gini laughs, nodding her head in agreement. "He is definitely handsome."

Elira steps closer to me. "Anyhow, we know that you guys just met tonight. And I'm sure it's shocking. But we can guarantee you that he isn't going to hurt you. We are like a family, okay? And we all protect each other. And love each other. The men would even die for each other and for us. We don't always get to choose our family though, do we? All we can do is make the best of it. So, even though you did not technically choose him as a husband, I have faith in the two of you. You agreed to marry him, but the truth is, this life chose you."

"Look"—I shake my head, not interested in hearing nonsense about fate and God—"I'm not sure how much you guys know or don't know, but—"

"All we know is," Elira interrupts, "you're doing Leo and our family a huge favor by marrying him. American citizenship has been his dream as well as a lot of ours since our births."

"It's amazing of you, Talia. Thank you." Gini smiles widely, like I just gave her a winning lotto ticket.

"You must be religious." I do my best to say it in a nice way as opposed to what I really feel, which is fury.

I'm not here of my own free will. I'm here because I was threatened by their fucking husbands! This *meant to be* bullshit drives me nuts on a regular basis. But coupled with my current circumstance, I refuse to smile and pretend to be okay.

"I'm spiritual. And I do think everything happens for a reason. One day, I'll tell you about Darius and me. Or Elira can tell you about her and Nico. Some things are written. And maybe you and Leo are too." Her voice is so hopeful that it turns my stomach.

"I don't trust in fate. I make my own. Now, if you two will excuse me, I need a moment." I walk away, through the front door.

I realize running would make no sense. These men would track me down in two minutes. Still, I find a bench on the corner and plop down, taking a huge gulp of air.

10

Leo

JESUS CHRIST. As I take shot after shot of tequila, all I can think about is whether or not this is a trick.

I already found Nico, pulled him aside to tell him that this was a mistake. He basically told me to shut the fuck up because he knew more than I did.

"Trust me, I know these things. She is perfect for you. You'll make it work, and she'll get you your citizenship." He smiled at me then and walked off.

I look around the room, noticing that most people are sitting down and eating. But where is Talia? The girl is so full of herself. Sure, she's beautiful. But beauty is more than just a face and a body. Beauty is grace, like Daisy. Talia's tongue is acid, and she borders on arrogant. Actually, *borders* is the wrong word. She is stuck up.

I chuckle, remembering when I came to America and heard the line, "She thinks her shit don't stink." I didn't understand it completely then, but I do now.

They must have threatened her good to get her to marry me. A girl like her definitely doesn't need the money. She looks like she doesn't have a care in the world with her expensive schooling and the freedom to be a musician. Typical American, waltzing through life without knowing anything about how others live. She probably couldn't even point to Albania on a map.

I need a smoke. I go outside and light up, immediately spotting her on a long brown bench. Her curly, long hair is becoming wilder from the humidity. A few minutes pass, and she throws it all up in a bun on top of her head. I can see her profile now, and I take a moment to stare. Small, straight nose with a tiny gold loop through one nostril and full lips. She has a dress on with thin straps, and I can see a tattoo on one of her shoulders. I have nothing against ink; I've got tons of it on my own body. But I've never cared for it on a woman. I quickly adjust my hard-on because, clearly, my body disagrees with my mind. She's gorgeous, and that's all there is to it.

I finish my cigarette and then walk over to her.

Could I have met a girl more opposite from Daisy? I don't think so.

She doesn't stand up when she sees me, but she glances at me from the corner of her eye before focusing on her phone. "Yes?" she says out loud.

I exhale, gathering my wits. I don't want to have a problem with this girl. I don't need an obstacle in my way to citizenship. "I realize that this is awkward. But I'm committed to this. We are married, and at this point, we can either be miserable or we can be friendly. I'm not expecting anything more than that. I don't want you thinking that I would come on to you or take any liberties. You don't have to be afraid of me."

"Fear you?" She laughs, standing up. The girl barely reaches the center of my chest, but she has no fear! "Leo, all I'm giving you is the bare necessities so that you can get your citizenship. If you even tried to touch me in a way I didn't want, I'd snap your neck. But in return for my going along with this, you'll need to promise me that when you're finally an American, you will help me speak with Nico to get out of this."

"You mean, divorce?"

"Yes. As soon as possible." She lifts her head up.

I lick my lips, knowing this is a touchy subject. Divorce might or might not be possible, but frankly, I couldn't care less about the paperwork claiming we're married. I never plan to marry for real, so what do I care? Still, she might be more amenable and calm if I let her think that our relationship will definitely terminate. Right now, peace is what I'm after. A little lie to smooth the situation over isn't a big deal.

"It shouldn't be a problem," I state as confidently as I can.

"Okay then," she says and puts out her hand.

I take it in mine. It's small and warm. I have to say, I'm surprised. I would have thought her hand would be more like sandpaper—to match her personality.

"We should go inside now. I'm sure the party is ending, and we should take more photos together."

She nods, and we walk back into the restaurant, a healthy distance between us. A cake is brought out, and we smile as a photographer snaps pictures. I do my best to look like we're a couple, but she's as rigid as a board. Everyone is clapping to the traditional Albanian wedding song, and I try to go with the flow. I offer her a piece of cake, and she tells me she hates chocolate. I bring her a few cookies instead, and she makes a face. She's rude to everyone who welcomes her. It doesn't take long for that small moment of peace we shared to become history.

When enough photos have been taken, I sit down to eat. The liquor I had earlier has seemingly left my system, but all I feel now is miserable. To live with such a shrew for a few months feels like it will be torture. Haven't I been through enough?

Everyone starts to leave, and Nico sits by me. Smiling, he tells me he wants to give me some marriage advice. "When things are shit at home, just work more."

"Thanks a lot," I deadpan, digging back into my food.

~

MY CAR IS PARKED RIGHT in front of the restaurant. I open the trunk and place her bag and cello inside before getting back into the driver's seat and buckling up. "Ready to go home?"

She secures her seatbelt. "Sure. I'm on—"

"No." I shake my head, turning on the radio and putting the car in drive. "You live with me now."

"Um, what?"

"Yeah. We have to live together. What did you think?" I expertly weave through traffic.

"I don't think so." She shakes her head. "Not yet. I don't even know you."

"Trying to delay the inevitable, eh?"

"Something like that. I'm on Houston and Wooster. My things are there."

"Looks like we're in the same neighborhood." I glance to my right. Her legs are crossed, and so are her arms.

"Where do you live?" she asks.

"Avenue B and Second."

She rolls her eyes. "Well, you'd better find a new place. Because now that we're married, I refuse to live in that area."

I shake my head, feeling my blood boil. "Not good enough for you, princess?"

"Nope." She shrugs without apology. "It's dangerous there."

"Well, get this. You're going to be living with me in my small and *dangerous* one-bedroom for as long as I say. And if you complain, I'll move us. To an even smaller place. In the Bronx maybe. Away from your fancy university. And maybe you'll have to commute, eh? Take the subway. Like regular people do."

She turns toward me. If we were in a cartoon, steam would be billowing from her ears. "I have my own money. I will live the way I want to live."

"No. You will live the way I live. You will eat with the money I bring us. You will learn to be happy with what your husband can provide." Before I can stop myself, I let the threats fly. "And if you don't? I'll let Nico know that our relationship is over and that you are no longer necessary to our operation. And you know what that means, don't you?"

I want to break her. I want to ruin her life the way mine was ruined.

What is Daisy doing right now with my piece-of-shit brother? Just the thought has me flexing my fists.

"Leo, I am working hard. I am studying, so I can play for the New York Philharmonic. It's been a dream all of my life. Don't do that to me." Her voice shakes, anger and worry mixing together to turn her face red. "I understand I can be tough and that we're stuck in this relationship right now. But if you just give me some time, I can—"

I pull over to the curb, unclicking my seat belt and leaning over to her. I get into her space, loving the fact that I'm twice her size. "You can *nothing*. You will live with me, as you've been told to do. You will move into my home like any wife would. Am I being clear?"

In a flash, her arm shoots out, twisting mine behind my back. Her other hand finds my neck. "Listen, motherfucker. You think you can threaten me? You think I'm one of these girls who will say, *yes, sir, no, sir*? Well, get this: I will ruin your life if you even try to get in my way. And I have no problem killing you in your sleep. Who will people believe? The sweet NYU student who plays the cello or the gang-banger from Albania who isn't even a citizen? I'm doing this because I have no choice. But if you ever try to manhandle me again?"

She squeezes my neck, opening her mouth to continue speaking. Before she can, I tug my hand from her grip and twist her bicep.

I don't hurt her, but I want her to know that she can't hurt me. We breathe hard, nose to nose. My eyes roam her face, and for maybe the first time, I get a nice long look at the woman who has been driving me insane ever since I spotted her playing the cello at the club. She has strong features—high cheekbones and a sharp jaw. She isn't feminine, like Daisy, who is all soft curves. Talia's eyes are dark and tilted up at the ends, like a cat. And those lips, pink and lush. Her hair is wild and curly, soft to the touch.

I look up again, and we lock eyes. Both of us are finally silent. We stay in this awkward hold until I can feel her temperature lowering. Or maybe heating. But in a different way.

She wants me. I can't help the smirk growing on my face. The ice queen still finds me attractive.

I lower my guard, and before I can even take a breath, her body turns rigid. With her free hand, she slaps my face, straight across my bruised eye. I grip her wrist again, my face thumping. I won't give her the benefit of knowing she surprised me. But, shit, she's strong!

I lick my lips, as though her slap was nothing more than a fight from a child. I can tell it infuriates her. "We have to prove that we have been living in married harmony for three years. Living together would be better, so we can get to know each other in the ways we need. Plus, if you want to get out of it, we should be able to tell Nico that we tried to manage together but couldn't. If we never lived together, he might force us to try. Believe me, after I saw you, I told him that we were wrong. He seemed to think otherwise. It's a matter of months until the interview for my citizenship. We can live through it. Once I get my passport, I'll find a way to let you go in the eyes of the shqipe. But if you aren't convincing or if it doesn't work and if, for some reason, I'm denied? I will never divorce you."

"Okay." She shakes her body out of my grip.

"Okay?" I look at her closely, surprised she gave up. "How did you learn to protect yourself like that?"

"I'm sure that is something you'd love to know."

"True. So, how did you learn?"

She straightens her face, refusing to reply. I blow air from my lips.

Merging onto FDR, I drive a few miles before getting off at the Houston Street exit. I drive west.

"I'm at 160 Wooster. The white building, up ahead. Aroma is the restaurant on the ground floor."

I spot it quickly and pull up in front of her building.

"We'll go upstairs and get your stuff. I will arrange to have one of the guys put your furniture in storage and bring whatever you left behind to my place."

"Look at me and promise that you will try to get this marriage annulled."

I swallow hard, looking into the depths of her eyes. Some people have pools behind their gazes. This woman has an ocean.

"I seriously don't want this continuing after I get my citizenship," she adds.

"As soon as we can, we will terminate the marriage. But we have to pass the interview, Talia." I look at her pointedly. I need her to go along with this.

She opens the door and steps out.

I put the car in park as she slams the door shut. Risking a ticket because of my illegal parking spot, we walk into her lobby, complete with all the bells and whistles that a rich and spoiled American girl needs. White marble flooring with a huge light fixture hanging from a twelve-foot ceiling. One man to open the door and another guy to sit behind a large oak desk to collect packages. Of course, both are in uniform. I bristle, looking at them.

When I first moved to the city, I was doing small-time work for the shqipe and still working at the pizza shop. For a brief moment, I thought maybe I could get a job as a building super in one of those fancy buildings on the Upper East Side, similar to this one. But I wasn't hired.

"It's all about connections in that line of work," they told me.

But still, it burned. I'd had a huge construction business back home. And here, they told me I wasn't good enough to take a package from FedEx.

She says hello to the doorman and waves to the second guy, sitting pretty. I smile, looking forward to seeing her reaction when we get back to my place. She's going to flip out, and I won't say that I'm not going to enjoy it. I could afford a penthouse on Park Avenue, but I like my small apartment. It reminds me not to get too comfortable in my life. Revenge is what I'm here for, not a high end building with amenities and a view of Central Park. Once I kill my brother, I'd love to live large. Until then, the good life will have to wait.

Up to the third floor we go. When she opens her apartment door,

I keep myself in check. I don't want her to see any emotion from me. My first impression is the size. It's not enormous, but it's immaculate. The floorplan is open with a row of floor-to-ceiling windows spanning from the kitchen through the living room. The kitchen is white, filled with closed cabinets and stainless-steel appliances. In front of the kitchen is a circular black marble table that seats two, and in front of that is a white sectional. There is no television in the living room, but an area by the window has a black stand, filled with sheet music. A black chair sits neatly front of it.

"I'm going to pack. Give me a few minutes." Her voice is low.

She disappears down a hall, which is where I assume her bedroom is. I look on the windowsill and see photos of her smiling with whom I assume are her parents. Another one of her in what looks like a high school graduation uniform, her curly, dark hair flowing beneath her cap. She's smiling so happily here. A few photos with her playing cello on a stage.

"Ready?" She exhales, and I turn to her.

Her white dress is gone, and in its place are white sweatpants and a black T-shirt. Her hair is up high in a sloppy bun, face cleared of makeup. I decide in this moment that I prefer her hair up, face completely bare. Not that I care either way though. She can look however she wants to look.

She walks over to the door, and I move behind her.

She spins around, stopping me short. "Can we talk about personal space for a second?"

"What?"

"Yeah. Personal space. It means that you should not be walking on my heels like a *dog*." She looks up at me. And when I say up, I mean, she has to tilt her head so that her chin rises another forty-five degrees.

"You have some real balls, Talia." I spit out her name. "I realize how hard it must be for you to slum it with a man who builds with his hands and fights with his fists. But you should understand something." I puff up my chest, thrilled by the fact that this girl is finally silent. I'm burning over the fact that she just belittled me. "I'm just as tough as you think I am. I don't have a set of morals, like regular men do. I don't have a huge family to love me and feed me, and I don't have one woman who waits for me. I'm one of those men with nothing to lose, and that makes me very, very dangerous." I step into her personal fucking space and watch her shrink.

She shivers.

"I can be a decent man—when I want to be. Otherwise, I can be brutal. Let's get out of here." I walk in front of her, opening the door and not bothering to hold it for her.

My chest hurts. My fingertips tingle. I meant what I said, and it's all true. And while I do still have some humanity, it would be better for her to think that I have none. I refuse to be disrespected. It happened to me once in the greatest way possible, but I won't be made into the fool again.

Getting into the car, I blast my music.

Ten minutes later, we get to the front of my walk-up building, and I luckily find a parking space. I grab her shit from the trunk but ignore the fact that she is here. And this time, I feel her at the back of my feet as we walk up to the third floor. She must be freaking the fuck out to be in this shithole. I use my key to unlock my front door and swing it open, flicking on the lights. My apartment isn't much, but I pay for it with my own hard work.

"My bedroom is there." I point to the bedroom on the left. "The couch here opens into a bed. And as you can see, the kitchen is right here in front of us. Welcome to The Plaza *Motel*, Talia."

"Look, I, uh, I'm sorry. I've been a huge bitch. I guess we got off on the wrong foot and ..." She shrugs, pulling her hair from the high bun. It tumbles around her shoulders.

She smells like vanilla and flowers. I wipe my nose, not wanting her scent to invade me.

"Things keep going wrong," she continues, flustered. "I'm still in shock that we're married. And I'm not even sure what this means for me and my life. I'm not actually mean, Leo. Really, I'm not."

"Funny. You act like a bitch. You walk like a bitch. You speak like a bitch. But you're telling me that you're nice?"

11

Talia

I REAR BACK like I've been slapped in the face. Somehow, this man has managed to hit my greatest insecurity right on the head. I know I act a certain way, but it's not who I really am. "How dare you judge me! You have no clue who I am, where I come from, nothing."

He drops on his black leather couch, leaning back and crossing his arms like a king. The man has a presence—I'll give him that.

"So, tell me then." He lights up a cigarette, blowing out smoke like it's his fucking house.

Okay, fine, it *is* his house. But if I'm going to be living in it, then he'd better get used to me.

I walk to the coffee table, pulling out my own cigarette from his pack. Lighting it up, I take a drag. "Well, for one thing, I'm not a spoiled brat. I grew up in Queens and went to Bronx High school of Science." I slowly let out the smoke, willing myself not to cough. I never smoke, but I want him to know I can do whatever he does but better.

"Fancy private school, eh? Let me guess ... you went with ... what's her name?" He looks up at the ceiling, as though trying to remember. "Paris Hilton?"

I laugh. "No. It's a public school, but you have to pass an admissions exam to get accepted." I take a seat on the edge of the couch, ashing in his small black tray. "I also play the cello, as you know, at New York University."

"Scholarship, or does your dad pay your tuition?" He glares at me, waiting for the answer.

Suddenly, it dawns on me. *Does he not know about Jet? Holy shit. He doesn't know.*

I tilt my head, weighing my options. It's the lie versus the truth right now. He smiles smugly, and I know he thinks I have rich parents. He doesn't have a clue about my arrangement with his "brother."

"Yes. Full scholarship."

Waiting for his response, I decide that it's only a partial lie. Technically, a scholarship is a grant to study. I guess we can call Jet my benefactor. Whatever. It's just semantics! I hate lying, but telling the truth would turn me into the scum of the earth in his eyes. And for reasons I can't understand, I don't want him thinking so low of me. He might not be fancy, but he obviously works for every piece of food he puts in his mouth. How would he react if he knew that I'd had a boyfriend who paid my way through school? A boyfriend he doesn't seem to know about. A boyfriend in his crew. I shiver, feeling like shit.

"Okay then. So, how do you pay for your apartment, if not your parents?"

I blink, a rush moving through me. *He definitely doesn't know about Jet.* And now, here I go, skipping down the lying path. "I'm friends with the landlord's daughter. She's at NYU with me. I get preferential rent." I shrug, looking straight into his face.

I realize that I'm not the only person lying to him. Nico and Darius must have withheld the information about my history with Jet.

He exhales, putting out his stub. "Okay. So, I'm corrected then." Clearly, he isn't going to apologize or elaborate.

He just isn't that type of man, and even from our limited interactions, I can tell that he's not one to ever say sorry.

I nod, looking into his blue eyes. For a few moments, we don't speak, just look at each other. God, he is so incredibly handsome. Magnetic. That moment I saw him at the club, I felt the vibration of him all the way from my eyes down to my toes. Something inside me wants to fess up the truth. This guy is being lied to from both sides. Ouch. But, no, I won't tell him anything. Because why should I? I have a short amount of time to deal with him, pass this interview, and then it's *good-bye, Albanian Mafia,* and *hello, New York Philharmonic.* If I tell him something that Nico doesn't want him knowing, I could wind up hurting myself. It's not easy, being so tough, but sometimes, there just isn't any other way.

He nods, like we've come to some sort of understanding. "Why don't we get a drink somewhere? Or some food? I noticed you didn't eat much at the party."

Now, it's my turn to exhale and put out my half-smoked cigarette. "Yeah, okay. There's a Landmark diner—"

"On Grand Street, I know."

He stands up to his full, towering height. "One more thing before we move on from hating each other. I have no intention of letting you walk all over me. If I did, you'd lose all respect for me—I know your type—and it would probably make you worse."

I open my mouth to reply, but he puts his hand up.

"I will tolerate a lot of things. If you like to eat at a certain time for dinner, I can be flexible. If you like to sleep with the apartment colder than I prefer, I can make that work too. But the one thing I won't accept? Any sort of disrespect. Don't roll your eyes at me. Don't unleash your tongue at me. Don't lie to me. Don't try to make me feel small, stupid, or anything else like that because I am none of those things. You might be one of the toughest people I've ever met, but if you try to pull that shit with me, this won't end well."

I wait, knowing there's more.

"I'm sure you eat some of these men in America for breakfast, eh? Let me tell you, I pity them." He steps up closer to me. "But not me. Never me. Are we clear?"

I press my lips together, understanding both his words and how I'm already violating them. I don't know his relationship to the shqipe other than the fact that he is technically part of them. I also know that Nico's word is law, and if he told Leo to marry me, he would have to do it with no questions asked. Honestly, it's their business what they want to tell him or not tell him, right? I tell my guilt that there is no place for her in this situation.

"I hear you," I reply.

"Let me just change out of this suit. And then we'll leave. When we get back, I'll show you into the bedroom and where you can keep your things."

It only takes him a few minutes to change. Loose grey sweatpants and a white T-shirt. And for the first time in maybe my life, I am literally struck dumb. He's all powerful muscle, heavy but also lean. And so tall. A girl in the orchestra once ranted about how annoying it was when short girls went for the tall guys and took them away from the taller women who actually needed them. I laughed at the time. But there you have it.

"You ready to go?" He crosses his arms over his built chest.

My heart beats like a jackhammer as I turn my head and grab my purse, acting like I don't care. "Yeah, I'm ready." I will my voice to stay calm.

I hate this guy and my body for wanting him so fiercely. Yes, he was hot as hell in the suit. But this version of him, confident and comfortable? Off the charts.

THE DINER IS a good place for us to go. We both refuse the menus, knowing what we want to order. I get a cup of black coffee and the double-decker tuna melt with cheddar cheese, fries, and a Caesar salad. He looks at me in shock at my order, and I resist the urge to give him the finger. He gets the grilled chicken wrap with no mayo, and the waitress fumbles over writing it down, her eyes jumping between the pad of paper in her hand and Leo's face. I roll my eyes.

"It's weird how we both come here often but never overlapped." I take a sip of my water from the straw as the waitress sets my coffee on the table.

He lifts his cup of water. "I guess our hours are different."

"So, are you going to tell me about what you do for work? Other than killing people for the shqipe?" I smirk, and he takes my comment for what it is—a joke. At least, I hope it's a joke...

He continues to tell me about how he runs a construction company out in the Hamptons and goes to night school at Baruch College, learning construction management and also taking an architecture class. He doesn't look old, but he already lives a very adult life.

Caffeine prickles through my blood as I listen quietly, enraptured by his voice and the way he speaks. I haven't ever been with a man quite like him before. There was my high school boyfriend, Jacob. He was a studious and gentle piano player, who shared my love of music. And then Jet, who was never truly a lover in the way a girl would dream of. We had fun together, but there was always the *understanding* of what we really were—a transaction.

I glance around the diner, wondering what we must look like together to the other patrons. I'm not stupid. I know that I'm attractive—to a certain type of man. I'm not fine-featured or classically beautiful. I'm also not girl-next-door cute. But I'm strong to my core, I have talent, and I know who I am and what I'm capable of.

Does Leo look like trouble? The answer is definitely yes.

I adjust my hair over my shoulder, still chewing while also feeling his knee press against mine. I know that he isn't trying to touch me. It's just how long his legs are. But touching him feels so good.

I blink, realizing that we've been quiet. "What are you building now?"

"I'm doing five homes out in the Hamptons." He nods, so confident in himself.

"So, is this your long-term thing? Construction?"

"Yes. Construction is my birthright. It's what I grew up doing in Albania. I have a busine—"

I wait for more, but he doesn't continue. Something came up in his head though because his blue eyes turn dark. The waitress arrives with our food, and I decide not to press him about the construction he did back home. Clearly, it's a "hot-button topic," as my father always calls it. And frankly, I don't need to upset the guy more than I already have. Hey, even I know when shutting the fuck up is in order.

We eat silently, and I'm so exhausted from the day that I can barely bother to speak. Still, I can feel his stare. And the weight of his leg, still pressed against mine. And I would be lying if I said I didn't feel the tingle in every part of my body. Even his neck is hot. The movement of his throat as he chews his food, tendons popping as he swallows his water.

We manage to finish our meal without any more bickering. My stomach is finally full, and I have to admit, I do feel better.

～

SILENTLY, we walk back to his place. I look around the apartment, not sure where I'm going to sleep.

"Follow me." He walks into the bedroom, and I trail behind him.

He flips on the lights, and I can barely believe my eyes. Two single beds are on either side of the room with matching wooden desks set against the wall, in front of each bed. It's like a dorm room, but better.

"So, you must have known for a while that this was happening?"

"About a week."

"And you set this all up?" I swallow hard, shocked that he went out of his way like this.

This is nice. Like, really, really nice. He could have thrown me on the couch. Or blown up an air mattress.

"Don't think too much of it. You're on the left." He points to my bed, covered with a light-blue comforter. "I already cleared out the bottom two drawers in the dresser. And half my closet. If you need more room, let me know."

"You set up my desk?" I swallow hard, surprised at his thought-fulness.

"Nico told me you are a student, and I figured you'd need a place to study."

"Well, that was really cool of you. Thank you. Can I check out the bathroom?"

"Go right ahead."

I look around, glad that the place is so clean. For a man so young, he definitely takes care of himself. I open up the door to the bath-room, and what I see literally has me shocked.

"Holy shit!" I exclaim.

"What's wrong?"

"This bathroom is amazing. Is that a sauna?"

"I told you, I do construction. Sometimes, I wind up with extra materials, and I use them. Wood for the desks—"

"Wait." My eyes dart to the bedroom. "You made the desks?"

"Yeah." He nods, like it's nothing. "Talia, speechless? I didn't expect that to happen so quickly."

"Well, there you have it. I'm a sucker for a nice bathroom and a desk made by hand. I'm going to unpack the things I brought and take a hot shower."

I want to say more, but I can't. He's talented. Really, really talented.

"Sounds good to me. I'll use the bathroom quickly and then watch some TV."

I do as I said, unpacking the few things I brought. All of his clothes are neatly folded, and at this point, I'm not surprised. I place my pajamas, socks, and underwear in one drawer and T-shirts and long-sleeved shirts in the other. I hear the faucet turning on in the bathroom, and then he quietly exits the room.

When I get to his closet, I roll my eyes. He literally has five black button-down shirts, all identical. If he wears a gold chain, too, I'm going to force him to remove it. I understand that he probably thinks it's cool, but it's not.

On the hangers go two pairs of my jeans, a long black dress for concerts, my shimmery dress I wear when playing at the club, and two blouses—one black with loose bell sleeves and a cream button-down. Lastly, I hang my black pants and a black silk camisole.

When I'm done putting my clothes away, I bring my toiletries with me into the bathroom. Pressing my lips together, I organize my makeup and creams in the bottom drawer of the vanity. I will not be here long, and I'll survive this. Sure, I haven't ever lived with a man for longer than a weekend. But I'll make it work.

I hear a buzz and realize he left his phone in here. I take a glance and see a text message.

Sabrina: Hey, Leo. Miss me yet? So much fun last weekend. Let's fuck at my place tonight?

My mouth immediately dries out. I shouldn't care, and yet somehow, the text has me uncomfortable. I leave the phone where it is, not wanting to touch it. Taking off my clothes, I think about the obvious. Leo and I aren't actually together. But does he think he can bring women here when I'm sleeping in the next bed? I wouldn't be okay with that. We'll have to discuss this.

After my hot shower, I put some cream in my hair to tame my curls before putting my pajamas on—a matching pants and long-sleeved black jersey set from Victoria's Secret. I put my laptop on my desk and organize my textbooks, making a mental note to buy book-ends for them.

Hands gliding across the soft wood, I'm amazed that he made this. It's just such a thoughtful thing to do for someone you don't even know. If he had known it was me, he probably would have put me in the fucking trash room.

I hear the television on in the living room and wonder if I should wander out. Or maybe just stay here. I crack open the door to let him know that he can come back inside, if he wants.

I take out my cello and pull out the desk chair, turning it around to face the window. Some people read before bed; others watch television. I love to play. Closing my eyes, I let the music overtake me. I always begin with my scales, and then I find my favorite chords. From there, I wander into different melodies. Eventually, my body starts to unfold. It's been a crazy day.

When I feel the tiredness set into my bones, I open my eyes. Setting down my cello, I stretch as tall as I can go and pivot, almost falling backward when I see him. "What the hell?!"

Leo is here, sitting at his desk and watching me.

"What are you doing here?" I wrap my arms around my waist, defensive.

"Listening." He licks his lips, fully confident.

I move my hands to my sides, feeling strangely vulnerable. "Well, fine. Next time, do me a favor and let me know when you come in. Knock or something."

"Calm down. This is our shared room now, isn't it? You left the door open, and I figured it was cool." He stands up and peels his shirt off his chest before grabbing a mat from the bottom of the closet and setting it on the floor between our beds. He drops to the ground.

I want to ask what the hell he's doing, but before I can, he starts doing push-ups. I swallow hard, my throat constricting. Watching this man move his body in the way God probably meant him to is a view to behold. The temptation to throw myself onto the floor and beg him to screw my brains out is high, but I've never been one to give in easily. I ignore the tightening in my abdomen and climb into bed, acting like it's nothing. Like his incredible body and all those mouthwatering tattoos and those hands that build and his eyes that smolder are all just run of the mill.

He continues working out, and I do my best to ignore him. But when he walks to the doorway where a pull-up bar is set up, I realize that I'm about to have the perfect view of him from where I lie. I try not to groan as I watch his shoulders flex along with a hard line down the center of his back.

Kicking off the sheets, I ask, "Is there no air in the apartment? It's hot as hell in here. You are literally steaming the place up."

He laughs, dropping to his feet and heading back to the closet. He pulls out a belt with a weight dangling off it and closes it around his waist.

I eye the weight, shaped like a kettle of all things. It looks really heavy. "Aren't you afraid for your back? Disc problems are real, you know."

"Terrified," he deadpans, reaching back up again to the bar. He brings himself up and down again, back muscles rippling.

I finally stop trying to fight it. I'm watching, dammit. I'm watching because he's hot as fuck and working out in front of me. I can resist temptation, but my eyes are on strike, refusing to leave the scene.

When he's finally finished with his workout, sweat coats his skin. He turns to me, and I shut my eyes, feigning sleep. Seemingly satisfied, he turns off the room light before walking quietly into the bathroom. It doesn't take long for the water to turn on and then shut off.

He steps out, light streaming in behind him as steam billows into the room, like a cloud. A towel is draped around his waist. He turns around and shuts off the bathroom light. Even though the lamps are off in the room, New York City is never completely dark. The neighboring buildings and the cars driving on the street illuminate him in a golden glow. I can make out the spikes of his wet, dark hair and the shape of his built body. He pulls out some clothes from the drawer, and I hold my breath.

Is he going to change ... here?

He undoes his towel, as if in slow motion.

It drops.

On my life, I believe God must be helping me out because the fact that I don't gasp out loud is a miracle. Even in the dim light, I can tell his dick is utter perfection. Thick and long. My pussy clenches as I squeeze my eyes shut.

12

Leo

I GET MYSELF INTO BED, glad to have the day over with.

Talia. I say her name in my head, bouncing it around a few times.

Closing my eyes, I picture her on the stage at the club. Her utter devotion to the cello is incredible. To be honest, I have never met a woman with so much drive. I'm sure that women back home might have been more driven if it were socially acceptable for them to be. Daisy never planned on working, nor did she have any passions outside of looking her best and getting married. At least, not that I knew of.

"Are you up?" Her voice squeaks in the dark.

I throw my arm off my eyes. "Talia? You're awake?"

Shit. I changed in this room. I guess if she saw me, she saw me. What the hell do I care anyway?

"Yes, I'm awake." She snorts. "Obviously."

I wait for her to elaborate. This isn't a girls' sleepover, where we're going to open our hearts to each other. This isn't love, where I'm going to hold her. And this isn't even a late-night fuck, where we're going to feel each other. It's nothing.

"When did you immigrate here?" she asks quietly.

"A few years ago."

"Do you plan on going back?"

"Yes. But just to take care of some business and see someone I used to know."

"A female someone?" she questions.

"Yes. She's a woman I once knew back in Kosovo."

"She's been waiting for you? All this time?"

I press my lips together, not wanting to answer. But as I've learned about Talia in the short time I've known her, she doesn't stay quiet. Ever.

"Leo, I asked you a question. This girl—"

"Daisy. Her name is Daisy." He says her name with a perfect Albanian accent.

"Okay. This Daisy." I pronounce her name with as much New York as I can muster. "She's just there, waiting for you to bring her here?"

Under my breath, I mumble, "It is what it is."

"You're not making sense, Leo. Well, what about the fact that you're married to me? I mean, I know in Islam, a few wives are acceptable, but I would imagine that she—"

"Talia, stop the smart-ass comments. Daisy is none of your damn business." The venom in my voice shocks even me.

"All right, all right. Talk about a hot-button topic. Jeez ..."

"Well, get used to it."

"Will you at least tell me what she's like?" She sits up and turns on the lamp beside her bed.

There's something passing through her face, but I don't know her well enough to understand what it means. I exhale, imagining Daisy. I ignore the woman I know her to be today and think about the girl I knew before.

"She's beautiful."

"And?"

"And soft. Kind and gentle. She barely raises her voice."

She laughs out loud. "Unlike me."

I laugh, not unkindly. "Definitely nothing like you."

"I bet her skin is fair, without any blemishes." She rubs her face self-consciously.

Talia has some small marks beneath her cheekbones. Light acne scars maybe. But it doesn't do anything to detract from how pretty she is.

I close my eyes, picturing Daisy and me walking in the park. It was the day before the disaster with her father. She was wearing a hat to cover her skin from the sun.

"Yes, her skin is perfect." I picture her eyes blinking up at me, noise around us but nothing between us. My arms wrapped around her tiny waist, bringing her into my chest.

"And obviously, she's the perfect height. Not short."

"Daisy is tall, but not too tall. A lot taller than you, though."

"Great." She stands up from the bed, clearly agitated. "Well, good for you. I hope you manage to bring her back. Little Miss Perfect, a beautiful Disney princess who does no wrong and feeds birds and mice in her spare time."

"Don't call her that. And I don't need your hope." I sit up on the side of the bed.

She stands in front of me now, so we're almost level with each other. I'm still a few inches taller than her, even seated.

"You just need me to pretend to be your wife?"

"That's right." I cross my arms over my chest.

"So, is Sabrina some enjoyment while Daisy sits pretty in Kosovo?" She tilts her head questioningly.

My heart stutters. "What?"

"Sabrina. The girl you're fucking?" She has a laugh in her voice, like she is busting my ass.

I stand up, pushing the sheets off of me. I want to jump out of my skin. "How the fuck do you know that?"

"Oh, calm yourself. Your phone was in the bathroom while I was in it. It buzzed, and I checked. She wants to see you tonight, by the way."

"I'm a man. What I do in my spare time is none of your business."

"Oh, sure. Love-of-your-life Daisy is away, so you're keeping busy with—"

"That's enough, Talia," I cut her off, but I feel exhausted.

She calmly takes a seat at the desk, unaffected by my anger. "I'm confused. And as your wife, I think I deserve some answers."

"It's a long story." I walk into the kitchen, filling up a cup of water from the sink. I quickly chug it down before going back into the bedroom. Something strange is coming over me.

"Well?"

"Well, she was stolen from me." The admission is a relief.

"Stolen? Like disappeared or taken?" Her eyes flash with worry.

"Not exactly." I sit down on the edge of the bed, my stomach sinking, and drop my head in my hands.

She gets up, moving beside me. She is so small, her body maybe half of my width. "Tell me. I want to know. I *should* know, to be honest."

"Should?"

"Yes. As your wife, there are things I'd like to know about you. Not even about this story maybe, but I'm sure it will be telling about the kind of man you are."

Before I can think on it more, I open up. I'm not sure why. I barely know this woman. For all intents and purposes, I can't stand her. And yet I tell her about my twin brother and our lifelong rivalry. My parents. I take her all the way through me landing in New York. Hiding in the auditorium of NYU, and listening to the orchestra play. Finding work at Famiglia. She listens quietly, taking it all in. I can see her mind is working as she listens.

Most women would be shocked at the story or might even chime in. But she doesn't make a move.

"So, now, you're silent?" I'm annoyed.

I don't even understand why I care what she thinks or doesn't think. She and I are nothing, and that is what we will always be.

"You must have seen us playing."

"Huh?"

"The day you came to the auditorium. You listened to music and slept there, right? That's the orchestra I play for."

Suddenly, it comes to me. The cello player I couldn't see. The long hair. It was her. I turn to my side to face her, and she does the same.

"It was you." *Of all the players, I noticed her.*

I study her face, wondering if that could be possible. She had no idea how much her music affected me at that moment in time. I thought I would be homeless. My life had been stripped from me. And there she was, her energy radiating. She looks up, and for once, she lets me see what she's feeling. It looks like sadness—for me.

I hate pity.

I turn away, going back into the kitchen for another glass of water.

When I get back in the room, she's no longer gentle for me. "Okay. So, he took your woman. Your business. Your life. And now, you're here, with the shqipe. And let me guess ... you're returning to Kosovo for revenge?"

"That's right."

"But you need citizenship to move freely. Hence our marriage."

I look at her, squinting my eyes. She's clearly smart, but I have to say, I'm surprised at the speed at which she picked it all up.

"It seems obvious." She shrugs, opening her mouth like she wants to say more. "Well"—she flips her hair to the side, and I notice it's still slightly damp and it smells like citrus—"I guess just moving on isn't an option for you."

"Of course not!" I yell, putting my cup on the desk. "Daisy was supposed to be my wife. That business was supposed to be mine. He stole it from me. He took my fucking life! Did you not hear a word I said? My mom, my own mother—" I stop, unable to go on. My blood? It boils.

She looks around the room, unfazed by my anger. "But look at what you managed to accomplish here. You are working. You have friends. You are studying. It's obvious to me that you're living the American dream. You are achieving great success here, Leo. This apartment sucks, and sure, you're involved in the Mafia, but clearly, you've done well if you're building massive homes out east ..."

I get up, pacing the room. *Who does she think she is?* "Clearly, you're deaf."

"I'm not deaf. I heard you loud and clear. You're the one who isn't listening to reason! You're above your old life."

I want to grab her. Shake her. Instead, I loom above her. "I will kill that motherfucker if it's the last thing I do. And I will look at Daisy with my own eyes and let her know that she is the scum of the earth, moving from me to my twin. Nothing matters more than that. Not even my life."

As I've officially learned, Talia doesn't cower. She crosses her arms over her chest, looking me dead in the eye. "If it is what you want to do, I have no doubt you'll do it. But what if she's happy? What if she has a child? What if everyone has moved on from you?"

My heart thumps. "They will have to figure it out. Kids are adaptable."

She bites her full bottom lip. "Okay. So, there are children?" Her words are slow and measured.

"Yes, there are kids. There was a wedding. There was everything!" I flip my desk over, and it crashes onto the floor. "My business is also booming in Kosovo. My business, not *his* fucking business!" I shout. "She has to be miserable with him. He is pathetic!"

I decide I can't sit here anymore. Not with Talia questioning me. I put my shirt back on, forcing my feet into my unlaced sneakers.

As if to pacify me, she puts up her hands. "Listen, Leo. I get it. Calm down."

"Calm down?" I need to get out of here before I shred my apartment. "I can't fucking calm down. My life—" My voice cracks, and she grabs my arms.

How this tiny thing thinks she can touch me right now is shocking. I should step back and pull away or throw her off me, but I don't. Instead, I'm breathing hard, staring at this woman who barely reaches the center of my chest yet holds herself like a queen.

"You aren't scaring me, so stop trying. I understand, okay? I get it.

I'll help you. We will pass the interview, and you will get your citizenship, so you can go back to Kosovo and break some heads—if that's what you want."

"It's what I want." I shake myself out of her grip.

"All right then." Something flashes in her eyes, like she doesn't quite believe her words.

I OPEN my front door and step out, slamming it shut behind me.

Walking the city streets, there is no one out but bums. Streetlights line the corners. The smell of hashish permeates the air. A man, full of grime, is sprawled on the hard concrete. I cross the street to avoid him, knowing that he likes to grab people's ankles. He's a usual around here, and he doesn't mean any harm. Still, I'm not in the mood.

With each step I take, I relive the hell my brother and mother put me through. I imagine lying in bed with Daisy and her father walking in. Entering my home to see my mother and brother waiting for me with phony news.

A homeless man groans on the sidewalk. I could have been one of these bums had luck not entered the picture. What would I have done if I hadn't taken the Uber and never met Yosi? What would I have done if he hadn't given me his card? Where would I have slept if I hadn't bumped into Nico and Darius at the restaurant?

I kick a piece of trash. It's a red can of soda, and liquid sprays against a graffitied wall.

Meeting the men of the shqipe was my luck. More than luck, they have become my family.

After I met Nico and Darius, I was nervous about whether or not Darius really would come to get me. At nine o'clock in the evening I walked out of work, flour on my hands, and there was Darius, presumably waiting for me in his Mercedes-Benz. I walked to the car as he pulled down the front passenger window. "I'm here to take you home," he said.

I entered without asking any questions. We drove to what was to be my apartment; it was furnished with the bare necessities, but it also included a laptop, a new cell phone, a bed, and a couch along with some milk, bread, and peanut butter in the fridge.

One year after staying there and working at Famiglia along with doing some random small-time jobs for the guys, the shqipe must have begun to trust me. Darius handed me a file, and told me not to open it unless I've got a hard drink beside me. I read that Albi had married Daisy six months after my exodus. They now had two sons. My mother lived with them in a beautiful new house with an enormous garden in the front. Business was thriving as Kosovo continued to grow, and my construction company was at the forefront of new development.

I read the notes, stared at the photos, and downed a half of a bottle of whiskey. I swore that I would get my revenge and take back what was rightfully mine.

And when I swear, I always follow through. Always.

Not long after that, Nico invited me to a dinner in his home. With nothing left to lose, I went. He explained to me that the shqipe was a family and they always protected what was theirs. I let him know about what had happened to me, and he promised that, one day, he would help me complete my revenge.

And yet initiating into the brotherhood was something that I naturally fell into, separate from my quest. Parties with the crew, along with friendship and support, came at a much-needed time. I was alone here in America, and I was alone in the world.

But the men of the shqipe speak my language. They dress as I do. They eat as I do. It feels right, rolling with them. I'm a decent man, but I've always been physical. I'm not one to sit in a library and study. I prefer to work with my hands. If someone fucks with me, I will always stand up and protect myself and my loved ones—with force, if necessary. I'm a good fit with the shqipe, and they all knew it.

I crack my knuckles, wishing I could hit fast-forward. My American citizenship is a boulder in my path. But there is no other option.

After my revenge is complete in Kosovo, I must be able to return to the States without a headache.

I stop walking, pulling a cigarette from the back pocket of my jeans and light it up. Talia is so sexy and whip-smart and plays the cello like a goddess. Upsettingly beautiful. Her dark eyes are nothing short of overpowering. All of that is undeniable. But she's just so tough! Breaks my balls as easily as a walk in the park. Stands up to me. Fights me. Cuts me down with those eyes of hers. Honestly, I think she's the first woman I've ever met who isn't slightly afraid of what I can do. Even Daisy often felt afraid by my energy. I'm hard, but I don't lack self-awareness. I understand that my temper is extreme, as is my will to fight. I've always been this way. But Talia barely feels it. Or if she does, it doesn't scare her.

A smile pulls at my lips.

One thing I know for sure is that I need her to be agreeable. Without her getting along with me, we might not pass the interview, and then I can't get my citizenship. Love is not on my map, and it never will be. But revenge is the main goal, and I will do what I have to in order to get it.

I pause, vowing to be better to Talia. I need her to like me. I need it to look and feel like we truly are husband and wife.

I turn the corner, finding myself back on my street, and head to my building. I unlock the front door and walk up the stairs to my apartment. Opening the door, I kick off my shoes and walk back into my room. I check to see if she's sleeping. And this time, I *really* check. Dropping to the floor next to her, I gaze at her face and swallow hard. Pouty lips, slightly open. That tiny nose ring, woven inside her nostril, glints. Wild, dark curls are splayed across the pillow. One shapely leg is thrown over the covers. Her twisted white sleep shirt shows the deep curve above her hip. I want to lift her shirt to see that tattoo on her shoulder. She could walk around in a set of rags and look gorgeous.

She blinks her eyes open, at half-mast. "You came back?" Her voice is scratchy.

"Yes. This is our home, right?" I exhale, hoping that we can just turn the corner.

She sits up, her eyes suddenly gentle. "I'm sorry, okay? For real. You've been through a lot. I get it. I'll help you."

I lift her hand and kiss her knuckles. "I'm not a good man, and I have nothing to give a woman like you. My heart, at this point, is ice. But while you're with me, I will protect you like my own. And when this is done, you'll be free."

I'm lying.

I have no idea if Nico will tell me that we can actually end this paper marriage. But if it helps her to calm down, so be it.

She gently nods, her eyes glittering, as though through a veil. "Thank you, Leo."

I press my lips into a hard line, wishing that I didn't have to screw her over like this. "Good night, Talia."

Pulling off my shirt, I change into my sleep pants in the bathroom before washing my face and hands. The city is nothing if not dirty, and I'm not getting into a fresh bed with clothes that have been outside. I leave the bathroom and hit the lights.

Beneath the sheets, I exhale, sweat from my walk beading to the surface of my skin. I'm hot.

That night, I dream of Talia playing her cello on an empty stage, the red curtains parted. Except, this time, instead of sitting in the audience, listening, I'm choking. But she can't see me or hear me. Instead, she just plays as I collapse to the floor, eyes rolling back.

13

Talia

Leo: Will you be around tonight?
Talia: Sure. After rehearsal. I'll be back by seven.
Leo: Sounds good. Let's eat at home and then go out for drinks. Have you been to Apotheke?
Talia: No, but I've always wanted to check it out.
Leo: Let's do it then. I'll reserve a table for us. See you back at home.

I IMMEDIATELY SEARCH up Apotheke and find out that it's a mixology bar with burlesque shows every Thursday, Friday, and Saturday night. The reviews are amazing, and frankly, I'm intrigued.

Leo and I have been dancing around each other nicely over the last few weeks in a calm and quiet rhythm. Every morning, he drinks coffee with skim milk and two sugars. He showers twice a day. He works almost constantly but exercises in the bedroom about thirty minutes every evening. He is always short on the phone when someone calls—unless it's a subcontractor. The only time I've heard him scream since that night he told me about his past was when the foundation piles got messed up on one of his new Hamptons houses. He went crazy on the phone, threatening the poor guy's life.

I find myself feeling suddenly warmed by my thoughts. Okay, not warm. *Hot.*

"What's up, cello?" Brian throws an arm around me.

While I play in the orchestra, he is a drummer in the band. He's pretty good-looking, if you like his type. Shaggy, dark hair, darker eyes, and two deep dimples on either side of his cheeks. But what I like best about him is his talent. The man is seriously good. We met in first-year music theory and have been friends ever since.

"I'm good, drums. Now, get off my shoulders; you're too heavy when you lean on me."

"God, Talia, just once, I want to see you smiling, carefree, and in a positive mood."

I look up at him, and he's smiling, dimples on display, obviously being cheeky. "I'm in a great mood."

"This is you in a great mood?" He stops walking, looking like he's about to laugh out loud.

"Yes."

"So, all this time, I thought you were playing hard to get, being tough, but really, this is you happy."

"Exactly." I nod, unable to hold back my own smile.

In another life, we might have been close friends. But it's hard to maintain a friendship when you're keeping enormous secrets. Like the fact that I've been tangled up with the Albanian Mafia since I was in my first year in college.

"Because you're in such a great mood"—he elbows me lightly in the ribs—"you want to get dinner tonight? I want to run some ideas by you. I might leave school soon."

"Oh yeah? It must be a pretty big deal if you're considering leaving right before finals and graduation. Can't you push whatever it is back until after the semester is over?"

"It is. I got a call from Heretic Pope. They're touring Europe and Australia, and they want me to come along."

"Holy shit! That's a huge deal! They're, like, the biggest band right now. They had the *Rolling Stone* cover last month, right?"

He smiles proudly, no words needed.

I adjust the strap on my backpack. "Well, that is an amazing offer."

"Maybe not. I need the education, you know? And like you said, I'm so close to finishing. Touring won't last forever. But let's talk about it over dinner."

"Oh shit." I bite my lip. "I want to, but I can't. How about next week?"

"Sure. I'll call you."

He walks away, and I head over to orchestra practice.

While I practice, I finally take a mental load off. There is nothing more relaxing than getting lost in the music.

When it's over, I walk out with Ronna and Leora, the violinists I play with at Wild Orchid. "What are you girls doing tonight?"

"Paper to write for music theory. Are you done yet?"

"No. I've outlined, but I plan on pulling it out of my ass when it's closer to the due date."

They laugh.

"Are we playing again Saturday night?" Ronna asks.

"No." I shake my head. "I think we're on for the following Saturday."

Leora smiles. "Okay, cool."

We wave good-bye.

I head back to the apartment, oddly looking forward to tonight with Leo.

To be honest, what he's been through is pretty sad. I know life is tough and that he always tells me how strong he is. But to be screwed over by your mom and twin brother? That's really, *really* bad. I've spent enough time with him at this point that I think his toughness has more to do with post-traumatic stress and anger after what they did to him, than anything else. And who can blame him? But I think it's all good now—between us at least.

I get into the apartment and can already smell food cooking in the kitchen.

"Hi, honey. I'm home!" I shout.

I can hear his laugh from behind the bedroom door.

"Just a minute while I freshen up!" he yells, clearly pretending to be a housewife. It's funny to hear him be playful.

I take off my shoes and put down my heavy backpack, massaging my left shoulder with my right hand. If only they could put all these textbooks online, I would save not just my wallet, but also myself from back problems that will surely plague me for years after this.

He walks out with a small smile dancing on his lips. "I cooked."

"Is that right?"

"Yes. This Albanian can cook Italian." We walk into the kitchen, and using black oven mitts, he pulls out a steaming Pyrex dish from the oven. "It's baked ziti. I learned how to make it when working at the pizza shop."

"Oh my God." I'm in shock and awe right now. "It looks amazing."

The cheese bubbles at the top, making a crispy crust over the noodles.

He bends down again and pulls out a tray of French bread. "Garlic bread."

"I mean ..." My words fail me. "Let me just wash my hands, and then we'll eat."

"I didn't make a salad. I hate washing lettuce."

"That's what the mixes are for. They're, like, washed three times or something."

"I have no idea what you're talking about." He looks at me like I've lost my mind.

I step beside him and turn on the sink before pumping soap into my hands. "You can buy prewashed lettuce. No one likes to wash it, so you pay a few extra bucks, and they wash it for you."

"But how do you even know it's clean?" He hands me a towel, and I swiftly dry my hands. "Maybe they washed it, but then the bag was dirty. I don't trust it."

"This is America. We just trust everyone here. The bag says washed three times, so who am I to argue?"

I open the refrigerator and take out a few cucumbers and tomatoes. It only takes me a few minutes to peel and slice them. Back into the refrigerator, I take out a lemon. A quick slice, and I stick a fork in it before I squeeze the juice out into my hand, making sure to catch any seeds.

Adding some extra virgin olive oil, salt, and pepper, I say, "*Voilà.* We've got salad, no lettuce necessary."

He chuckles, and I rinse my hands before we both sit down at the small glass bistro table.

"Let me serve you," I tell him, standing up and putting food on his plate. "Who knew you'd be a man of so many talents? Other than forcing women to marry you, you build homes and cook."

He laughs, shaking his head at me. "Not women. Just one woman."

He sits back and lets me handle the plating. I look up after I give him salad, and he's watching me intently. No. It's a stare that I can feel from my toes up to my cheeks.

"I like your nose ring." He taps the side of his strong Roman nose.

I take a seat. "Thanks." I go ahead and put food onto my own plate, ignoring his weird compliment.

"And your tat," he continues, "I want to know about it."

I take a huge bite of the buttery garlic bread. "This is really good, Leo. Thank you."

"My pleasure." He eats his pasta with his fork and keeps the bread in his other hand, alternating bites between the ziti and the bread.

"The tattoo is of music notes. It's from the first song I composed."

"That's cool. How old were you?"

"I did it two years ago, when I was twenty. How about all of yours?"

"I've got a bunch."

"Yeah, I've noticed."

He laughs. "Most represent an aspect of the shqipe, and some are just personal ones I wanted along the way."

"There is this tattoo artist; he travels the world." I pull out my phone and open up Instagram before passing it to him. "You see?"

He scrolls. "Holy shit. He's unreal." He moves through the feed, eyes widening.

"Yeah. One day, I want him to draw something on me. I'm not sure what yet."

"Nico has some guy from Hungary who comes to New York City every few years. See this?"

He lifts the sleeve of his shirt, showing me his forearm from across the table. It's a gorgeously realistic eye in black and white, but inside the iris, I see an outline of two people.

"I've got my eye on *them*." He clenches his jaw.

"What's on your other forearm?" I quickly focus back on my food, not wanting to accidentally say something that would piss him off.

"Oh, that's the Albanian eagle. We all get it."

"Was it weird to join them?"

"The shqipe?"

"Yeah."

"No. It was the most natural thing in the world for me. I've told you before, I'm not a good man. Maybe in some ways but not in others. I work hard, and I run a decent business. But I also support my brothers above and before anyone else. They're family in the truest sense. Thicker than blood."

I swallow hard, feeling guiltier than ever that I'm not telling him about my history with Jet. I want to punch Nico in the face for not being truthful with him. He seems to notice my mind working because his head tilts to the side.

"Well"—I chuckle, wanting to change the subject—"out of curiosity, how much money does the shqipe take? Because if you're building like you say you are, shouldn't you be living somewhere nicer? No offense."

"I like this place. First off, I don't need more. Second off, until I get my revenge, I don't feel like living large. Anything special I might get would feel tainted. But once I crush them, I plan on moving."

"Jesus, Leo. You sound depressing."

"It's the truth."

"I wouldn't want to be on your bad side—that's for sure."

"Sweetheart"—he puts his fork down, smiling, blue eyes twinkling—"I wouldn't want to be on yours either. I might be the Mafia man, but you're ..." He blows out air, shaking his head.

"I'm what?" I know I have no right to be offended because I know who I am. But what the hell?

"You're unbelievably sexy. When you're mad, it's just off the charts."

I can feel my blush reaching my roots. "I'm going to change for our night. We're still going, right?"

"Yep." He takes a look at his watch. "I'll clean up, and then we'll head out. Be comfortable to walk but dress sexy."

"What?" I narrow my eyes.

"We're going somewhere nice. There will be a show. I want you to look hot. Is something wrong with that?"

"I don't operate like that, Leo."

He rises from his chair and steps close to me. I can smell his cologne when he's this near. It's masculine and woodsy. God, I love it.

"I'll make dinner, and I'll even clean up, on occasion. But when I tell you I want you to wear something specific, I mean it."

"I'll pretend you said, you want it to look believable that we're married. And it wouldn't be believable for your wife to come out with you, looking unsexy."

"If that's what it takes."

I walk into the bedroom calmly, like I have no care about time or about looking hot to amuse this man. The moment the door closes, I'm on speed, rummaging through my closet. I can be tough, but I'm still a woman. I need to look gorgeous but like I didn't try. I want to look incredible, but I want him to think that it took next to nothing to get me there. Okay, fine, I want to look hot, dammit. But I don't want him to know how badly I yearn to please him.

I take out a pair of low-rise dark jeans and a black silk camisole. In my desk drawer, I remove a set of ten gold bangles that I bought from a street vendor in SoHo. They're annoying with all the jingling they do, but I love the way they look, sparkling on my wrist. Setting it all out on the bed, I head into the bathroom for a quick shower. I sing some old Elton John song as I scrub my hair and shave my legs. I know they're hairless, and I know that no one will be feeling them tonight, but I want to go over it again.

Out of the shower I go with my hair literally sopping wet. I rub my Deva Curl hair gel into my palm before running it through my strands with my fingertips. I turn on the sink and cup my hand beneath the faucet to catch some water, adding it to my hair and scrunching up. There needs to be enough water mixed with the gel to ensure that my hair comes out soft and controlled, not crunchy. I did the *wet curls* look for years, and let me just say, I'm glad it's behind me.

Some CeraVe body cream on my arms and legs, a little pink blush from MAC on my cheeks, and a swipe of Laura Mercier pink lip gloss on my lips, and I'm done with my routine. The clothes come on next, but my problems begin when I take a look at my shoes. Sexy high and strappy heels are a no-go since we're walking. But I really don't want to be short tonight either. I rummage around and finally decide on a pair of black booties I got on sale from Rag & Bone. They are casual and only give me two inches, but at least they aren't totally flat.

When I leave the room, he's sitting on the couch, an arm draped across its back, watching Fox News.

I clear my throat to get his attention. "Ready?"

He stands up and turns around, staring at me. His eyes roam from my legs up to my face.

"We need to get you some new tops. This is nice, but I like sexier. Let me just change quickly."

He heads into the room, and I curse him. Any sexier than this, and I'd look like a streetwalker! Okay, maybe I'm exaggerating. But I refuse to play this part he's expecting. I won't let him dictate my clothes. When he comes back, I'm telling him that!

Minutes later, he walks out in—surprise, surprise—a black button-down shirt and a dark pair of jeans.

I want to make a joke about his outfit, but the moment I see his face, my mouth dries, and all rational thought leaves my head. He's unbelievably hot, and it's annoying as hell! The frustration he's pulling out of me? I want to throw it back inside my chest, where it belongs, and tell it to stop pounding around my midsection like a starved animal.

We leave the apartment and walk together toward Avenue C. The bar is probably about a twenty-minute walk away, but I'm realizing now that we have to go through some really shady areas to get there. Each consecutive building keeps getting worse.

"I don't usually walk these streets." I look around at the darkened buildings, a few lights sprinkled on in square windows.

When we pass the Blue Houses, I take a pause, not knowing if I should stop or hightail it. The Blue Houses are widely known as a crime-ridden and dilapidated housing project.

"Anyone who wants housing to be run by the state should take a look at this. Maybe live here for a week and see how good the state is doing at playing landlord," I whisper, loud enough for him to hear me but quiet enough not to draw attention.

With a laugh in his voice, he tells me, "Don't tell me *you're* afraid?"

"It's called self-preservation. This place is bad, Leo. Really, really bad. Maybe you don't realize because you're not from this country" I smirk and he shakes his head, clearly understanding my dig. "But this area is gang central."

"Don't tell me you forgot that I am gang central too."

"Ugh, don't remind me."

We continue to walk, but my fear is increasing.

"So, how did you fight me in the car like you did?"

"It was Krav Maga."

"MAGA? Like Make America Great Again?"

"No," I retort, a laugh bubbling from my chest. "MAGA, as in Make All Girls Amazing."

He stops walking, seemingly confused. And then he laughs—a real one, straight from his belly. He realizes I'm messing with him, and he likes it. "Talia, Talia, Talia ..."

We turn the corner. It's really dark here. Dirty cans lie on the broken concrete along with discarded cigarettes and other random pieces of trash. A park is ahead, and I can see the outline of gray swings blowing back and forth, as though someone were recently on them. I'm sure I can hear them creak, although I know it must be my mind playing tricks. I shouldn't be able to hear that, and yet I do.

I swallow hard, thinking about every step I take.

"Be comfortable to walk," he told me.

I'm wishing now that I had put my sneakers on. Even in the dim night, I can see the windows in the Blue Houses have bars across them. I shudder. It feels like a prison, not people's homes.

He steps closer to me, grabbing my hand. His palm is so warm. "Don't worry, Talia."

I look up and see a soulful gaze.

"When you're with me, you're safe. If something happens, just follow my lead."

I am warmed by his sentiment, and yet confused. *Is he insinuating something?*

It's like God is laughing because, after those words, a group of men starts prowling toward us. I know that it's all in real time, but I'm so afraid that it almost feels like slow motion.

"Leo, those guys are—"

A man shouts, "Yo, *ese*."

The wolf pack walks closer. I can see their faces now. Gripping his hand, I want to tell him to run. But before I can speak, he grips my palm harder, letting me know, in no uncertain terms, that we aren't going anywhere. This is on, his grip seems to say.

The leader steps up to where we stand, snarling, "So, what are you doing here, eh?" He raises his chin.

There are five of them. Tight white T-shirts, gold chains around their wrists and necks, low-slung jeans, and slicked-back black hair. If I were watching this in a movie, I would roll my eyes and say it was a cliché. But this isn't me watching from my couch. This is real.

Leo lets go of my hand, cracking his knuckles. He's acting casually, but a *don't fuck with me* vibe is written all over him. "Carlos, nice to see you again, man. It's been too long. How was prison?"

Carlos brings his phone to beneath his chin, the flashlight turned on. Four tattooed red teardrops line each of his beady eyes, raining down to his thin upper lip. "Prison was good to me. Not so good for others." He smiles again, a golden tooth shimmering.

I can feel the blood drain from my face. I'm light-headed, my mouth dry. I saw a prison documentary once, and they explained how some gangs would draw tears on their faces for every kill they completed.

"Look at the piece you brought." He smirks. "Little gift for me?" He momentarily glances at my face before zeroing in on my breasts.

I have clothes on, but I already feel undressed. My body is at once hot and cold as dread filters through my bloodstream.

I could run but where? I should look at Leo and figure out what the hell is going on, but I can't move. Nothing works—not my eyes, not my legs.

"This one is mine." Leo possessively puts an arm over my shoulders, bringing me closer to his enormous body. "We're headed to dinner, but I wanted to say hi to you boys first. Make sure things are moving smoothly these days. Nico is going to be in touch."

"Everything is smooth. Tell Nico I send my regards, and I'd love to speak with him about anything at any time."

They shake hands.

"When he's ready to talk, he'll find you." Leo's body is rigid and tall. He isn't afraid. He is dominant, and every single man here knows it.

They walk away first, and then we finally take our leave. He squeezes my hand, and I look at him. I want to bawl him out, but I still can't speak.

We keep walking until we're out of the Blue Houses territory.

"The fact that you didn't pass out is a testament to what you're made out of. Good job, Talia."

I stop moving, and he turns around to face me. That's when I punch and slap his chest and kick at his shins like a crazy person. "How dare you!" I scream. I have zero calmness. I can't even think.

But I know he put me in a dangerous situation, and I won't stand for that.

He throws me over his shoulder like a sack of potatoes. "Come on, Talia. Relax. They weren't going to hurt you."

Using my fists, I punch his back, screaming, "Who do you think you are? How could you? You'll pay for this!"

"Calm down. We're leaving the area. Just calm the fuck down."

I can tell he is getting angry at my outburst, but I can't slow myself.

"I will *not* calm down! Do you realize what you just did? They could have taken me!"

We finally get to Avenue B, where the streets have some ordinary people walking down them. He sets me down at a bus stop bench. Bright lights surround us now.

"Look at me!" he yells, grabbing my hands so that I can't use them against him. "You have to trust that I will not let you get hurt. Those guys do work for us. I had to stop over and see them. That crew, they're like dogs. You have to show your strength often, or they start to think they can take care of themselves. Still, you being with me keeps things light. When they see a woman by my side, they know that it's casual and not threatening. But it still gets the point across."

"And you didn't want to at least tell me what we were doing?"

"You wouldn't have agreed."

"That wasn't okay, Leo. That was fucked up! You can't just bring me into gang territory—"

"I am gang territory. You live with gang territory. You eat dinner with gang territory. Don't be dense." He keeps his grip on my hands, locking them together in front of me. With his free hand, he touches the side of my face. "Talia, calm down. I only took you because I knew you could handle it."

"Just because I have a big mouth doesn't mean I can handle Carlos in the Blue Houses," I pant.

Suddenly, tears well up in my eyes. The reality of my life hits me hard. I'm married to a Mafia man. Visiting gangbangers at the Blue Houses is part of his life and, apparently, mine too.

"You can't put me in those situations without letting me know. I don't like being lied to. I refuse to accept that."

"You're right. I will tell you if I ever need you in that way. For what it's worth, I barely interact with losers like them. But sometimes, it is what it is."

With his thumb, he wipes beneath my eyes. I can feel wetness seeping, but I refuse to admit that they're tears. I don't cry. I'm not a crier. Nope.

"I like how strong you are. When I was standing there, it felt good to have a woman by my side who wasn't going to run away, screaming. I won't ask you to use your Krav Maga skills on them, eh? Even if it did make you amazing."

He gives me a genuine smile, and I find myself nodding. I can't laugh, but I understand that he's trying to take the heat level between us down a few notches.

But still, I feel cold and clammy, the stress settling into my chest. He pulls me closer to him, warming me. When we're face-to-face, his thumb moves up my cheekbones, down to my lips. We're so close. A rush of heat blows through me as I stare into his blue eyes.

"I'm your new backup?" My voice is breathier than I intended.

"Yeah." He nods, bringing his forehead to mine and swallowing me up in his arms.

I can smell his breath, and I open my mouth to take him in.

"You were my second out there. I'm not used to having a woman hold her own. It was ... good."

He moves back a few inches. We're still so close, and it feels so right. His hands, heavy and hot, are against my back.

I settle my head on his chest, letting myself calm down. He's got me, and I'm okay.

When I'm finally steady, I let him go and stand up. There is a lot unsaid between us, but for now, we're going to keep it cool.

We spend the remainder of the walk talking about my parents, who work so hard and sacrificed everything to support my dreams of music. I tell him about taking a year off between high school and college, working at a music school to save money for my first year at

NYU. He tells me about his amateur fighting career in the city, which isn't serious but fun.

"Have you ever had any real injuries?"

"Nah, not really. A cracked rib once. Some stitches."

I look up, noticing the bright lights. "Oh, we're already here!"

A neon glow shines from above the building. Apotheke. To the left and to the right of the club, it's dark. We skip the entire line, and the bouncer says something in Albanian. The two men laugh and bang their fists together in the way guys do, and we walk straight inside. Perks of being with a man in the shqipe, I guess.

The room is red and black, sultry in velvet. A tall woman in a red dress meets us at the front and brings us straight to a table in the back corner. Drinks are immediately brought out and set on our table.

"So, that's how we're doing it tonight?" I lift my shot glass, not sure what's even in the thing. It's gray and smoky-looking.

"You know it. No more fighting. Just some fun."

"Fighting?" I put the drink to my nose, trying to smell it. "And all this time, I thought it was foreplay."

He laughs out loud, and we tap our glasses together before gulping the contents down. I might be an orchestra geek, but I know how to handle my alcohol.

My eyes widen as my taste buds dance. "The drink is absolutely delicious. Wow."

Clapping begins, and I look around the room. Everyone eagerly angles their chairs toward the stage.

"I'm excited for the show!"

"Yes." He nods. "When it's over, the place turns into a club."

He leans back into the plush couch, doing that king thing again. He just has this vibe about him. Like he's very important. Very rich. Very powerful.

Six women begin to dance in a line. They look nearly identical in short blonde wigs, dancing in tandem in their black lacy lingerie. It's a fun song with a downtown beat. Until the music stops, and one woman steps in front of all of them. She's tall with long black hair that reaches her hips. She's holding a black whip. Suddenly, the music turns back on. It's dark and sexy, in a language I can't place. The strip truly becomes a tease as she dances, twirling the whip in the air as she undoes a tie in the front of her bra. It opens, showcasing perky white breasts. From here, I can see the glint of rings through her nipples.

My mouth dries.

I'm turned on, my own nipples hardening to peaks beneath my silk top.

I turn to Leo, assuming he's watching the stage but he's not.

He's watching me.

A server walks to our table in a short red dress, whispering something in Leo's ear. He nods, and she scurries away. I put my focus back on the dance, eyes widening as I see her seductively swirling her hips. I shouldn't be so surprised, considering what I see when I play at Wild Orchid. But these women are on another playing field from the girls who dance in cages at the club. They're a lot sexier and a lot more serious about dance. Steaminess aside, they're really talented.

When the server comes back to the table with a bag in her hands, she gives it to Leo.

"Talia," he whispers in my ear. His breath is so warm. "I have some gifts for you. And I would like you to wear them."

He hands me the bag, and I look inside. "What's in here?"

"Open it."

I pull out the first box, my eyes widening when I see the brand. I whisper, "Cartier?"

He nods.

I undo the bow and open the box, only to find another smaller box inside. I want to be neat with the wrapping, but there is no dignity or sophistication right now. There are women dancing, basically nude, onstage, and the hottest man I've ever seen is in front of me with gifts. It is what it is.

I open the box and then immediately shut it. "What the fuck is this?"

"Diamond earrings."

I want to reply, but I can't. I have no idea how big they must be because I have no understanding of these types of things. The good life is one thing, but diamonds are a completely different level. I thought maybe he got me something simple, like a *welcome to my life* gift. But this isn't that.

I decide I might as well see what's inside the other boxes first before I yell at him for being so excessive.

The next box is also from Cartier. I open the double box and see a diamond bangle. I want to touch it, but I can't. It's gold with round diamonds set evenly apart around the bracelet. The light in here is dark, but I swear the diamonds are sparkling. I might not know diamond sizes, but the Cartier Love bracelet I know.

He moves close to me, putting his lips to my ear. "My wife should wear the best."

"No." I snap the box shut and stuff everything back into the bag it came in. "These aren't for me."

"Actually, they are for you."

"Did Nico tell you to do this?"

He laughs, like I'm joking. "Absolutely not. This is for you and you alone. And it's from me because I want them for you."

"Why would you spend this much money on your fake wife? Am I supposed to wear it until our eventual divorce? Wait." I pause. "Are you doing this, so I'll sleep with you?"

A few people shush me, and I realize I'm being too loud.

He stands up, grabbing my hand, and pulls me outside. I hope he took the bag with him because those jewels must be worth a few hundred thousand dollars—at least!

We get outside, the warm air filled with cigarette smoke and perfume.

"Take these gifts." He thrusts the bag back in my hand.

"No!" I push the bag back into his.

"Jesus!" he exclaims. "What is wrong with you? I want you to have these."

"I don't want to be bought!" And the truth is, I really don't. I've been there and done that. And frankly, I don't want to be that girl ever again. Just the thought of Jet and our relationship makes me feel like shit. "Nico is paying me really well for this arrangement," I continue. "I don't need anything more. My school is paid for, and I don't need a man to support me. Never again."

He tilts his head to the side. "What do you mean, a man to support you, never again?"

My eyes flash. "It doesn't mean anything. I just don't want to be your whore."

"Whore?" He shakes his head. "Trust me, you aren't my whore. We haven't even fucked."

My mouth gapes open.

"Ah, speechless Talia. A rarity." He smiles, his eyes dancing.

"This isn't a joke." I cross my arms over my chest, feeling defensive.

"All right. Let's just go back inside. Don't take the jewelry, okay? I didn't think it would make you upset. I thought it would make you happy. Maybe make this whole thing between us easier. But if it bothers you, you don't have to keep it. I have other whores who would happily take it."

My eyes widen in shock, but when I see him laughing, I slap his arm, trying not to laugh myself.

"There is one thing though that I would like you to wear." From his back pocket, he takes out a small box. I open my mouth to say something, but he cuts me off, "Don't worry." He flips it open.

It's a yellow-gold wedding band. There are no diamonds. Just simple, thin, and clean.

"I wasn't sure what you would want as an engagement ring or what style. But you should look like you belong to me."

I put out my hand, and he slides the ring onto my ring finger. It fits perfectly. "How did you know my size?"

"I notice things about you. From the first time I saw you. Maybe it was even when I watched you play the cello at your practice. Or at the club, when you played onstage with those violins. But I notice you, Talia."

This time, I'm stunned silent. I'm not sure he meant for our conversation to take this turn, but it has. The silence between us grows, but it's still not quiet. I want to tell him that I noticed him too. I want to tell him that I feel the same way. It's something in his eyes, but it's so much more than that. We've got a strong connection between us, and it's undeniable. But I know better than to just trust feelings.

"You know what? Feelings are bullshit."

"Is that right?" He chuckles, rolling his eyes like I've ruined the moment.

"Yes. I'm serious. Feelings are full of random things, like hormones and excitement and lust. It wanes. It moves up and down. They aren't to be trusted."

He takes out a pack of cigarettes from his back pocket, lighting one up. I watch as the smoke wafts around him, his full lips taking inhales and then slow exhales. Even though it's dark, his blue eyes are bright. "So, what is real?"

"What's real is a deeper level of intimacy and understanding that should go beyond just the physical excitement of things. It's about satisfying each other and growing an actual bond. Leaning on each other. Trust and friendship, which must be built over time. Knowing someone's dreams and caring enough to support them. Putting them first. That's real."

He looks at me closely, swallowing hard. "So, what's this then?"

"This is the start of something ... enjoyable. Maybe."

He drops his cigarette on the floor, a small smile on his lips. "Let's go back inside. Enjoy the night."

He grabs my hand, and we get back to the club.

The show must be over because everyone is up and dancing. Red smoke fills the area, and Bad Bunny plays on the speakers. In true New York City fashion, it's so random, but it all works. Leo takes a seat at our table and pulls out his phone. I move a little to the music when I spot Ronna and Leora walking toward me.

Leora exclaims, "Hey, Tal!"

We kiss on both cheeks.

"I can't even believe you guys are here. How great is this?"

"The show was insane." Ronna smiles.

Leo stands up then, towering over the three of us. "Hey."

Their jaws? They drop. Literally drop. A few giggles, and it makes me laugh out loud. To see these two beauties be in shock over a man is very surprising.

"Ronna, Leora, this is Leo." I look up at him. What the hell should I introduce him as?

"I'm her husband," he shouts, loud enough for everyone in a five-foot radius to hear.

"What?" The girls start laughing. Clearly, they think it's a huge joke.

I laugh, too, because the situation is just too absurd to explain.

"Excuse us. I'm going to dance with my wife."

Leo pulls me into a throng of people. Normally, I worry about going to the center of a crowd like this. I'm not so tall—okay fine, I'm short as hell—and I can easily get swallowed up. But with Leo, there is no worry. He's so tall and strong, almost like a rock in the midst of waves. No one can push him over or get into his space. *Our* space.

I let the music take over, and by the way he is dancing, he does too. We get into an unbelievable rhythm together. The man can dance. Holy shit, he can move. I don't have to lead, like I normally do with guys. I spin and drop and let myself have fun. Because what else is there to do?

We laugh for no reason, enjoying the music. A girl walks around with a tray of shots for five dollars each. He pulls out his wallet, takes out a twenty, and hands me two before taking two for himself. I guess it really is going to be that kind of night! We both drink up quickly, and I let the burn open my heart.

I exhale, smiling, and then take a look at my left hand. I've got a gold ring on my finger, and it's a joke, but it's not. I'm literally married. The laughter bubbles up, and he just goes with it, laughing with me.

And then, suddenly, a slow song comes on. Everyone is awkwardly looking at each other because what on earth is a slow song doing in the middle of a club? Before I can think more on it, Leo pulls me toward him. I wrap my arms around his neck. We let ourselves stare at each other.

"What's real is this moment, Talia." He licks his lips. "I know it's not easy. You've been put in a fucked up situation with me. But I want to thank you for taking a chance on this and on me." His eyes blaze. "I need this citizenship," he adds almost hesitantly.

"Yeah." I want to speak, but nothing else will come. Somehow, I feel disappointed. I have no right, but I do.

The music changes back to something upbeat and fun, and I push my emotions aside as we continue to party.

By the end of the night, a black car comes to pick us up. I have no clue who is driving us, but if Leo feels comfortable, I should too. When we finally get back home, we both hastily change and fall into our respective beds. It would be nice to sleep next to him. But I remind myself, feelings aren't real.

14

Leo

OVER THE NEXT TWO MONTHS, we get into a routine. Our schedules are different, but we manage to overlap for breakfast and, most nights, for dinner too. We talk about ourselves a lot, which is something we need to do. We have to know each other well enough to be able to convince someone that we're actually married, and it seems like, somehow, we are on the right track for that.

Last night, I took her to the famous Rainbow Room for dinner. After taking the obligatory photos together in front of the magnificent New York City views, we enjoyed our night. She talked more about her family. I told her about Kosovo. I wanted to tell her about the war, but I felt badly about bringing that shit into such a nice conversation.

Surprisingly, she's really funny. And smart. And completely laser-focused on her cello and schoolwork. The most surprising thing about her is that she cooks a lot. For a woman who is as tough as she is, I didn't expect her to be so good in the kitchen. Of course, she doesn't make fresh bread like Daisy did for her family. But she makes us eggs every morning and lots of salads and grilled fish for dinner. I scratch the back of my neck. She might even be better than fresh bread.

Her words from our night at Apotheke, about feelings being bullshit, keep rolling in my head. It made me think more on Daisy and what we had. We had a secret romance, which kept things very hot all the time. We had sex, and to me, a young kid, it was the greatest feeling I had ever known. We talked but mostly about what could be. I wouldn't say we shared more than that.

I'm a man now, in the shqipe. All of this, Daisy has no idea about. What I felt about her was strong, but I was a child. I had no idea about what life would bring me. The fact that she turned out to be a gold digger? It was shocking, but maybe it's not. We never had a chance to be real together, out in the open.

When everything is a secret, it's always charged. Not that I don't still despise her for what she did to me. Young or old, deception and lies are not tolerable.

A FEW NIGHTS AGO, I made eggplant Parmesan with loads of cheese sprinkled on top, just like I learned during my short time of working at Famiglia. Talia laughed over how good it was before devouring it. She'd even picked up a six-pack of Corona beer before dinner and taught me how to open the top using the side of the counter! I'm not used to seeing a woman this way, so laid-back and unconcerned with her appearance. Talia looks gorgeous because she is gorgeous. Not a stitch of makeup. Natural hair. Clean, short nails. She's just ... herself.

And that night we met with Carlos and his gang at the Blue Houses? I still can't believe how she held her own. I know she was scared as shit. But she did it. Until that moment, Talia and her beauty and toughness had been the center of lustful thoughts. She had been a woman I wanted to enjoy carnally, before it all ended. But that night, she showed me how much more lurked beneath her surface. I felt protective over her when Carlos walked toward us. And when we left the scene, I wanted to hold her. Then, she surprised me when she refused the jewelry.

I never imagined a woman could be this way. She is amazing.

When I told Nico about the Carlos meet over lunch, he laughed out loud. "Made of tough stuff, that girl."

It was obvious he respected her. I asked him if they had any history together, and he said it was all arm's length.

"You have any plans for her, within the shqipe maybe?" I leaned forward, wondering if there was more to this than I knew.

"Nothing in the works. I figured she'd do well by you. The girl is all business. You don't have to worry that she'll bloodsuck you." He folded his arms, leaning back into the chair. "Just focus on your path. Get your citizenship and get your ass to Kosovo to kill that motherfucker."

"Yes, sir."

He lit up a smoke before lifting his head to mine. "Any feelings developing between the two of you?"

Without hesitation and with full confidence, I told him, "No. My focus is on my work and getting to Kosovo. She's nothing to me."

"Good." He took out his phone and read something, seemingly serious. His brows were furrowed as he furiously typed something out, the cigarette hanging from the corner of his lips.

I had lied, but Nico was too preoccupied to notice.

Something big was happening between her and me, but I wasn't ready to bring it to his attention. Not yet.

He stood up, signaling that the conversation was over.

We shook hands on that, and I left.

With Nico, you take what he gives you. There is a lot of trust I put him in, but he deserves it all. His history speaks for itself.

THIS MORNING, I'm making coffee while Talia showers. I know that she prefers it black, in her pink coffee mug that reads, *Cellos do it better.*

She walks into the kitchen, smelling so damn good with her wet, long, dark hair. I've obviously smelled her body wash in the shower, but it isn't quite like her smell. Maybe it's a mixture of the wash and just her own natural scent. Whatever it is, it's good. Too good.

"Hey, Leo. Or shall I say, *good morning, husband of three years*?" She pours coffee into that pink mug and takes a deep inhale of the steam. "Smells so, so delicious."

"Busy day today?"

She shrugs. "Sure. I've got school and rehearsal. You?" Looking down at her phone, she scans her news app.

"Heading over to the job site. Lots of random shit happening today."

"Mmhmm." She takes a seat, reading something intently.

"Any good news this morning?"

"A woman was raped on the 6 subway train, and New York City is still broke." She lifts her head. "All these taxes we pay, and where does the money go? The streets keep getting filthier. I understand high taxes if it means more services but high taxes and no services? What the hell are we paying for?"

I smile, liking how opinionated she gets. I want to push her, so she talks more. "Why not just go socialist and let the government run it all then?"

"What?!" she exclaims, heating up. "I mean, why would I trust the government enough to literally run my life, choose what I need, and feed me? I work hard, I study hard, and I take responsibility for myself. I don't trust my government, or any government, to hold that kind of power over my life. I love my freedom, thank you very much."

"It's true. But when you're struggling and someone tells you free school, free healthcare, free everything ... it's easy to want that."

"I have one word for you: Russia. My friends who left in the '90s tell me about how their lives were run." She shivers, like the memory of it is too much to bear. "America needs to do a better job of teaching kids history. I'm not saying a colorful one but the truth. People don't understand that socialism doesn't work, and I have to assume it's because they never learned about it."

"And what's the truth?"

"There's no such thing as a free lunch. Not under socialism. Not under communism. Not under democracy. One way or another, payment by the people is due. At least under democracy, we can try to control how it goes for ourselves. I want my life to be the one I make. Even if it's a horrible one, I want it to belong to me. Democracy isn't perfect, but it's much better than the other options. Oh, and the greatest example of all is North and South Korea!"

I swallow hard, listening to her go on. Trying to describe how I feel right now, watching her talk about something she feels passionate about, would be impossible. And it's not just that I can't find the words, but also because she's just so bright and beautiful that it's showstopping.

"North Korea. They are always hungry, and their economy is run by a military dictatorship. And then you have South Korea, which is a liberal democracy and one of the most advanced economies of the world. Countries lose when there is no freedom."

I'm quiet. I could let her talk for hours, but I can tell that my silence is confusing her.

I lift my coffee mug in the air. "Well, God bless America!"

She smiles, lifting her own cup. "God bless democracy."

We lock eyes.

"God bless beautiful women who are willing to marry men for citizenship."

"And God bless crazy-sexy Mafia men who will do anything for citizenship."

"Crazy-sexy, huh?"

She rolls her eyes. "You know what you are. I married you for a reason, didn't I?"

I tilt my head to the side, feeling the air fill my lungs. I dare her, saying, "Tell me what I am."

She doesn't speak. But she looks. And God almighty, I feel it. I want her, and she wants me. I know this as a fact. She turns her head away and focuses back on her phone. This tension between us is building—fast.

I empty my cup and rinse it out in the sink before grabbing my wallet off the counter. "Will you be home tonight? I'll make dinner."

"Mmhmm."

She waves me off, and I leave the apartment, smiling.

I FINISH CHOOSING THE MIELE, Sub-Zero, and Wolf appliances for three of the new homes I'm building and check the time. I've got about two hours to get home, wash up, change, and grab a bottle of wine from the liquor store on my block before getting some dinner ready.

I'm learning quickly that the happier I keep Talia, the more likely I can reach my goal. I ignore the fact that our time together has turned enjoyable. Or that she's on my mind constantly. We keep all of our conversations general, neither of us digging too deeply into how our feelings are evolving. And it's been working.

Swiping my MetroCard, I navigate through the tunnels and hop onto the 4 train just as the doors begin to close. It's packed with people leaving work, and not for the first time, I'm glad to be as tall as I am. I wonder how bad riding the subway must be for Talia during rush hour with that huge cello in her hands, her face barely reaching most people's chins. Something stirs in my chest. She really shouldn't take the subway at all. It's gotten much more dangerous lately. I don't take the subway to save money, but because I despise sitting in New York City traffic. At least the train gets me where I need to go quickly.

A few men push onto the train, elbowing their way into spots that are already filled. The result is a cluster of people packed like oiled fish with barely any room to breathe.

I look down, noticing a woman trying to twist her way around, likely in an attempt to get some air. She has a baby attached to her stomach in some sort of colorful blue-and-orange sling, a look of exhaustion and heat on her face. The baby starts to scream, and there is collective groan of annoyance from the riders. I grab the mother's hand and pull her to where I stand. At first, she's shocked, but when she locks her eyes with mine and notices that my spot is better than where she was, she calms. I enforce some room for her, and people try to keep their distance.

She exhales, looking up, and whispers, "Thanks."

I don't reply, just nod.

Luckily, my stop comes, and I walk off as quickly as I can. The streets are not too busy, but I basically run back to my building. Up the stairs I climb until I reach my apartment. When I unlock the door, it swings open. I'm met by a scent. Not just any scent. It's Talia. She's actually taken over the space in more ways than one. There are white candles on the window. A few flowers sit in a vase on the coffee table.

I pull off my shoes and set them beside her slippers. One thing we have in common is keeping a clean home. Both of us don't like to walk inside with dirty shoes, and she always switches to these little slippers with fur inside. They're ugly as hell, but even I have to admit, they look comfortable. I pick one up and look inside. UGG.

I put it back down and walk into the bathroom for a shower, trying to move as quickly as possible.

Fifteen minutes later, I'm at the liquor store on my corner, picking up a bottle of wine. I spot Talia's favorite red in the back, a cabernet sauvignon from Israel. Before I can get to the cashier, I notice a woman browsing the cold wines in the refrigerator. Long black hair reaches the center of her back. And the height, the shape, the way she sets a hand on the side of her hip.

Could it be Daisy? I swallow hard, feeling beads of sweat rise on my forehead. *What would I do if it were actually her? What would I say?* A torrent of feelings swirls in my chest. *If it were her, would it make me happy?*

I breathe in and out, trying to regain my control.

She turns around, and I have no choice but to lean against one of the tables to keep myself straight.

It's not her.

I pay for the bottle of wine and get home, showering for a second time because I need to calm down. The moment the shampoo is in my hair, I can feel my anger rising. It's bad enough that Daisy did what she did. But for her face to now haunt me? Fuck that. I want to move on from this. I need my revenge. I also refuse to ever let a woman have this kind of power over me again. Never.

I make dinner—some grilled chicken and pasta with tomato sauce. I like to have salad, but I can't bring myself to chop any vegetables or wash lettuce that has apparently been washed three times already. My phone buzzes on the counter. It's Talia, and I hit Accept.

"Hey."

"Leo? It's Talia. I have so much going on at school tonight. I just don't think I can leave. I have a paper due tomorrow in music theory."

For some reason, her excuse sounds exaggerated. *Could she be lying?*

"Oh, come on, Tal. I left work early. I already bought the wine, and I've got food on the stove."

"I can't possibly leave. You know how important school is to me."

Her tone pisses me off. Aside from the fact that I could have been the one with the same excuse had my life turned out differently, it's also disrespectful as hell.

"So, you're saying that you aren't coming back for dinner? Even though I changed my whole schedule to get back here?"

"Don't put it like that. I feel terrible about it, but school is school. It has to come first."

"I'm the one who should come first." The words spill from my mouth before I can stop them.

She sasses, "You? Um, I don't think so, Leo."

Every masculine cell in my body turns to fire.

She must understand that my silence isn't positive because, quickly, she adds, "I'll make it up to you somehow."

"Oh yeah? And how do you plan on doing that?"

I can sense her hesitation by the shortness of her breaths. She's silent, but I've got an inferno raging inside my chest.

I hang up on her before she can get another word out and lean against the counter.

Fuck this. I should have stayed late on the building site, and I would have if Talia hadn't told me she was coming back for dinner. I'm sure the electrician messed up some lighting, and I wasn't even there to deal with it.

Clearly, Talia doesn't give a fuck about me and my time.

I shoot off a text to Dren, seeing if he's around tonight to party. He says he is.

I unceremoniously dump the food in the trash bin. There are plenty of bars and restaurants around New York City who know us and will service us—in more ways than one. It's time for me to have a little fun.

She does what she wants to do, so I'm going to keep doing what I want to do. I'm not even sure what I thought was happening between us. She and I are fictionally married—nothing more.

~

THE BACK of Harry's Bar and Grill is a strip club. No one knows—unless they do. And the shqipe definitely knows.

I walk in and find Dren at the restaurant bar. We embrace before I take a seat next to him. "Need a strong drink tonight and some decent food."

"Looks like we're in the right spot for that."

The bartender steps over, smiling. "Long time no see, handsome. Macallan 18, one rock?"

I smile back. "That's right."

Dren lets out a groan as he shifts in his seat. "I tattooed her name on my ass last night. I can barely fucking sit." He slowly adjusts himself like an old man would.

"Whose?"

"What do you mean, whose? Vesa's, obviously."

"Why the fuck would you do that?"

Vesa is his long-term woman. I know he loves her, but he's never been faithful either. It seems they have some kind of understanding though because he doesn't exactly hide it and she is still around.

"I was drunk. She wanted a commitment. I wasn't about to propose, but I had to pacify her."

"But now, you have her name tatted up on your ass!" I laugh out loud, clapping, as if his life were theater.

He rolls his eyes, his heavy cheeks flushing with embarrassment. He grumbles, "Should keep her quiet for a while at least."

"Well, I would hope so. I always knew you were a closet romantic."

The bartender puts my drink in front of me. "If you want anything else, after dinner, just ask for me."

"Might take you up on that, thank you."

She's sexy, and I know firsthand that she can give head better than anyone else in New York City. But tonight, she just isn't for me.

The hostess walks over in a short black dress, pretending to be shy. I've seen her many times before. She's one of these strange women who has a different hairstyle every time I see her. Sometimes, it's short and black, other times long and blonde. Tonight, it's wavy and brown.

She brings us to the table, and Dren and I take our seats across from each other. As usual, he likes to face the front door. Some habits are hard to break. The waitress follows right behind her and takes out a small white pad of paper.

"Are you ready?" She lifts a brow, and I don't miss the double meaning of her question.

I immediately order a bone-in rib steak with mashed potatoes and spinach on the side, and Dren asks for the same. Two more drinks, and we're ready to enjoy the meal before the meal. He's always been the one who loves to talk, so he tells me about the drama at the mechanics shop, also owned by the shqipe. He goes off on a tangent, and I try to follow his story about some Italian Mafia guy, son of Anthony Borignone, who ran off to Utah to build a casino.

It doesn't take long for dinner to be finished and for me to get comfortable on one of the plush private couches. One of the waitresses, Star, works quickly, and it isn't long until she's grinding against my cock like the queen of a rodeo, complete with heavy red hair and jeans that are open at the crotch and ass and held up with black leather garters. I focus on her fake tits bouncing because I really don't want to put a face to what's happening right now. But I catch a glimpse and decide to shut my eyes entirely before I lose my hard-on.

What I wouldn't give to teach Talia a lesson for ditching me tonight ...

I sink lower into the couch. I might as well face it; Talia is a girl who puts the right shit in life first. But if she would just soften up a bit, things could go so well between us. The fantasy comes at me in flashes, and the atmosphere within my chest shifts to molten heat.

Talia's long hair brushes against my chest. She's in a gold dress, her tits so full—too full for her top. We're back at the club, the night I met her. In the dark back alley. Only I get there first. But she walks up to me. She tells me she was waiting for me to step outside. She's vulnerable, and I want to protect her. I want to show her who I am. She pulls down the straps of her dress, her eyes praying that I like what I see. She's absolute perfection.
I press her against the wall and lift her. She's so tiny, so perfect. Her legs wrap around my waist, and my hands move beneath her dress.
Smells so good. Feels so good.
Shiiiit.
Her nails dig into my shoulders, her long throat exposing itself to me. I lift the bottom of her dress to her hips. I can feel the pulse pounding in her pussy, beating against my cock. No barriers. I shift her, wanting to hit that right angle for her. She moans, and it's deep and guttural. I lower my head, latching my mouth on to one pert nipple, drawing it into my mouth and sucking until she shakes.
I can feel the climax building behind my eyes. Talia has the sweetest pussy on earth, and I know it to be true. With the hottest hands, she holds on to me like she might die if she doesn't. I grab her plump ass, pumping so hard that I might break her. She's soaked—I can hear it.

I'm about to burst, sweat breaking out across my chest. I can feel and hear how close she is, as her pussy clenches me like a vise.

I open my eyes. *Oh fuck.* I pull Star off of me, and she squeals, but I keep my face away from hers. Thank God I didn't come in my pants. I just want to get out as quickly as possible. The feeling of guilt rises in my chest faster than I could have imagined.

It was just a lap dance, and yet I know that if Talia knew what just happened, she'd fucking kill me. Nothing like Dren's woman, who looks the other way. And she's nothing like Daisy either, who clearly goes where the money is. Talia would never stand for such a thing, and if I were being honest with myself, I wouldn't want her to.

15

Talia

WITH A HOT LARGE BLACK COFFEE, I get my bagel scooped out and toasted with cream cheese, lox, tomato. Rachel is late, as usual. She and I have been friends since childhood. She studies at the Fashion Institute of Technology, learning fashion marketing. You see, the thing about Rachel is that she has a scholarship. A *real* one.

As I wait, my mind drifts back to last night—or I should say, this morning. It was intense. So intense that I'm not sure how to process my feelings. What happened between us makes me ... hot. Also slightly disturbed and completely confused.

I got back to the apartment around one a.m., dog-tired with my eyes burning from staring at the computer screen for so long. It had been peaceful at the library when I was in my own cubicle. I'd written about the origins of human appreciation for rhythm and discussed how listening to your mother's heartbeat in the womb was your first understanding of music.

Bah-boom. Bah-boom. Bah-boom.

I came home, looking forward to sharing what I'd learned with Leo. I knew he was angry that I'd ditched him, but school is a hard line for me. I had gotten myself into this mess because of my dreams, and the only way to play for the New York Philharmonic after I graduated is to finish at the top of my class. So, sue me. I am an obsessive pursuer of As. I have to try my best at everything I do. The weather had been lousy, too, and I'd had a good seat in the library. I couldn't just give it up! Library seats are rarer than diamonds, particularly before midterms and finals.

I had a whole dissertation in my head about how I would explain it to him. Get him to understand the seriousness of school. The women he knew probably hung on his every word and would let go of whatever they were in the middle of just for a few moments with him. I still hadn't been to a shqipe party, but I could imagine it all. Hot, wealthy, powerful men who were utterly devoted to each other. Women on call. But I had a life too! I wasn't one of those girls.

Still, I couldn't deny the fact that I felt ... guilty.

I'd had a general outline for the paper, but I didn't realize where my research would take me. And once I recognized that it would be all night, I let him know. I hadn't thought about the fact that he was setting up dinner. But the truth was, he wasn't just setting it up. The man was cooking—for me. And he'd left work early—for me. I understood why he was furious. Not only that, but sometimes, I thought he resented me for my schooling. God knew it had driven him insane when I told him where I studied that first night we met. Clearly, it was still a real thorn in his side.

I felt ready to deal with him. I looked around, noticing he wasn't there. I washed the frying pan he'd used in the sink and took a look into the refrigerator to see if I could reheat what he'd cooked. It was empty. I opened the trash to throw away a random piece of Bounty lying on the counter when I saw exactly what he had made. Chicken breast lined the trash. He'd dumped it!

I sat on the couch, wondering if I had any right to text him. Thinking about texts made me think about that girl who'd reached out when I first got there. He was a man with needs, and I wasn't fulfilling them—that was for sure. I wasn't the type of woman Leo was used to. And I wasn't like him or his friends. And yet my heart sank with each moment I realized that he was not here, so he must have been with someone else. It felt bitter. Awful even. I watched the entirety of Clueless *for the millionth time but still could not sleep. By two thirty a.m., I washed my face and changed into a second pair of pajamas. But sleep was still impossible. I got back up, went into the bathroom, and decided to do a hair mask. After waiting twenty minutes—five more than the directions said—I rinsed it out with ice-cold water and then decided to do a face mask. Close to three a.m., and he was still. Not. Home. I changed for the third time, into a shirt and shorts, and then I decided I wanted to wear his clothes instead. I rummaged through his neat drawers, making a mess, and picked a pair of boxers and a white Hanes T-shirt. And then I realized that he was going to think I was a psycho because why would I be wearing his clothes?*

Oh, fuck that. So what if he thinks I'm crazy? Where the fuck is he?!

I sat with my cell phone in my hand, wondering what would become of me. What if he got into a fight somewhere and was lying dead in some underground fight ring? I knew he sometimes fought in his free time.

I paced the room, listening to the AC whir. And then I sat by the window, watching cabs drive through the night. Waiting for him to get out of one. That was when he came through the front door. Or at least, I thought it was him. It could have been the creep from the Blue Houses—Carlos. I heard the clunk of shoes hitting the wooden floor. But would Carlos pull off his shoes before entering? Obviously not.

I looked down. I was wearing his clothes. My skin was probably red from the mask. My hair was a ball of frizz because I had no product in it. When he finally walked into the bedroom, he ignored me and went straight into the shower.

I took a nervous breath at how he'd prowled through the room. His intensity was off the charts. Was he going into the shower because he had been with another woman? Was it perfume I smelled on him or just my imagination playing games?

I sat there in bed, worrying and anxious. His temper. God, it was awful. He finally exited the bathroom, a towel wrapped around his trim waist. His eyes moved to my body, widening when he noticed that I was wearing his clothes. I couldn't read whether or not he was pleased or pissed.

When he came to the side of my bed, I could feel the heat radiating off his body. Droplets of water dripping down his chest. The scruff on his beard, dark and harsh. Bending down, he removed my shorts. His shorts from my legs. I was shaking so hard that I was sure he'd noticed.

But that was nothing compared to what happened next.

His palm, so hot and rough, went straight to my pussy. I clenched in surprise and then liquefied. Legs spread, I held on to his wide back as he fingered me until I shook. Pulled off my shirt. Sucked on my nipples so hard that I thought I would die from the pleasure. One finger turned into two.

I shut my eyes tightly, trying not to shudder. Just the memory alone has my mouth drying out.

When I came, I moaned so long and hard. The shock of it—

Rachel unceremoniously sits down at the table, breaking me out of my reverie. "Hey, Tal." She throws her long blonde hair into a high bun.

Gathering myself, I tell her, "I know it hasn't been too long since I've seen you, but we have so much to talk about."

"Yeah. Like shouldn't you be en route to the Hamptons with your Mafia man?" She unwraps her sandwich, taking out her bagel and biting into it.

I drop my head into my hands. "The man you're referring to and I are done."

She leans her elbows on the table, getting closer to me. "Spill."

And so I do, in word-vomit form, barely taking a breath.

She raises a pointed brow. "So, now, you're married, pawned off to a different but much hotter Mafia guy?" She looks at me incredulously.

"Yep. But Leo doesn't seem to know about me and Jet. I feel like a liar, by the way. Or worse."

"You mean, you don't want him to think you're a whore?"

I roll my eyes. "Can we not? For God's sake." Heat rises in my chest. *I'm a whore.*

"Don't be so sensitive. I expect more from you. You know you're not a whore. You just fucked a guy for money and now married a different one—for more money."

My jaw drops, and she laughs out loud.

"Come on. Make light of it. You wouldn't be the first or the last. We both know that sex and money are the way of the world. Who cares anyway? You're not fucking a million guys. You had a boyfriend, and he hooked you up. Now, you've got a new man, and you've been hooked up again. The end."

"Well, it seems that, now, I'm trapped. When I was with Jet, I could have pulled the cord at any time. But this time, I'm locked. And I have a marriage certificate and ring," I lift up my left hand, "to prove it."

"Well," she continues, "if you can get divorced in the end and it's only a few months of your life and five million dollars? This is amazing, if you ask me. Take the money and never think about it again. Can we take a trip when it's over? I'm dying to go to Ibiza."

"But what if they don't let me leave him? How do I know we'll be able to get divorced? Jet told me that there is no divorce."

"Well"—she exhales—"you have a point. Maybe Leo is just promising you an end date—"

"So I shut up and do my best during the interview? Yeah, I agree. But another part of me feels like maybe this is turning into more between us." I drop my head in my hands.

She takes another bite. "How much more?"

"Well, we've been spending a ton of time together. And he's gorgeous and successful and smart. The first time I saw him, we had that connection. And sure, things got testy. But then we've had so much fun ..."

"It won't happen. He will find a way out."

"Are you sure?"

"Yes. It's because of that girl he's obsessed with, who screwed him over." She shrugs. "I think that he'll want you out of his life. I mean, this man has been through a lot of shit. He must be damaged as hell. There is no way he wants you in his world and by his side—no offense. And thank heavens for that. He might try to convince Nico to let you out because he wants you gone. Trust me on this. He doesn't want marriage."

"The man is hell-bent on destruction. He's got a grudge like I've never seen before." I shiver, acting like I'm scared. Key word? Acting. The truth is, I'm not scared at all. I wonder what could be so wrong with me that just the thought of Leo angry gets me horny?

"Grudges are hard to let go of. I still despise Ryan Landau for telling everyone I got my period in the seventh grade."

"Truth. Fuck him. I hate that asshole."

"But let's get back to this impending divorce," she continues. "If he is this dead set on revenge, then why are you even worried about the two of you growing feelings? Let him hold on to the grudge. Much more likely for him to get rid of you when it's all over and you aren't useful. And in the meantime, enjoy your time with him."

"But I'm not even sure Nico will allow us to end it. I'm really not. That man is like Big Brother. He knows and sees everything, no matter what. And who knows what his plans are or why he chose me to marry Leo?" I look around the store, wondering if one of their thugs is following me. "I want to get married for real. I want kids. And love. I can't be stuck with Leo for life."

"You should talk to him. Nico, I mean. Have a dinner. Find out the deal from his mouth. Not Jet's and definitely not Leo's. Just ask."

"You do realize who he is, right? Nico is the head of the Albanian Mafia. The man is a killer," I whisper-yell.

"Sure. But he won't hurt you." She tilts her head to the side. "Well, at least I think he won't. He chose you for Leo, didn't he? He wants you for some reason. Maybe it's as Jet said—that you are okay with the life and you can hold your own." She shrugs. "Someone once said that the simplest explanation is usually the right one ..." She raises her head to the ceiling, trying to recall the name.

I put up my finger. "I am *not* okay with the life."

"Well, you did live it. And you happily took the money." She raises a brow, quickly lifting her hands in front of her chest. "Not that I blame you."

I groan.

"Go and find out what it is. It sounds like Leo is a very good-looking guy. I'm sure many women would have married him without the drama. Don't these guys have all those hang-around girls who would marry them?"

"Exactly!" I nod.

"Anyway"—she takes another large bite of her bagel—"let's recap our conversation. Nico chose you, and now, you're married. Leo and you are enjoying your time, right? So, have fun and stop overthinking everything."

"Maybe you're right."

"I am definitely right. Be happy and relax. It will work out in the end." She crumbles her tinfoil over her bagel and stands up. "Sorry to have to leave so quickly, but I've got class in half an hour. Love ya!"

She struts off, slinging her bag over her shoulder.

A guy, college-aged by the looks of it, taps my shoulder. "Are you almost done? If not, can I join you?" He gestures to the empty seat, as if he's hoping we can sit together.

I stand up, shaking my head. The last thing I need right now is another complication. "It's all yours."

On my way out, I decide that I'm going to let this thing between Leo and me run its course. There is no end other than him leaving back to Kosovo for his revenge. So, why not enjoy whatever it is we have, for however long we have? I'm smart enough to keep everything in check. I can have sex and leave my feelings at bay. I'm not a girl who can't keep track of what's what in a relationship. If anyone can draw a firm line, it's me.

I DO some early food shopping and schlep it all back to the apartment. By the time I get through the front door, I'm panting. The steps to get up here aren't a big deal on their own, but add a load of weight, and it's like the StairMaster on steroids.

Leo is sitting at the kitchen table, a laptop open, along with what looks like sets of home plans. The sheets of paper are enormous, almost as long as my body, and spread along the table and the floor.

"Hey." I drop the groceries on the floor and take off my shoes before sliding on my UGG slippers. I wonder if it's going to be weird, seeing him after our night.

He stands from his chair and takes the groceries from the floor. "You don't need to pick these up. I actually have a credit card for you to use for everything home-related."

"But—"

"No. This is the home I provide, and in this home, anything we buy comes from my work. It's how I am. I've been meaning to tell you this since you got here, but I know it's not easy for you to let me take control."

I should argue—because feminism! The problem is, I can tell that I have no choice but to say okay right now. Beneath his relatively calm exterior, there is restrained dominance. I've seen pieces of it. And sure, I have seen him rupture, but the truth is, I know that I've barely cracked the surface. If I push too hard, he could likely unleash a serious force on me. The way he's breathing, his muscles are so tense. I guess that I have to give in—sometimes.

I look into his resolute face. "Okay."

"Okay?"

"Yes. Okay." I shrug, feeling strangely vulnerable.

I let my eyes roam from his legs upward. He's wearing soft blue jeans and a black T-shirt that hugs his perfect chest.

Without another word, he takes my hand, running it across his length over his pants. I should be shocked, but instead, I'm melting. Everything about this moment feels right.

"Another thing you should know: I don't mind your feisty mouth. But when we're intimate, I'm in charge. No negotiation. Do you understand?"

"Yes," I whisper.

His alpha personality is nonnegotiable. It radiates off of him. And maybe it's something I noticed from the start. With this man, I'm not the one driving. I don't call the shots. And somehow, in this setting, I love it.

He's so thick, hard, and long. I want to feel him without the pants.

He takes my hand, and we walk to the couch. He unbuttons his jeans before he sits down, legs spread, and I kneel before him. I hold the top of his jeans with my hands, silently asking permission. He lifts his lower body up and slides his jeans down, his underwear with it.

Holy shit.

It's so big. I'm dazed by it. Dizzy.

I wrap my fingers around his dick, saying a silent prayer I do this right. Although something tells me God doesn't want to get involved in this moment, I need his support right now. I let out a shaky breath.

He groans deeply. "You are so beautiful."

The veins in his neck and forearms strain as he clenches his fists, trying to stay under control as I finally move both of my hands up and down.

"I almost never feel like this unless I'm in the ring, ready to brawl. This is how crazy you make me, Talia. Since the moment I saw you, you've been driving me fucking insane."

Those are the last words I hear before I purse my lips and take him into my mouth.

"Ohhh fuuuuck."

I feel no fear. Nope. I feel powerful. Alive. Strong. He's shaking now, completely at my mercy. I move up and down on him, enjoying this moment more than I thought possible. He's delicious.

"I'm getting close. So close ..." His words are a prayer, and he chants them over and over again.

I don't let up on him. I continue to suck, rolling my hands up and down. I gasp as he gets even bigger down my throat. He finishes with a roar until I feel his vibrations in my core.

"Take off your shirt," he pants. "I need to see you naked."

I release him, my lips feeling wet and puffy. Without hesitation, I pull my shirt up and off and unzip my jeans, kicking them onto the floor. I let him take his fill of my body.

"Take everything off, Talia."

I take my panties off, not wanting to blush, but it's impossible. It's in the way he's looking at me. I know I'm a damn good cello player, but I also know that I have a lot of physical imperfections. I'm too short, and I have big breasts and an even bigger ass. Well, what-the-fuck-ever! I'm in this, and he's in this. And if he likes what he sees, who am I to argue? I unhook my bra and toss it into the pile.

He swallows hard, eyes darkening as they rove around my body. "You are a vision. I never thought you'd be this perfect. From the moment I saw you on that stage, I wanted you. And I still want you."

I sit on his lap, facing him, with my legs spread, straddling his. And then he kisses me. I hum into his mouth, and just the taste of him has me quickly tumbling into bliss. I'm unable to stop, and neither is he. He sucks my lower lip into his mouth before moving to my neck, and I lift my face, wanting to give him access to anything he wants. I grip the bottom of his hair and lean back as he takes my nipple into his mouth. Ahhhh, I can feel the jolts straight down, like an electrical current through me.

I don't think it's possible for me to get any hotter, but I'm churning, grinding into an inferno. We're panting. Sweating. We're all but fucking on this couch. I meet each of Leo's grunts with my own, our feral noises growing stronger. The neighbors can probably hear us, but I couldn't care less. If he would just slide it in. I groan, trying to maneuver myself on his lap. His hands grip my ass, slowing me down.

"Wait, what?" I pant, breathless. "I don't want to stop this."

"Yeah?" He pulls me back from him, so we can look at each other, eye to eye. "I need to make sure you really want this. I said I'd never take advantage."

Breathlessly, I assure him, "You aren't."

He plays with a lock of my curls, stretching it out to its full length before it springs back into a coil. "I can get very territorial. Dominating even." His face is straight as he explains himself. "After everything I've been through or maybe even before that. I'm the type of man who needs you to understand that I'm the one in charge. When we're fucking, it's my way. Understand?"

I look into his face, understanding plain and clear. "Just in bed, right? Because I don't think I can handle that kind of dominance in our actual life. I've got a lot to say, you know."

We both burst into laughter.

"No shit. Talia, you've got more to say in your pinkie than anyone el—"

I cut him off with a kiss, but he quickly takes the lead. And that's when he takes the proverbial driver's seat. Lifting me off the couch, he brings us straight to his bed.

And, God, but the man takes his time when he wants. Licking, sucking, driving me insane with his tongue. Places I never knew were so sensitive, he finds and exploits. When I moan, he understands. When I slightly twist to get him into another spot, he understands that too. He takes me on and off the brink of orgasm over and over. When I'm finally so out of it that I can't see straight, he stands up, taking out a condom from his drawer. Before he can tear it open, his phone rings.

It's a different ring than usual, and he moves to pick it up.

He's completely serious when he answers. "Hi, Darius."

I watch him as he listens to the caller. His gorgeous profile. Thick neck. Ripped abs down to a sharp V. Perfect dick, utter perfection. Hard. Strong, muscular legs. If this man were music, he'd be Bach's Cello Suite No. 1.

I start to giggle over my dorkiness but then stop. Because his eyebrows are furrowed together, lips tight.

"Be right there."

He hits End and puts the phone down before opening the closet, presumably to dress.

"Leo?" I pop up from the bed.

"Sorry, Tal. I have some business I need to deal with." He throws on a pair of jeans, no underwear, before opening his side table drawer and pulling out two small black handguns.

Holy shit.

Let's get one thing straight. I'm not from the South, where guns are as common as underwear. I'm not from the ghetto either. I'm a nice girl who grew up in middle-class New York. I play the cello, for God's sake! The worst weapon we had in my apartment, growing up, was an old baseball bat that my dad kept in the coat closet by the front door. A gun? No way. Guns scare the shit out of me. When I think of guns, I imagine Columbine and other crazy shootings. To think, I've been sleeping near one, and I didn't even know it!

"Leo, you have guns here?" Anger rises in my chest.

He casually slides them into two holsters, as if he's putting on something as mundane as underwear. And then he puts a small pack on his belt.

I grip the sheets to my chest. "What is that?"

"Ammunition."

"Leo, look. I can't deal with this." A buzz runs through me, and it's not the heat from earlier. It's cold as death. I'm scared.

Nonchalantly, he replies, "You've been dealing with it, and you will deal with it. Just relax. I'll be back later."

"But—"

"No buts." He kisses my head. "Emotions of steel but afraid of a gun."

"Look, it's not fear exactly ..."

"Uh-huh." He shakes his head like he knows I'm lying.

"Believe it or not, my great uncle brought me to a range once to make sure I knew how to protect myself, but I hated every second of it. I was so nervous. I came home burning up with fever. And when I told my mom where I was, she flipped." I admit. "And what do you mean, emotions of steel?" I cross my arms, feeling annoyed. "I don't need to live beside a weapon. What if you get angry at me one night and-and-and shoot me?"

He laughs out loud. "You're crazy."

"No. You're crazy!"

He walks over to me, sliding a black T-shirt over his chest. He smells like clean laundry. I look up, nervous.

"Listen. I was born in the aftermath of the war in Kosovo. Read up on it; it was in the 1990s. Suffice it to say, I know how to shoot, and I know how to protect myself. For me, it's nature. I'm a member of the shqipe, right? I have to have protection on me. Understand?"

I nod my head slowly. I get it, but I don't like it.

"I'm not typical. I'm nothing like the men you know. We're dangerous. And when I go out to do work for the shqipe, everyone knows they have to be cautious."

I want to admit that I understand his life better than he knows. Not that Jet ever gave me any details, and not that I asked or wanted to know, but it was still there to see. I saw him come back to his apartment once, with stitches over his eye. Another time, blood on his shirt. But I can't get the words out of my lips—it feels impossible to say.

If I thought it was hard to keep my relationship with Jet to myself before, it's nothing compared to the guilt I feel now. But every second I wait to tell Leo the truth, the harder it is. I swallow hard, ready to just come clean. I can do it.

"You look like a lost puppy. I'll be fine, all right?" He smiles, unguarded. "This is my life, and it's under control. Soon, you'll get used to it. Probably quicker than anyone else in the world, huh?"

I drop my head, not wanting him to see my eyes lest he saw the storm brewing in my chest. "All right," I reply, staring at the comforter. "But lock it up ... or something."

"Yeah? So, if someone comes into my house with a gun, ready to kill, you want me to turn the dial, open the safe, pull the gun out, fill it with ammunition, and then what? It takes too long."

"Jesus Christ." I exhale, looking up at the ceiling.

I want to give him an earful, but he looks at his watch.

"Prayer is good. Protection is better." And then he's gone, sauntering out like the devil he is.

16

Leo

Leaving my apartment building, I step straight into the shqipe's black Escalade, driven tonight by Dren. Jet is here, too, with Armand, a newer guy to the crew.

"You spoke to Carlos recently, right?" Darius lights up a smoke, leaning back in the front seat.

"Yep. Went with Talia. Carlos was his usual fucked up self."

"Not sure they were scared enough. We've got to exert more pressure. Big deal they're doing for us next week, and Nico needs them to understand that we're all cool. But if they fuck it up, they'll be in big trouble."

"Nico told me he wanted a calm hello. Brought Talia with me to keep it cool."

"Makes sense," Dren replies, nodding.

"So, where are we headed?"

"We're going to a bar they hang out in. We picked out of a hat who has to go, and sorry, brother, you're in." Armand, sitting in the back row, taps my back. "Hope we weren't interrupting something with Talia, eh?"

The guys laugh.

"Hope you're enjoying that. She's smoking hot. Darius," Armand calls out. "You think Nico can set me up with a wife that hot? I could use citizenship, too, you know."

Before I can get a word in, Jet pipes up with a loud, "Shut the fuck up!"

Darius exhales smoke out the window, and it jets by my window.

I turn my head around to Jet. "What's wrong with you? Shit, man." It's almost as if he cares about what they say about her.

He spits, "They shouldn't talk about her that way."

"And what's it to you?"

Silence descends in the car. It's heavy. I know by the look in his eyes that he wants to say something.

"I asked you a question," I push, cracking my knuckles. *What the fuck is going on?*

Darius bangs on the front of the car, getting our attention. "Can you all shut the fuck up? We all have to know who we're hanging with when we get there. Leo, you're with me the entire time. Everyone else, be cool and hang around, always staying close to one another. And don't fuck with any of their women."

"Way to ruin a good time." Dren chuckles.

"This is business, not fun."

I smile. Darius has always been so serious.

"How's your ass, by the way?" I chime in, tapping Dren's shoulder.

Everyone laughs as we pull up to a corner bar in Hell's Kitchen.

Walking in, Carlos's gang, the Snakes, get quiet. There must be about fifteen of them hanging out in here. Bar to the right, pool table in the back. Bright Exit sign to the right. I know all of us are quickly figuring out the place, calculating.

They look at us, and it's obvious they know to be cautious. We're far too dangerous, way above them in the ladder of the underworld. We're also much bigger than them in physical size.

"Carlos is in the back," the bartender adds. She has long, dark hair and an enormous pair of fake tits. She acts like she has nothing to fear, but she does.

Darius and I take a walk to find him, and the rest of the guys get drinks and say hi to the few guys they know.

I don't come with Darius too often but often enough. The truth is, we're a good team when we go places together.

"We have to make a serious statement, Leo. Let's get him praying on his knees that he runs the drugs through the night without a hitch. Because if he steps in the wrong place at the wrong time, he'll be walking into the edge of my knife."

There is a door at the back, and someone opens it for us. He's small, probably one of their newer members. We enter, and I let Darius step up. He's the talker, and I'm the muscle here. Darius is more than able to take care of himself, but the shqipe would never let him go into a full-blown meet like this alone.

Carlos is sitting behind a desk. The fact that he's trying to make himself look legitimate is laughable. He's nothing but a bottom-rung drug dealer—king of his shitty Blue Houses castle. Frankly, he's so beneath us that it makes me sick. No wonder Nico never comes to see him.

"Just want to make sure you boys are ready for tomorrow night."

"We're ready. Why do you always have to fuckin' babysit us, huh, *ese*? You're sending Leo to us with his woman. Now, you all come together?"

Darius loses his patience—this time, faster than usual. He grabs Carlos by the neck. "Are you blind? You think we will ever trust scum like you? You're our dogs. Our snakes, eh? Do the dirty work, and then we throw you back in the cage you belong in."

Carlos turns red with anger.

"I will never hesitate to fucking kill you, *ese*." Darius spits the word back at him. "We have no affiliation. This is a drug deal that you're helping us with for a price. If you fuck with our money, we will kill you and all of your men. And Leo here will bury you under concrete. Maybe he'll get his woman to help, huh?"

Fire runs through me, and I let it roar. When Carlos looks at me, he knows that there is zero hesitation in my face. Darius is my brother, and I take my loyalty very, very seriously.

When he seems to understand, Darius gives me a head nod and we head out.

I itch to check my phone to see if Talia has messaged me, but I have to always have my focus when we're doing business like this. I glare at the guys hanging out. One by one, my crew jumps behind us, and we leave the place.

"Should we go out tonight? Party?" Dren asks excitedly.

Darius replies, "Gotta get home to my woman. Maybe Leo does, too, huh?"

"Home for me too."

Talia and I were in the middle of something, and I'd like to get back to it as soon as possible.

I turn to Jet, and he's fuming through the ears.

"Yes. Let's go out. Our club. What about you, Leo, huh? Looking forward to seeing your *wife*?" He spits out wife like a curse, and straight up, I'm getting sick and tired of his attitude.

"What the fuck is up with you, man?"

"With me? What the fuck is up with you? I never thought you were the type to take seconds—"

"Cut the shit!" Darius yells.

I have no idea what he's talking about, but now isn't the time to ask.

Ten minutes later, I'm back in front of my building. I get upstairs, hoping that Talia is still awake.

When I open the door, she's relaxing on the couch, watching a home makeover show on HGTV. She's wearing my boxers and a T-shirt, which makes me laugh. It's cute how she's been doing that. It's also hot as hell.

"Hey!" she greets, smiling.

"Hey back."

"Oh wait. Can you take the guns off your body first, please?"

"What if you took them off for me?"

"Oh no. I don't want to touch them."

"Maybe you should." And then I realize that I want her to. "These are going to be living with you. You shouldn't be afraid of them."

She worriedly shakes her head. "I told you that I've shot a gun before. I know how to use one, lock and load it. But that doesn't mean I don't hate them."

"Sometime soon, let's go to a range together. I want you to learn how to use my guns. And I want you comfortable with them."

"Can we cut the talking? Get rid of your weapons, and let's go back to happier times."

I shake my head, chuckling, and walk into the bedroom, putting them away before washing up. I hate the smell of bars, and that place was rank. When I'm in the shower, I decide that I want to finish what we started. Badly.

I open the glass shower door and shout, "Yo, Tal. Can you help me out for a second?"

I hear her step inside. "What do you need?"

"I need you. Naked and in here with me. Now." There's no room for negotiation in my tone, but with Talia, I'm sure she would find a loophole if she wanted to.

I watch her undress slowly, each article of clothing dropping to the floor. And when she enters the steamy shower, I pull her into my arms for a searing kiss. There are a million things I want to do to her. I want to make her come. I want her screaming my name. I want her clawing at my back, begging me to give it to her harder.

For a moment, I let her go. We're breathing heavily, steam billowing around us. Her eyes look wild. I let my fingers trail down her sides, feeling her wet skin and the goose bumps pebbling on her flesh. My hand finds her pussy. It clenches and floods with heat.

"Not here. I'm afraid I'll pass out," she whispers.

I turn off the water and lift her into my arms. Pushing the shower door open with my free hand, adrenaline shoots through my veins. I set her warm and wet body down onto the bed, ready to feast. I let two fingers slide in deep and thrust, curling upward. I want this woman so primed for me. Covering her mouth with mine, I swallow her moans. My hands move around her as my cock presses between her legs, wanting to enter. I force myself to slow down as I make my way across her body. I lick and suck until she's begging for it.

With a ridiculous amount of strength, she pulls at my back. I lift my face to her.

"Fuck me already. I can't take this!"

I make my way up, licking my lips. "You want it so bad, huh?"

My dick rubs against her clit, and she gives me a low moan.

I grab a condom from the bedside table and slide it on before raising myself up on my hands. I focus all of my energy on slowly entering her. Do I want to fuck her brains out? Yes. But I also want to make this last, and I want to make her mine.

I ease in all the way, pull back, and then slam in deep.

Talia cries out, and it does nothing but spur me on.

After a few minutes, I pull out, lift her legs, and flip her around to her stomach. Pinning her thighs together, I thrust back inside. I pound her hard, my hips hammering as I find her clit with my hand. I keep the pace until she's melting, her pussy clenching so violently that it spurs on my own climax.

When we're both sated and sweating, I can hear her swallow.

"You're really, really good."

"How hard was that for you to admit?" I turn a bit to the side to be able to see her.

She's flushed and still trembling.

She doesn't reply. Instead, she flips over and pulls me to her lips. Her hands touch my face as she entwines her legs with mine.

When our kiss finally breaks apart, she exhales. "A lot easier to admit than I thought it would be."

That night, we order two boxes of pizza and a six-pack of Corona Extra. What's extra about it? Neither of us is sure. But we drink and eat and laugh. Have sex a second and third time. Listen to Leonard Cohen's *Hallelujah*, and agree it's one of the greatest songs of all time.

And at the end of the night, she delves into a textbook for one of her classes, sitting at the desk I made for her. I ask if I can borrow one of her books. She gives me *Advanced Orchestration: Screen Scoring*. I sit up comfortably in my bed and start from the very first page. I want to focus on it, but it's boring as hell.

I look at her instead. Living with Talia is … good. I've been trying to keep focus on her despite the chaos I'm always feeling inside me. But if I'm being honest with myself, having her with me in my home has been a solace. Somehow, even with our forced marriage and her big mouth, her tough nature and sharp wit, and despite the fact that she is literally nothing like what I thought I liked in a woman, she makes me happy. I also love her body …

She shuts her book. "What the fuck, Leo? Stop staring at me."

I laugh at her. "You want to go outside for some air?"

She presses her lips together. "I have work to do."

"You can do it later."

She exhales, scratching her neck. "Some air might be good."

She puts on one of my sweatshirts and a pair of old sneakers, and I do the same. I lead her down the stairwell, her small hand in mine.

We walk through the streets, talking and laughing about everything and nothing. I can feel the outline of my ring on her hand. She's been wearing it ever since I gave it to her, and even though it shouldn't, it means something to me.

"You know," she starts, looking up at me, "we've got our interview next week."

"Is it really that soon?"

We pause at a red light between Houston and Wooster, no one else on the corner with us.

"Yeah, I guess so." Her eyes fill with question. When I don't reply, she keeps going. "You know, you used to tell me how dangerous you are. But I don't think you're so bad."

"No?" I smile.

"No. I think you're afraid to be vulnerable after what you went through. And maybe you're a guy who does some shady things. But you're a good man, Leo."

I don't respond. Her sincerity washes over me in a way I never could have imagined. It also fills me up when I didn't even realize I was empty.

17

Talia

I INVITED Brian over today to study for our aural comp in music IV. We were supposed to study together at the school library, but every single study room was taken. We even went to NYU's law school, but there were no rooms available there either.

When we got back to my apartment, I ordered some Chinese food off of GrubHub before quickly changing into comfortable sweats. Without any small talk, we immediately got to work, spreading our textbooks in front of us and our printed notes in our hands.

We have studied together countless times throughout our three and a half years at school, and we have a good thing going. We basically study on our own, and then we ask each other questions we have. By explaining things, we solidify what we know. And by asking the other questions, we learn the things we don't.

After we read through the first half of the notes, Brian turns on the music, so we can listen to recordings, identify the different musical forms, and try to hear the overtones.

When the front door opens, both of us are surprised. Leo is happy —but then he sees Brian. His face goes from light to dark.

Oh shit.

"Hey, Leo!" I greet, trying to keep things cool. "This is Brian. We're studying together for our final."

He walks toward us, not even taking off his heavy brown work boots. His faded jeans are stained with dirt, and his white T-shirt isn't exactly clean either. He smells like sweat and sun. When was the last time he shaved? Scruff lines his jaw. He prowls to where we sit with the energy of a caged animal.

Brian stands up, his fear palpable along with his utter confusion. *Who the hell is this?* he pleads with his eyes.

Leo crosses his enormous tan arms over his chest. His tattoos bulge on his forearms.

Not for the first time, it hits me that Leo is huge. He looks even bigger, standing next to Brian. And with his boots on? He must be close to six foot five.

"Sorry to interrupt you guys. Studying?" He eyes our books. "Tal, get me a glass of ice water, would you?"

I move my ass into the kitchen and fill the tallest cup we have with ice. Grabbing a bottle of Poland Spring from the fridge, I pour it into the cup.

Leo calls out, "Aren't you going to introduce us?"

"I thought I just did." I laugh shakily and hand him the water. He wouldn't actually hurt Brian, right? "Brian plays the drums. He is considering leaving school early to play with Heretic Pope. Super talented drummer," I add.

He drinks the water, each gulp long and heavy. His Adam's apple bobs with each swallow.

"I'm her husband." He wipes his mouth with his left forearm and hands me back the glass before putting out his hand for Brian to shake.

Brian gives his hand to Leo, like he's handing over his firstborn.

I'm sure he wants to ask me a million things, but I exhale and turn away, not sure how to get out of this awkward situation.

"I'm going to get into the shower. I assume you're done, no?"

"Yes. We're done. Now. At this moment." Brian stuffs his bag with his notes and computer and recorder. "Thanks for the study session. I'll see you soon, Talia." In a flash, he's out the door, practically tripping over his own feet.

"Leo!" I yell when the door closes. "What the hell?"

"Me?" He points to his chest. "What did I do?"

"Well, you basically came in here—" I pause, suddenly out of breath.

"Uh-huh."

"You-you came in here. Didn't even take off your shoes. Towered over him. Bossed me around. Scared him to death!"

He shrugs calmly.

"Well, you scared him," I continue. "And I have this test coming up in—"

"I can walk into my own home with my boots on. And I can ask my wife for a glass of water after a long day, no?"

I'm stunned into silence.

"Brian is my partner," I retort.

I'm grasping at straws, trying to stop myself from feeling this attraction to him. An unbidden heat curls low in my belly. Everything about him turns me on to no end—from his dominance to the fact that he is the one man, maybe on this earth, who both gives me my freedom and yet doesn't let me disappear from his view. At the same time, I won't deny the fact that I want to kick him in the nuts for pushing Brian out of the house.

I open my mouth to yell at him, but he cuts me off.

"You have one partner." He points to his chest, harder this time. "It's me. You have one man you answer to, and it's me," he repeats. "You were embarrassed I told him we're married—is that it?"

He tilts his head to the side, and while he seems pretty calm, I know he's fuming.

"No, of course not. I'm not embarrassed, but you're so, so ..." I look him up and down, furious and wanting him so badly that it hurts.

He raises a brow, waiting for me to continue.

"Messy."

"Well"—his gaze moves from my feet up to my face—"it looks like you like me messy." He crosses his arms again, and the muscles in his biceps bulge.

"I do not!" I reply a little too defensively. "You're making a mess in the house. The floor is probably caked with dirt from all the job sites, and ..." I swallow hard, taking in his body and his warm blue eyes. I hold on to the top of the couch, trying to get a grip. My strength is leaving me because all I can see is Leo.

His smile spreads across his face. "Oh, Talia ... if you only knew how glad I am to finally be able to read you. Your voice spells anger, but your body says something different." He pulls the straps of my tank top down, kissing my right shoulder while unhooking my bra from the back. "You're mine. You live in my house. You wear my clothes to bed. You study at the desk I made, sleep in the bed I provide, and you love spreading your legs for me. You're my wife, do you hear me?"

I want to speak, but God help me, no words come. Not one measly word.

By the time he's entering me, I can barely even call out his name. All I can do is pant.

THE INTERVIEW IS TODAY, and then we have a party with the crew later on. It's Elira's birthday. I haven't seen any of those guys since I met Leo, not that he hasn't asked. But between schoolwork and spending one-on-one time with him, I guess the right moment just hasn't presented itself. There's also the issue of Jet, who I have been hoping to avoid.

Earlier in the week, I bought a green photo album, filling it with photos of Leo and me. It chronicles everything from our relationship. It's amazing how many memories we've made over the last few months. Dinners, both at home and at restaurants. One with me smiling as I show off my cucumber-tomato salad. A few with Leo and his famous baked ziti and other Italian dishes. A bunch of photos on the dance floor at Apotheke that night we went out.

And of course, from two nights ago, when I went to play at Wild Orchid. Leo hung out at the bar, watching me up onstage. Undressing me with his eyes. And it wasn't that different from the first time we'd knowingly laid eyes on each other—except this time, the charge was higher. I played for the entire crowd, but we both knew that it was all just for him. I even wore my gold lamé dress that drives him so crazy. When I was finished with my set, we danced and drank together, barely noticing there was anyone else at the club.

And when we got back to our apartment, he insisted on fucking me hard but slow, no matter how much I begged for more. My dress was still on, and I came with an intensity I'd never known existed on this earth.

I shake from the thought, my insides clenching from the memory.

And photos of some walks we took in the evenings. Down in South Street Seaport and around our neighborhood.

"I can't take another photo! I'm done with the constant pictures." He turned his head away.
"Just smile. Look at me," I begged. "I like taking pictures of you."
He crossed his arms, pulling out a cigarette from his back pocket. "I'm not looking at you." He lights up, the waiter setting menus in front of us.
"Look how the tables have turned. Two months ago, you had to drag me into a picture. Now, you're the one who is getting annoyed?"
He turned to face me, cheeks sucked in, smoke wafting around his face. And I snapped. "Got ya!"
He leaned across the table to grab the phone and spilled water instead.
I stood up, laughing loudly, my crotch soaked with water. "Happy now?"
"Very." He smiled, wagging his brows. "Let's go home and get you out of those shorts."
He wrapped a heavy arm over my shoulders as we walked back to the apartment.

I swallow hard before opening the green tube of Great Lengths mascara. It doesn't even matter anymore, right? Because once we pass this interview, he's leaving for Kosovo.

My hand trembles as I coat my lashes one, two, three times. More than ever, I need to look like the kind of woman that Leo would marry. I even removed my nose ring. My tattoo is covered with a short-sleeved white sweater. I'm wearing a bra with a pad inside to give me that round shape the Victoria's Secret models have. I look sexy but in a different way. Mature. The way a wife of a handsome, successful man should look.

I stare at myself harder. The real me isn't what he wants. This is probably what Daisy looks like. And who knew that I would fall for him as I have? He's so smart and hard working. Hilarious. He sees me —really, truly, sees me. And not only do I see him, but I love what I see.

I close the mascara tube, feeling furious at my sudden drop in confidence. I hate how he has this power over me. I like who I am. I like how I dress, dammit!

But ... what will happen now?

You'll finish school and have a huge amount of money in your bank account, my conscience reminds me.

What about after that?

You'll play for the New York Philharmonic and have an enormous bank account.

But what about Leo? I'm falling for—

Put him out of your mind. You'll forget him in time. Men are disposable!

God, I really am a tough bitch. The decent part of me wants to get louder, but I don't let another word come out of her mouth. It is what it is.

My stomach? It sinks.

I put the tube away, realizing that there are a few logistics I've overlooked. I have to find somewhere to live. I guess I can stay here in the apartment while he's gone, but when he gets back, I should be moved out.

I swallow hard, imagining his future. *Is he going to bring Daisy back here? What if she sees him and how successful he is and wants him back? What if he changes his mind and decides to stay there?*

Leo opens the bathroom door, looking clean-shaven and smelling perfect. "Ready?"

To the mirror, I reply, "Uh-huh."

I want to beg him to notice how good we look together. He is so big behind me, bright blue eyes and tan skin. We're opposites physically, but we also fit so well.

"Look at you, all prim and proper. Is that the term Americans use?" He ribs me and smiles, tilting his head to the side, in that way of his.

"Yeah, that's it." I want to joke back with him, but I can't manage it.

He taps the side of my nose. "Put your ring back in, please."

"But I won't look as—"

"When I look at you during the interview, I want to see you. Not a fake version of you." His tone is no-nonsense, and I nod my head, happy to oblige—for once.

I open the drawer and pull my ring out. On my tippy-toes so I can lean closer to the mirror, I slide it back through my nose. I look at myself in the mirror and nod. *This is me.*

He bends his head for a moment before placing a necklace around my neck. It's a heart-shaped diamond on a shimmering gold chain. I'm in shock as I see it sparkling on my skin. I never thought that diamonds would suit me, but this one does.

"I saw this and thought of you."

He closes the clasp, and I adjust it so that the stone sits right beneath my clavicle. "It's beautiful."

"No. The necklace is just pretty. You're the one who is beautiful." He pulls a few errant curls stuck beneath the chain.

I turn to face him. I want to ask, *What are we doing? Why are you still leaving for Kosovo when you have me here? Why can't you choose me over destroying them?*

But I don't say a word. I can't force him to pick me.

WE ARE silent on our drive to the naturalization interview, located at the United States Citizen and Immigration Services office. We enter the building and head up to the fifth floor. There are four rows of black chairs filled with applicants, but we find two together at the end of the second row. Leo's leg won't stop bouncing, and I put my headphones on, listening to music.

They call his name, and we rise. Taken to a small cubicle in the back, we sit down.

An officer asks Leo to raise his right hand and swear to tell the truth during the interview. Of course, he does it easily.

The officer reviews Leo's N-400 form, the application for naturalization. He goes on to ask Leo several questions about his application and all of the supporting documents.

Leo has been reviewing every detail of his application for weeks. Messing up an answer or having any inconsistencies would jeopardize his citizenship. Some people might be nervous, but Leo is absolutely calm and collected.

Since he filed on the basis of marriage to a US citizen, I also had to bring proof of my own citizenship as well as leases with both of our names, tax returns, bank statements, and of course, the photo album. They ask us to show our apartment keys, and we both take them out. Mine from my purse, him from his pocket. It doesn't stop there. They ask about each photo, where we went, when it was. They ask what each of us likes to drink in the morning. Frankly, I shock myself with how much we know about each other. It's an act, but it's also all truth.

I try not to laugh when the officer tests Leo's ability to read, write, and speak English. Only because I know how smart and competent he is. I know English is a hard language, but Leo is at the point where he dreams in English. Luckily, he answers all of the questions with flying colors. All he has to do now is pass the written exam, and he can finally get sworn in.

The officer commends Leo, "Your English is excellent."

"Thank you, sir."

That's when he walks into another room to take his citizenship exam. I make my way into the waiting area, hoping that he passes. Maybe I should want him to fail so that he can't leave me, but I don't. I can't. I want him to be happy.

He walks back into the waiting room, smiling. "Everything is approved. I just said the Pledge of Allegiance. It's done, Tal. I'm an American." He lifts me into his arms and spins me around.

I'm so thrilled. I find myself laughing. "Let's go out for an early dinner to celebrate!"

"Yes. I'm going to text the crew, let them know that the party tonight should be extra good. Citizenship, Tal! We did it!"

He pulls out his phone and smiles as he messages the shqipe. I'm so sad, but I'm also extremely proud. Still, I'm losing him.

One of the shqipe hang-arounds is waiting for us in a long black Escalade with tinted windows. He drives us to the best Italian restaurant on the Upper East Side of New York City—Elio's.

Leo opens my car door, and I ask, "Do we have a reservation?"

"Of course not." He winks.

We walk inside and are immediately hit with noise. A tall woman swings her black Chanel bag, and Leo bats it away like a fly, stopping it from smacking me in the face. He's about to have words with her, but he looks at me first. We both look furious before bursting out in laughter at the absurdity of it.

"I need to wear higher heels. My height is a liability."

"I like you this way." He bends down, pressing a delicious kiss on my lips.

I follow him through the crowd to get to the maître d', standing behind a small wooden podium. Leo shares a few choice words with the stuffy, suit-wearing Italian, and within minutes, we're sitting at the star table in the front of the restaurant, by the window facing Second Avenue. No menus are given to us, but the waiter lists what feels like twenty special appetizers and entrées before asking what we'd like to drink.

"Wine tonight?" Leo asks.

"No. We're going out late, so let me just start with what we'll be drinking later. I'll have a Reposado on the rocks."

"I'll have the same."

"Yes, sir," the waiter says, nodding his head before walking away.

Leo takes my hand across the table. "What should we eat?"

His thumb slides across my knuckles. I look at his nails, clean and without any dirt beneath them.

Funny enough, I gave him a manicure last night so that he would look as professional as possible during the interview. For reasons I cannot comprehend, I wanted to memorize his hands and the shape of his nails. Every groove and scar I committed to memory. He laughed through it, but I loved every second.

"We should order everything." I smile, feeling a small tickle in my nose. I will not fucking cry. And yet the tears well up.

"Tal?" He leans closer to me.

"It's nothing. I'm just so happy for you. You had this dream, and it's yours now."

The waiter returns with our drinks, and Leo asks him to send a sampling of appetizers before the filet of sole with white wine and tomatos, and the special rib eye.

"Are you sure you want them choosing our food?"

"Yes. It will be amazing, trust me."

Leo goes on to tell me about the test. His pride is evident. I don't let go of his hand. I want his happiness. And more than anything, I realize, I want him to love me.

Our dinner is delicious, and even though I know he's leaving, I make a mental promise to myself that I won't mention what's to come —not tonight. Tonight, I want him to enjoy the fact that he reached his goal.

We leave the restaurant, full and happy. I'm a little tipsy from my two drinks, but the truth is, we're both high on life.

The same black Escalade is in front of the restaurant. Leo opens the rear door for me, and I slide in. When he gets inside, he slams the door shut and pulls me to the center seat, so we can sit close together.

It doesn't take long for us to start kissing. My hands in his hair, his hands all over my body.

"Leo," I pant. My brain reminds me that we aren't alone in the car. "The driver—"

Leo shouts, "Pull over and get out. Now!"

The car swerves to what I assume is the side of the street before the driver's door opens. He throws the car in park, jumps out, and slams the door shut.

Hallelujah!

My traitorous body pulls him closer, begging to absorb all of his hot energy. He nibbles on my neck, and I just need *more*. I climb over his big body, pressing him down into the seat. My skirt, which was meant to be prim and proper for the interview, is now up around my waist.

"Fuck your underwear," he complains into my mouth, his fingers finding my clit.

I thrust against his hard dick, and I know that if I keep this up, I will definitely come. Between my grinding and his fingers, I can tell my orgasm is imminent. "Maybe we should turn around. Go home."

He doesn't reply. Instead, he pulls my top down along with the cup of my bra. His hot mouth trails from my neck down to my breast. "Fuck, Talia. You smell so fucking good."

Heat roars through my body. His fingertips slide through my wet folds before focusing on my clit. I arch against him, wanting to scream. Instead, my mouth opens in a silent moan as I come so hard that I see stars.

"Look at me," he demands.

I obey his request, coming down from my straight-up glorious orgasm, and immediately get lost in his eyes. I want to tell him that I love him. I want to beg him to stay. Instead, we're quiet.

It takes us a moment to straighten out our clothes. I adjust my bra and fix my skirt. My underwear is soaked, so I pull it off.

"Talia, what are you doing?"

For whatever reason, I feel like playing with him. "Here in America, we call it going commando."

He laughs out loud. "I know what going commando is. But I don't like the idea of you without your panties at a party filled with my crew."

"Well, I don't like the idea of walking around in panties that are soaked through."

"Give them to me then."

"What will you do with them?"

He doesn't answer, just stuffs them into his pocket. "Safekeeping."

"That's gross!"

"Remember last night, when you came all over my tongue? Was that gross?"

"I can't with you." I roll my eyes.

He shoots off a quick message on his phone and a few moments later, the driver returns. I set my head on Leo's chest, and close my eyes. I want to take him in.

We get to the club, and the driver stops right in front.

Leo walks out of the car first and then opens my door. We walk to the door of the bar just as the bouncer tells a bunch of guys that the place is shut down tonight for a private party. Leo and he do a fist bump, and we walk inside.

Before we enter, I'm not sure what to expect. Maybe a party filled with Albanian men doing cocaine on glass tables with hookers of the Eastern European variety as arm candy. Look, I'm not saying all Russian girls are hookers. But I know the type these men like, and it's them.

Well, I am glad to say that I was wrong. The bar has been transformed into a black, white, and red wonderland with low tables filled with candles and red roses and bottles of fancy vodka and tequila in large silver tins. Against the wall is an enormous American flag—slightly out of place, but the sentiment is awesome. The moment I see it, my face brightens.

It doesn't take long for the guys to realize we have arrived. They all run over, swallowing him up and clapping his back with congratulations. He doesn't let go of my hand, not for one second. Two younger-looking guys hand both of us drinks, and Leo and I maintain eye contact as we take them back. Everyone keeps asking questions, like what the officers asked him or if there were any questions that we couldn't answer. Leo happily replies to everyone, clearly proud of his new American status.

Finally, we make our way to one of the small tables. The same guys who offered us the drinks stand within earshot distance. I glance at them before looking at Leo. Their deference to him has me wondering what the hell is going on. Maybe he is a more important member than I know.

"They want to join up with us. Just ignore them unless you want something."

"They really want to impress you, huh?"

"Sure they do."

"I never asked, but are you a big player in your crew?" I scratch the back of my neck, understanding for maybe the first time that I wish I knew more about the shqipe.

He lifts an eyebrow. "I'm one of the bigger moneymakers. My business does really, really well."

"Like, how well?" I'm being nosy, but whatever.

"Let's see." He shifts me so that I'm on his lap. "Imagine one house. I buy the land for three million. Build a house for another three. Sell for twelve."

My jaw drops. "Are you serious? Well, don't you have loans? Construction loans and all that?"

He laughs. "The shqipe doesn't do loans. It's all cash."

"Holy shit. And aren't you doing five houses right now?"

"Yes." He nods. "And the Hamptons is the hottest market too."

I blink, acting passive, as if I didn't know all about the Hamptons and how much the shqipe loves to hang out there. I let out a shaky laugh. "Well, color me impressed."

"I have to bring you sometime. To see what I'm building."

"Yes!" I exclaim excitedly. "You know, I watch all the shows on TV. When they build and design. I feel like I could do it."

"I know you do." He chuckles. "I bet you would be good at it. Maybe for the next house you can help me choose finishes."

Before I can reply, his hand starts moving under my skirt. I throw my palm on top of his, stopping him from moving up any farther.

Into my ear, he whispers, "Let them all know that we're together. This isn't a game, Talia. Let them know you belong to me."

My heart thumps.

"There is so much I want to tell you." His warm breath in my ear has my mouth drying out. "But it can wait for tomorrow, right?"

"Right," I whisper back, leaning my head on his chest and letting his hands take their fill.

I want to laugh because the old me would never have allowed a man to declare me in this way. But Leo makes me do crazy things.

Elira and Nico must come in because the entire place erupts again. Everyone jumps up to stand, not kissing or touching her, but welcoming her and wishing her a happy birthday. She is nothing like some of the other women in here. She is the queen.

My attention is quickly averted when I feel Leo's cock grow under my ass. This is wrong. We are in public, for God's sake! And yet my body begs for it. Yes, *again*.

I wiggle myself downward, and he groans, letting my butt tease him.

A big guy with bulging muscles walks up to us.

"Dren," Leo says.

"Hey." I smile, a lot more nicely than I did the first time we met.

Leo has mentioned him a few times, and I know that of all the guys in the shqipe, they are the closest.

Dren takes a seat beside us, and the two of them shoot the shit, mostly ignoring me. His hand is still roaming beneath my skirt, but it's harmless now.

Some other guys walk over to us, speaking in Albanian, none of which I understand. I should have Leo teach me because otherwise, I'm totally out of the conversation. I don't want to just sit here in the dark. I need to be able to converse in his life. Seeing as I can't understand a word out of anyone's mouth, I take the time to scan the crowd. There must be about fifty people in here now. The women are dressed like slutty models, and the guys range from greasy and tough to clean and smart-looking.

A girl in a short black dress walks up to us with a tray of shots. I take only one and hand it to Leo. I have to pace myself so that I don't get too drunk, too soon.

He takes a sip and then hands it to me. "Finish it."

"I shouldn't."

"I said to finish it."

I glare at him. He knows I hate doing what he says. We stare at each other, facing off. His eyes glance around the room, and I understand that he wants to piss on me in front of everyone. Normal me wouldn't allow this, but drunk and horny me apparently doesn't mind.

"Fine," I reply, smiling into his eyes. *I love this man so hard; it's unbelievable.*

I touch the side of his hair, loving the feel of it. He looks back at me, his hand touching mine, his eyes melting into me.

A scratchy voice calls out, "Looks like you've tamed the beast, eh?"

Both of us look up. My jaw drops. It's Jet, and he's glaring. He looks between us, a fire burning in his gaze that I never, ever saw within him, not in the time we were together. He looks lethal and furious. And me? I just want to die. It's like when you're in a dream and you know something awful is about to happen, but you are literally frozen to the spot and powerless.

From deep in his chest, Leo asks, "What the fuck is that supposed to mean?" His grip on my thigh tightens.

I jump up, feeling both self-conscious and utterly miserable. I look at Jet, my lips suddenly fused together. I want to yell at him, but then what?

Leo looks between us, knowing something is going on. But what should I say? And how can I explain myself now, in the middle of this party? I open and shut my mouth, wanting to fix this impending disaster but not knowing what to do. I plead with my eyes, but as Leo sees the distress in my face, he seems to understand that something is wrong. Really, really wrong.

Jet smiles smugly, and I want to murder him. I also wish I could push pause on this moment and redo the evening, never showing up here. How stupid could I have been? I was so dazed and in love and happy for Leo that I wasn't thinking straight.

"You're a real bitch, you know that?" Jet points his finger in my face. "I knew you were always in it for the money and your stupid fucking cello, but I didn't realize how easily you'd be able to bed-hop from me to him in less than twenty-four hours."

"Who the fuck do you think you are, talking about me like that?!" And then I do what any woman with self-respect would do when her ex-boyfriend talks shit to her new man. I slap Jet straight across the face.

He turns to Leo, laughing to himself as he rubs his cheek. "She's good, isn't she? Loves it when I put my dick in her a—"

Leo grabs Jet by the neck, and they're on each other in seconds. I want to get Leo out of this, but he is definitely the winner. Not only is he way younger, but he's also so much stronger. He gets maybe five major punches in when Dren finally uses his muscle to pull Leo off of him. I know that Leo likes to fight in underground bouts, but since we've been together, he's been clean of that. Clearly, the man hasn't lost his touch. Jet is on the floor, bloody and lying in the fetal position. His eyes are already swelling shut, his lip sliced and bloody. It's gross, and I'm mortified.

Arguments ensue between a bunch of the guys until, eventually, Jet is dragged into the back room, presumably to wait for some medical attention. Leo, on the other hand, is fine, except for the sheen of sweat over his face and blood on his knuckles. He's sitting back on a chair, Dren whispering something in his ear. He's clenching and then unclenching his fists, nodding.

I step forward to go to him, and he raises his eyes to me, stopping me dead in my tracks. His stare is glacial.

My stomach falls to the floor. "No, Leo, it's not what you're thinking—"

With his teeth gritted together, he says, "Don't come near me."

One of the guys hands him a cup of ice water or maybe alcohol—who knows? He takes a big gulp.

"No." I step over anyway, putting my hands on his sweaty, firm chest.

He grabs my wrists and pushes me away with considerable force. "Don't touch me. You were with him?"

I can't speak. I look around the room and see people staring at me. I feel like the world is shrinking inward.

Leo growls like an uncaged animal, throwing the table over. Glasses, along with bottles of vodka and tequila, crash onto the wooden floor like an earthquake hit the place. The entire room goes silent.

"No, Leo." I vigorously shake my head, not giving a shit anymore about anyone watching. "Let me just explain. Let's go somewhere. It's not what you think."

"Don't come near me"—he throws his hands into the air—"ever again. I promised you an ending to this fake marriage. Well, you got it. We are done now. Finished! Get out of my face."

His body is so rigid; it's as though I'm staring at a different man from the one I know.

He turns away, strutting out of the bar. I go to chase him when Dren grabs me by the upper arm.

"No, Talia. You're not going back there tonight. I've got a place for you to crash, and it's cool. My woman's apartment, here in the city. Vesa. She's got a spare room. Stay there until you get yourself set up."

"No, I've got all my stuff at our place. My books. My cello. I have finals coming, and I need Leo to—"

"I'll make sure you get your stuff," he interrupts. "But I can't let you go back there."

I find myself nodding as my limbs buzz. "This is a misunderstanding," I explain. "He doesn't know about my past. I should have told him, but it's complicated. I need to go to him."

"I won't let you out of my sight. He won't see you. Not now and maybe not ever."

"Can I at least walk outside to get some air? Or am I stuck in this bar for life?" I put a hand on my hip, wishing I had a knife. *Fuck Dren for trying to stop me!*

He grabs my arm again and walks me, like I'm his errant dog, to the front door.

When we get outside, I shake myself free of him and pull out my phone, tears streaming down my face. I call Leo one, two, ten, one hundred times. Who the fuck even knows how many times I dial? My voice mails go from mildly collected with begging to absolute desperation.

Finally, I decide, *Fuck this. I'm going to him.*

The moment I step out of Dren's line of sight, he jumps out at me.

"You aren't to see him," he yells. "Don't make me force you or threaten you. You're smarter than that."

I look to my left and right, knowing that I can't escape Dren. I need someone else to help me. I tap my foot on the ground, thinking. I need someone whose word is law. "I need Nico then."

He laughs, like I'm joking.

"I'm serious. Nico got me into this mess. Tell him I need to speak with him." With as much strength as I can muster, I add, "Now."

He shakes his head. "So, here's the tough girl Leo told me about. It's your death wish," Dren mumbles.

Back into the bar we go. I wait against a wall, my stance protective, as Dren speaks to Nico at a table in the corner.

Finally, Dren walks back to me. "He'll meet you in the back room."

I follow him through a throng of people. He's a rolling boulder, and I'm trying not to tumble in his wake. My heart feels like it's breaking. And it's not even for me—fuck me and my feelings. It's because Leo is out there in pain—I know he is. And I caused it. I need to explain and fix this.

We wait for Nico in a small, windowless room with a wooden desk and black chair. I couldn't tell you the color on the walls. All I see in my mind's eye is Leo's face, shattering from the realization that I'm a whore and a liar. What? It's the truth. It's what my actions have deemed me to be.

Finally, Nico enters. "Dren, wait outside. Thanks."

"Yes, sir." He leaves the room, shutting the door behind him.

Nico leans against the front of the desk. He's wearing a dark suit and crisp white shirt, and frankly, he looks angry as hell to be here.

"Why did you lie to Leo and not tell him about me and Jet?"

"Cut right to the chase, eh? No pleasantries. No *happy birthday to your wife. What a beautiful party you've thrown for her.*"

"No. I need you to help me fix this. You brought me into this life. I don't want to lose it."

He clicks his tongue. "So, you think the fake marriage turned into something real, huh?"

"Yes, that's exactly what happened," I agree.

"I'm sorry to hear that you feel this way. But if you care about Leo so much, why didn't you fill him in on your history with Jet?"

"You expected me to tell him? Of course I couldn't! You didn't tell him, so why should I have been the one to say anything? Aren't you guys brothers?"

He chuckles, laughing at my attempt to blame him. "Yes. And why should I have told him about your status? I told him I'd found him a woman who would help him pass, and I did just that. You fucking Jet for money before marrying Leo had no bearing on your ability to get him citizenship."

My jaw drops at his audacity. And yet shame hits me so hard that it's debilitating. "I-I couldn't tell him. I wasn't exactly proud of it. I did what I had to do at that time." I swallow hard, my hands shaking so violently that I have to cross my arms over my chest.

He stays silent, waiting for me to continue.

"I'm not a whore, Nico!" I scream. "It was one guy I dated, and when he offered to help with school, I said yes. I'm not for hire. I'm a musician. I have dreams!"

"But you *were* hired. By me, to marry Leo."

"Yes, I was hired. But I'm not for hire. I don't want to be for hire. And I did it out of fear, too, you know. What choice did I have?" Tears stream down my face. I want to die right now from the pain of losing him.

"I'm not a man who likes to explain himself, but I'll talk to you now. You took the job I offered, married him, and completed your work with flying colors. He passed his interview. Be glad all of this came out after his citizenship was granted. Now, you can leave with the money you earned."

"I don't want to leave, do you understand? I love him."

He crinkles his eyes, pity in his gaze. "Are you sure he feels the same way?"

"No." My heart races. "Yes."

"Leo is the best guy. Incredibly loyal. But he has a job to complete in Kosovo, and you were always a means to an end for him."

"A means to an end?" The words make sense, but I know that I turned into more than that. Just like he did for me.

"Maybe he was upset tonight that there was something about you he hadn't known." Nico shrugs. "But he fully intends on going to Kosovo and finishing his job there. I'm sorry you took your position in his life so seriously. I figured you were tough enough to keep it business. He doesn't need a woman falling over him. These other girls would have gotten pregnant—or something worse—to keep themselves in this life. I figured you were smart enough to do your job without complication and that, once completed, you'd leave happily."

"I thought you weren't going to let me leave. Jet had said no one ever leaves—"

He puts up a hand, shutting me up. "You're not a member, and you weren't a real wife. I'm sure Leo kept his mouth shut about anything that would implicate you, correct?"

I nod.

"I never meant for you two to stay married. You were picked to do your job. Now that the job is done, you're through."

Adamant, I tell him, "I might have started out as a marriage of convenience, but we turned into more than that."

He shakes his head from side to side. "He's leaving in forty-eight hours, Talia. I met with him recently, and he never mentioned you as anything more than a piece in his path for citizenship. He wanted to fuck you while you lived together. But he's already bought his tickets, and he's set to fly with Dren. Leo has a singular focus, and that's to get to Kosovo and finish off what he never even got to start. You think you're so important to him, but do you realize that he has been waiting for this moment for years? No one is going to ruin it for him. I won't let you get in his way or make him think that he doesn't need to complete his task. If you do that, he will never be able to get over what happened to him."

Nico steps closer to me, and God almighty, I see the Mafia king in front of me right now. He would kill me if I disobeyed him.

"No one is getting between Leo and his goal. I will die, protecting my men—and that includes both their lives and their interests. He's been waiting long enough and worked hard to prove loyalty to us so that he could go back there. It's time now that you disappear. And if you don't do it on your own, I'll make sure it happens. I never regret a hire, but I'm pretty close right now."

I feel like I'm in a terrible dream, falling into a dark hole. I hear Nico, but my mind doesn't want to listen. "H-he wants to punish them. I get it. But what does that have to do with anything else? He can want to hurt them, and still love me. These two things aren't mutually exclusive."

"Nice logic, but it's not the right answer. He doesn't love you. He needed you, and you were successful in your work. Nothing more than that. Now, get out of the man's way and let him do what he needs to do."

Salty tears settle into the corners of my lips. "I love him."

He shrugs, almost casual. "He does not love you."

"How do you know this?"

"We talked. I asked." He shrugs, opening his hands. "And he gave me a firm no."

I turn around on my heel, opening the door and running through the club. The moment I get outside, Dren is there, holding open the door of a black Escalade.

I hop inside, and the driver takes off. Where I'm going, I have no clue. But my mind is awash in so much pain that I can barely get myself to care. The car takes me to a small building on Eighty-Fifth and Second. We get out, and he escorts me inside. He says a hello to the doorman and then the concierge behind the desk, and we walk through the long white marble foyer into the elevator to apartment 19A.

He rings the bell, and a beautiful blonde opens the door. "This must be Talia?"

I step inside, and the driver leaves.

"You poor thing. Dren told me you were coming. Sit down." She walks me into her beautiful white kitchen and pulls out a seat at her table. "Tea or coffee? Food?"

"Just water."

She pulls out a glass and fills it with cold water from her refrigerator. Handing it to me, she takes a seat at the round table. "Dren told me this is about you and Leo?"

I burst into tears at his name.

MONDAY MORNING, I jump on the 6 train from 86th Street and ride down to school. I have finals this week and next, and a piece that I've been composing needs to get finished. Because I can barely sleep, I spend my nights writing music. During the day, I study to the point of exhaustion, followed by a series of triple espresso shots spaced three hours apart. This will likely be my most successful round of exams I've ever taken, which is saying a lot, considering the fact that I always study with my ass on the line. I'm putting my body through hell, but I just need to push myself long and hard enough to graduate with straight As.

I get to the library so early in the mornings in fact that I'm always able to get my own room.

And as kind as Dren's girlfriend Vesa tries to be, I just can't be near her. I can't be near anyone who has any connection to Leo or the shqipe. She has a spare room with a small bathroom, and I keep them as tidy as possible. I don't want to let her think that I'm staying here for too long, or getting too comfortable.

When I pause from my studies, I obsessively scan for apartments for rent on StreetEasy.com. I don't have any guarantor, but I don't need one—my bank account, now that Nico has wired the five million dollars, speaks for itself. I plan to pay a year upfront, and I'm sure one of these landlords will gladly take my cash.

I want to walk over to Leo's apartment to check and see if he's still home. I used to scoff at lovesick girls who wouldn't get the memo that their boyfriends had moved on. But here I am, one of those girls—maybe worse. If I could throw myself in his path, I'd do it. If I could beg him on my hands and knees, I would do that too. I know his schedule. I know his eyes. I know his hands. I know his body intimately.

I blink the tears away, wiping my nose with the back of my hand.

I have two major obstacles that I can't seem to get over. One is that Nico might literally kill me if I come between Leo and his vendetta. The other is that Nico might be right, and the love I felt for Leo was one-sided.

What is there to do?

Nothing, so I study.

"This isn't a twenty-four-hour bodega," the library's security guard reminds me. "It's time to get out."

I lift my head from the pages of my textbook and drag myself out of the building and into a cab, back to Vesa's apartment. I would have taken the subway, but it's shady as hell this late at night, and, hey, I'm no longer poor. My account now has millions in it. Nico even sent me a receipt for the "five-million-dollar cello piece" I wrote for him.

I get into the apartment's foyer and unceremoniously drop my backpack onto the tiled floor. Before I can even take off my shoes, I hear some laughter coming from the living room. I take a few tentative steps inside.

"Rachel?" I exclaim, shocked to see her.

She's sitting on the long gray couch with Vesa curled up on one of the brown chairs to her right. They're holding wineglasses, seemingly mid-laugh. I look at my watch; it's already after eleven. *What is she doing here?*

Rachel stands up after setting her wineglass on the coffee table. "Get your ass over here. I've been calling you nonstop. Finally tracked you—"

"Tracked me?"

"Yes. Find My Phone. Remember?"

I slowly nod. When we both moved into the city, we decided to track each other in case of emergencies.

"I found you here last night, but it was too late to show up. I knocked on the door about an hour ago and met Vesa. She opened up a bottle of wine, and we've been waiting for you." Loudly, as though to make sure Vesa hears, she adds "she's great, by the way. Works at Saks. You think she can get us discounts?"

"Probably." I shrug. I know she's trying to lighten the mood, but I don't feel like talking. "Did she fill you in on my whereabouts?"

I walk into the kitchen, washing my hands with soap. Even without taking the subway, I still feel gross every time I get home. The city can get so grimy.

"No. All she said was, there was a fight between you and Leo, and Dren dropped you off here. She has instructions to keep you comfortable until you find your own place. You should have called me—"

"I couldn't." I pump more soap into my hand. "I have had a crazy week, and my last exam is tomorrow. Dren dropped all my shit off here last week, and I couldn't deal with moving everything again in the middle of finals. And—" I swallow hard and then harder.

I don't want to cry. I don't want to see anyone who will ask me to talk. I just want to finish my test and focus on graduation and applying for auditions.

"Okay, I get it." She puts her hand on my arm. "Now, stop washing your hands; you're going to turn your fingers raw." Turning off the faucet, she hands me a piece of Bounty.

"I can't discuss anything now." I wring my hands with the paper towel. "I can't even get into it. I have so much to do. So much work to do for my last test ..."

She leads me into the living room, holding my arm like she's afraid I'll either break or bolt. Vesa is there, standing tall with a fresh, full glass of wine in her hand. Her blonde hair is perfectly straight and long, and for the first time, I notice that her makeup is amazing too. She gives the glass to me, and I take it. I don't miss the look of sadness on her beautiful face.

"Well, Talia," Rachel starts, "this is an intervention." She takes her seat back on the couch.

"I don't need that right now. I have a million things to think about, and I just need to finish the semester. Get to graduation."

I shake my head, annoyed. Out of all people, she should understand this.

Vesa clicks her tongue. "You have to talk to us. You look like you might not make it through this last exam. Over the last few weeks, you've hardly eaten, and you've barely spoken to me. You walk in and out of the apartment like a ghost. I feel just terrible for you. I'm so glad Rachel came over because, honestly, I didn't even know who to call."

"I'm trying to find a new place to live," I reply, exasperated. "I'm close on something—"

Rachel interrupts, "I came over, and we spoke. We have different views, but both of us think that you need to open up a little bit. Relieve some of this stress. Talk it out and let us help you."

"And I don't need you to leave," Vesa adds. "There is no rush. Living alone is good, but it's nice, having someone else here at night." She shrugs.

I take a huge gulp of the wine. Vesa is right about one thing—I have barely been eating. No doubt, this wine is going to go straight to my head.

"Well?" Rachel asks.

"Things are bad," I admit.

She exhales. "No shit."

I start with my relationship with Jet, getting Vesa up to speed. And then how I wound up being married to Leo. The forced marriage of convenience, it seems, turned into something much, much more. A few tears slip down my face as I explain how much Leo came to mean to me. All those months together, my heart was forced open. And how he accepted me. And how he truly saw me. Gave me my freedom but still kept my feet nailed to the ground in a way I'd always yearned for. And how smart he is. Gorgeous, too, but so much more than that. How the small omission about Jet turned into a big lie until it became too difficult to admit. My relationship with Jet was a stain on my life. *Is* a stain on my life.

Vesa fills my glass again. "Oh, honey, keep going. I know Jet. He treats his wife like shit."

I get to the horrible part about Elira's birthday. Jet showing up. The fight. And how Leo flipped the table over before casting me away. When I get to Nico and his threats, Rachel has her hand over her mouth, and Vesa looks worried.

When I'm done, Rachel yells, "Fuck Nico! That son of a—"

"Shh!" Vesa and I both scream in unison, and my eyes search the windows.

It might seem crazy, but if anyone were to have people listening to this conversation, it would be Nico. Clearly, we both know the power Nico has in this world, and he has eyes and ears on everyone at all times.

Vesa flips her hair to the side. Whispering, she says, "Nico likes to control everyone and everything in his life. And he's very protective of all the guys. But he's wrong, Talia. I heard the story, and I believe you. You both fell in love. And he's definitely hurting. And also furious."

"I have to agree," Rachel adds. "You aren't one of those girls who gets things wrong. If you felt the love and the connection, it's because it was real. It's because it was there. You don't make that shit up."

"But now what?" I look at them, forlorn.

"You're going to finish your exam; get an A, like you deserve; and wait for him to return, so you can explain the situation."

Vesa shakes her head. "I would try to reach him as soon as possible. What if he's going to do something terrible? What if he is so angry with you that he does something he will regret?"

"Like what?" My heart thumps.

"Like, who knows? Maybe bring Daisy here?"

Her Albanian accent when saying Daisy's name is so natural, and suddenly, it dawns on me. "Wait. You're Albanian?"

"Of course I am. What did you think?"

"Eastern European ..." I lift my brows, hoping not to offend her.

"You're hilarious." She waves a hand in front of her face, like she isn't the least bit offended. "I'm Albanian. I have known the men of the shqipe for all my life, and my older sister went to school with Elira. Actually, I still have some family back in Kosovo ..." She stops talking, but her eyes jump wildly. She pulls out her phone and quickly types out a message before hitting Send. Moments later, her phone dings. "She answered! My cousin, I asked if she knows Daisy. She says yes. Apparently, she has two sons. She married a very rich guy, Albi, who builds all over Kosovo."

"That's the one!" I exclaim. I scratch the back of my neck. "I don't think anyone knew about Daisy's relationship with Leo. He told me they had kept it a secret."

"I wish we could ruin her life. Tell everyone that she's a whore who jumped from one twin to the next," Rachel says in a singsong voice, sipping her wine.

"We shouldn't," Vesa replies firmly. "Then again ..."

"We don't even know what's happening there right now. I don't think we should get ourselves involved. If Leo wants to hurt or ruin his brother, then this rumor circulating could implicate him in whatever he's doing."

"Oh, good point! You're so smart." Vesa gives me a huge, genuine smile, and for the first time, I regret being so cold with her.

"We need a plan. And it starts with you finishing your exam tomorrow. Kicking ass. And then getting a message to Leo." Rachel nods, like her words are obvious. "Maybe through Vela's cousin?"

Vesa's phone rings, and she answers. "Send him up, please."

Rachel tells me, "We ordered some sushi. Figured it went with the wine."

Vesa skips to the door, signs a bill, and sets the plastic bag on the table. Methodically, she removes everything before bringing plates from the kitchen. "Come on, guys. Let's eat."

I drag myself to the table and take a piece of salmon sushi onto my plate. I don't want to eat, but hopefully it'll get the girls off my back.

Vesa takes a few pieces of tuna sashimi in her plate before clearing her throat. "The thing is, you definitely messed up. These guys are very big on love and loyalty. If he thinks you aren't loyal ..." She pauses, pressing her lips together, and then takes a piece of the shrimp tempura roll.

"How can I prove it to him though? It feels like a lost cause." I put down the empty wineglass and drop my head in my hands.

Rachel pushes, "Just get through tomorrow and do well on your exam. We'll brainstorm after that and figure out a way."

"But she can't just talk to him about it. He isn't a typical American guy, sweet and simple. He's a member of one of the toughest Mafias in the world. He grew up in war. He won't take her calls. He threw her out of his house! He isn't going to give her the time of day without something big."

"Vesa, you aren't helping," Rachel replies, annoyed. "Talia got herself into this mess because nothing comes before school and getting that audition to the orchestra. She can't just throw it all away for a man. Not after everything she's been through."

"Well, if it's love, then maybe she should."

"Absolutely not!" Rachel yells, standing up.

"Okay, okay." I stand up, too nervous to sit anymore. "I hear both sides. I'm going to think on it tonight while I review my notes for the test. I'll figure it out." I hug Rachel. "I'm alive, and you know where I am now, right?"

"School has to come first. You've worked so hard to get here, Tal. Don't forget it."

"I won't."

"Thanks for the food and wine, Vesa. I've got an early class, and I need to leave. I'll see you guys soon." And with those parting words, she picks up her purse and walks out the door.

I open my hands to Vesa. "It's just that she doesn't want me jeopardizing my future. She's been through a lot with me."

"I know. She loves you very much. But this life in the shqipe is one of real sacrifice. The men put themselves on the line for each other. When it comes to the women who love them, we must be behind them one hundred percent. If you don't want that life, then maybe Leo isn't for you. Love is an important ingredient in a relationship, but that's just one part of the puzzle. With a man in the shqipe, it's a commitment not only to him, but to the entire crew too. You have to deal with things. The secrecy of it all. The fact that these men live hard and dangerous, you know? There can't be lies."

I exhale. "I've got a lot to think about."

She picks up her empty plate and says, "I'm going to sleep. Eat something before bed, will you? I saw that you didn't touch the sushi. I have some fruit in the fridge and lots of cereal in the pantry cabinet."

I look around the apartment, noticing that there is no man's imprint on anything. "Is Dren ever around? I thought maybe I'd see him here."

"Actually"—she tilts her head—"he doesn't live here. He has a place a few blocks away. But right now, he's in Kosovo. With Leo."

Silence falls between us as my mind works. "Where are they staying?"

"At the Swiss Diamond Hotel Prishtina. It's by far the best hotel in the city."

THE NEXT MORNING, I move automatically. Brushing teeth. Putting on my black sweatpants, a white V-neck T-shirt, and my green Nike running sneakers. Grabbing my backpack and cello, I run out the door. I want to be nice and say good-bye to Vesa, but I'm sure she's still sleeping.

I walk over from Second Avenue to Lexington and then up one block to 86th Street to catch the 6 train downtown. It's filled, but I'm lucky enough to get a seat, plus a little extra room for my cello. I put my headphones on and focus on listening to the music. Someone tries to sing rap for money, pushing himself through the crowd, holding a hat. Normally, I'd throw something in there because, hey, us artists have to support each other. But right now, I don't even have the energy to open the zipper pocket on my backpack.

When I finally get into school, I flash my ID card at the front desk but keep my head down. I don't like any small talk before exams.

As usual, I take the third seat in the third row of the auditorium. Quickly removing my headphones and turning off my cell phone, I stuff them into the bottom of my backpack and take out my pencil case. The standard blue booklets are handed out along with a tape and a music player. It's old school, but it's the easiest way to rewind or fast-forward. The professor goes through the timing we have for each section, and then she tells us to begin.

But for the first time in maybe my entire life, I can't focus on the music. I look up at the clock, and I have two hours left to go. My composition has been handed in, and I know I've aced all of my other exams. But this one isn't coming together. I tap my pencil on the side of the desk, adjusting my headphones. I need to get my shit together, but all I can think about is Leo. I rewind the song to hear it from the beginning. But still, all I hear is him. His footsteps prowling the streets of Kosovo, the beat of his heart when he pants, his brow lowering in focus.

I Googled Kosovo last night because I wanted to imagine him there.

And now, all I can think about is, *What if he needs me?* Not that he isn't so strong. I know he can handle that part. But he's going through something serious. And I should be there with him.

I look around the room, wondering what I should do. That's when

I notice Brian's seat is empty. Holy shit, he must have left for Heretic Pope! He left school for that opportunity.

What if this is mine?

Sweat beads between my breasts. I'm nervous. Really, really nervous. *What if Leo's in a bind? What if something went wrong?* My knee is shaking beneath the desk. The tough part of my personality tells me to shut up and focus on the test so that I can make my way into the orchestra. But I can't listen to that bitch anymore! I need Leo more than anything else on this earth. I will figure out a way to finish this exam and get the audition to the New York Philharmonic, but it can't be now. It just can't be!

I slide my chair back, and the sound jars people. I know it's rude to make noise when people are trying to listen to sound, but it is what it is.

I run down the auditorium steps to see my professor. She looks up, confused.

"I have an emergency. I'm so sorry, but I can't finish this exam."

"But, Talia, I can't pass you unless you finish. Do you understand that?"

And with all the strength I can muster, I look her in the face and reply, "I do."

18

Leo

I SADDLE myself up with three guns, two knives, an enormous lighter, and my new mobile phone. Dren is packing all of that, too, but he also adds explosives.

Earlier today, we held a meeting with the mayor of Kosovo. The strength of the shqipe isn't lost on these streets, and I'm going to use it to my benefit every step of the way. It did not take long for him to understand that Albi should no longer be receiving any government contracts, as we'd heard a few of his prime buildings would be catching fire around two o'clock that afternoon.

"You see, Albi is already in big trouble with some very important people back in America," I added. "It wouldn't be good for the city to be involved with a man like him."

"Yes, yes, of course. We understand." He nodded nervously. "Nico is a legend here, even still. He already sent a message that you'd be coming, and we understand everything perfectly."

We stood up, shaking hands.
"That's good."
"Yes, sir."

We drive directly to a building that I started construction on all those years ago. It stands tall, about fifteen stories. Seeing it completed is strange. On one hand, it's part of my history. On the other, it's so small now compared to what I've accomplished back home. I touch a few red bricks, wondering how the building would have been if I had been the one to finish it. What would my world look like had I continued on with this life? Would I have been happy?

I pull out a cigarette from my back pocket and light up. Another man might feel badly about blowing up a building. Unfortunately, I'm not that man.

"Leo, is that you?"

A tall police officer in dark glasses walks over to me in a signature blue shirt, perfectly tucked in, his dark hair styled in a crew cut. His badge says *Azekaj*.

We don't speak but assess each other. Something about his name seems familiar. Do I know him? Our glances turn into shock when he pulls the frames from his eyes, and we confirm who the other is.

"Wow, man!" I exclaim. "How are you?"

We embrace, and he claps me on the back. He looks very much the same as he did in high school. Azekaj is still tall and lean with sunburned features.

"I hear you're important back in America, huh? Rolling with the shqipe." Clearly, he still radiates the same good nature.

"You know, just doing what I do."

We both start to laugh in that way when you see an old friend. Nothing is funny, but we're happy to see each other doing well.

"So," I continue, "a police officer, huh? I thought you'd go pro football."

"I was planning on it but got injured. You know how these things go. But it's all good now." He pulls out his phone and shows me a photo. "My family."

I hear some movement behind me and know that I need to move this along.

"It's good to see you. But I'm pretty busy here now, huh?"

I take out a hundred dollars in US currency from my back pocket and discreetly hand it to him. He looks at it, nodding in understanding. Some things in life go way beyond countries and languages. Money is one of those things.

"Let's catch up later, have a drink?" I add.

"Sure. It's good to see you, Leo. Been too long. Come visit us more, eh?"

He takes off.

Old friends haunt this town, and it's a strange thing to be back.

Dren joins me at the western corner of the building. He told people there is an electrical issue, and they needed to leave right away. We see businessmen exiting the building, one by one, walking quickly with bags and files in their hands. Dren does one more walk-through before telling me it's empty. I drop the explosives in the corners and then jog around, lighting them up. We exit just as the entire building goes up in flames.

We continue this for three more buildings. Yes, it's fucked up to ruin the city like this. But it's on Albi, not me. He filled up my gun with ammunition, and I just pulled the trigger.

With dirt and sweat lining his face, Dren tells me, "Let's sit and eat before we go visit brother dearest, eh?"

"Sure. I wouldn't mind washing my hands first either." I look up, hearing the sound of roaring sirens and seeing smoke in the air.

We head into a beautiful restaurant, painted blue. Imagine my shock when I see my old friend Liri walking toward us by the hostess desk.

"Leo!" he shouts, and I stand up, hugging him.

We went to school and played football together.

"Is this your restaurant?" I look around. The tables are full, and the space looks beautiful.

"Yes, of course it is. After you left to America, I didn't think I would see you again. What brings you back into town?"

"My brother has found himself in some trouble, and I'm here to check on him." I smile, keeping things simple.

"Well, sit down and relax. I'm going to send food over to you. Come. My best table." He claps my back, and we follow him to the left, to a corner table by a large bay window that faces a flower garden.

We sit down, and he runs off, presumably to take care of restaurant business.

"Let me use the restroom." I excuse myself and find it on the other end of the restaurant.

The moment I lock the restroom door, I wash my face and hands. Gripping the side of the sink, I wonder how Talia is doing. Did she finish her exams? Then, I look at myself in the mirror and tell myself to shut the fuck up. I'm here for a job, and she's a liar. My feelings are wounded. But wasn't she the one who said that feelings aren't real? What's real is the fact that she lied to me about fucking one of my brothers.

I stalk back to our table, cleaner but also angrier. As soon as I take a seat, Dren leaves to wash up. There is a cup of ice water in front of me, and I immediately drink it all down. When we're finally both clean and seated, two waiters set large white plates down at our table. It doesn't take long for Liri to fulfill his promise. I think he ordered the entire menu for us. The table gets so overwhelmed with food, the servers have to bring over a second table to set more food down.

Dren and I eat with absolute relish, dipping the warm bread into the various spreads. The level of freshness is off the charts, and that's something that is missing in American food. Even at the best restaurants, it's not like it is here. The bread was probably made an hour ago. The cheese is likely from Liri's mother's farm. The vegetables are grown out back. The fish recently caught.

When we're full, we light up our cigarettes and enjoy a hot tea with fresh mint. I've made this black tea for Talia, and she loves it. Suddenly, it tastes sour in my mouth. When I landed, I swore I would stop thinking about her. And yet I can't. How could she? After everything she knew I had been through—and now, it's time to focus on my revenge. I've been waiting for years for this moment, and all I can do is think about Talia.

Dren burps. "What are you thinking about? Don't tell me you're having second thoughts."

"No, of course not." I put out my smoke into the small silver tray and lift my phone.

"So, what is it? Talia?"

I light up another cigarette. "Yes. I can't believe I didn't know about her and Jet. I can't believe Nico kept it from me."

"I spoke to Nico about it before we left. He says Jet didn't want to bring her around everyone. You know him; he's a weird fuck. Likes to keep certain things separate from other things."

"Yeah," I add. "Haven't even seen his wife or kids in years."

Dren takes a sip of tea. "But Nico had met Talia and liked her for you. He thought she'd keep it all serious business, and when it was done, she'd leave easily. Remember what happened with Noel? He married that hang-around for citizenship, but then she got herself knocked up. Those girls all want to be wives. I guess Nico thought that Talia wouldn't."

"True." I exhale. "It's actually correct. She wanted out the minute she was forced in."

"Look, I hate to throw myself into your business ..." His eyes sparkle, and I can't help but laugh. Dren loves butting into my life. "But Talia lied to you. If you're still thinking of her, force yourself to stop. She's a bitch, just like Daisy—"

I yell, "She's nothing like Daisy!" I slam my fist on the wooden table, sending our plates an inch into the air. "She's an amazing woman. Dedicated to school. And she was dedicated to me." I point to my chest.

He squints his eyes in confusion. "So, what do you think happened then?" he presses.

"I don't fucking know. She had a past with him, obviously. And decided to keep it from me."

He tilts his head to the side, as if in understanding. "When should she have told you? When you guys met, maybe she figured you already knew. And by the time she learned that you had no idea, maybe she was scared to tell you. Seems possible."

"We were together nonstop for months!" I press my lips together, fuming. But beneath my anger is an ache. I know there must be a reason, but I can't hear it. The betrayal is too heavy, and it's taken up too much space within me. All I feel and see is poison.

Dren glances around the restaurant, shifting in his seat. "Haven't been back in Kosovo since I was a kid. I never came out to restaurants. There was too much war." He gets that faraway look in his eyes.

I know that the Serbs hung his father in the village square before raping his sisters and killing them too. When he found his way to America, the shqipe took him in.

You'd never know that Kosovo has been through so much, so recently. The tables of the restaurant are full, and the women are incredibly beautiful. Life goes on, even after devastating war.

"I'm ready to go." He waves his hand to get the waiter's attention.

The waiter comes running over. "No, no money. It's on the house."

I shake my head to Dren. Of course we're paying. I spot Liri by the register and walk over to him.

"The food was incredible, thank you." I hand him a wad of cash. "Maybe we'll be back tomorrow?"

"Oh, no. I can't take your money, Leo."

We go back and forth a few times about him accepting payment, but of course, he eventually relents. We might have been friends as kids, but this is his livelihood.

We get back into our car, Dren buckling his belt in the driver's seat.

"Ready?" He turns the car on but keeps it in park.

"I've been ready for years."

And the truth is, I have. I have thought about what I will do. I have thought about how I will end his life. How I will ruin him. And now, the day has finally come to put all of my plans into action.

We pull up to a white stucco mansion with green shutters, a large wraparound porch, and flower beds in front of balconies. There is a garden in the front. Two children run out, playing. His sons. I swallow hard. A woman walks out behind them, wearing white pants and a matching shirt. She's older, likely the nanny.

I get out of the car, and Dren tells me he'll come inside in ten minutes. I nod and stand in the driveway, taking in the scene. I dig into my stomach, wanting to pull out the pain of my past. I remind myself that Albi is now in this magnificent house that should have been mine. Two children, also should have been mine. I wonder what my kids would have looked like had Talia and I gotten that far. The thought of her pregnant has my mouth drying. I wish I'd gotten to see it. No. Not Talia! I look up at the sky. Daisy.

I walk over to where the kids play, clenching my fists.

"Hello," I tell them in Albanian.

I want to see their faces. They look up. One has eyes as blue as mine, and the other is a carbon copy of Daisy.

"Twins?" I ask the nanny, making small talk to keep her comfortable.

"No. They have one year of difference." She smiles at them fondly. "The best boys."

"I hope they are hardworking," I tell her.

"One spoiled, the other tough."

I laugh at the irony. "Is Albi or Daisy home?"

"Yes. They just sat for lunch."

Without any ceremony, I walk to the front door and open it. Daisy is by the sink, drinking a glass of water, and a man is sitting at the table, his back to me. She turns her head for a moment, opening her mouth to speak. But she sees me instead and freezes. The cup she is holding falls to the floor, shattering against the white tiles.

Albi stands up angrily, as though he's about to yell at her for breaking the glass, until he turns around and sees me.

"Is that how you welcome family into your beautiful home?" I blink, reminding myself that my weapons are strapped to me. I could kill him anytime I want. The choices are endless, and they are all mine.

"L-Leo," Daisy stutters. Her long, dark hair is perfectly smooth, not a strand out of place.

"Have you been enjoying yourself here, in this life? One brother, another brother—what's the difference if you get what you want?"

She vehemently shakes her head. "You left, and I was alone—"

"Cut the shit. I left, and you wanted the money. Your small house and your devout father would never have provided you with a husband who could give you this life of luxury."

She blinks, water welling up in her eyes. "We were kids, Leo. I did love you, but you left. And he offered—"

"Tell me what he offered. Jewelry? This new mansion?"

"It's not that. You are mistaken. That's not what it was." She swallows hard, eyes darting in a way that looks like she's embarrassed.

"Tell me the truth!" I yell.

"I told you the truth!" She blinks, the tears dripping down her face.

I roll my eyes. Daisy always knew how to turn the tears on.

"You left. And I was alone. My father, he was furious. What could I do?" She puts her hands out to me. "I was scared people would find out about us. My reputation could have been in question. Albi came, offered me marriage. My father practically drop-kicked me out of the house."

I stare at her as she speaks. And I realize I barely even know this woman. I did once, but I don't know her anymore. She is still beautiful. Still full of makeup. Her nails are still long. But presently, I have not one feeling for her. If anything, all I feel is pity.

I look across the kitchen and find an old bookshelf, identical to the one we had in our living room. I'm sure that all of Albi's favorites line the shelves. He used to eat through the classics like a fire. I shake out my shoulders, wanting to push the past out from my ribs.

I slowly walk over to Albi. Towering over him, I whisper, "You were my blood. We were different, sure. But you sold me."

"What did you want me to do?" He visibly trembles. "I wanted more. I wanted her." He nods to Daisy. "I wanted this life and business."

"You mean, my life and my business?"

"I knew you'd be okay," he replies shakily. "You've always been resilient."

I laugh darkly. "Did you? You sent me off, barely a teenager, all alone, to a new country. No money, no family, no nothing."

The door to the left opens, and my mother marches in, wearing a navy dress and low heels. Her hair looks very black, a sharp contrast against her pale skin. The smile is wiped off her face when we make eye contact.

"Oh, Leo!" She dramatically drops to her knees, as if this were a play and she were the star actress. "I'm so sorry." She puts her head down, lifting her hands in prayer. "I am sorry. I had to play along. It was Albi—"

Albi yells, "Shut up, Mother! This was your idea! How dare you blame me! You always wanted him gone."

They continue to argue, and I look at the scene before me. Pictures of their family on the wall by the white cabinets. In the first one, Albi is holding a baby in the air, and Daisy is smiling at them. I can't picture myself as him. That's not my baby, and that's not my wife. And the truth is, I don't want them to be.

In the second photograph, Daisy is posing in a tight red gown, her black hair around her shoulders and an enormous belly protruding. I want to laugh because Talia would never pose like that or wear something like that—not normally and definitely not during pregnancy. So showy. Mildly obscene.

I hear the children playing in the yard. Food is set on the table. They have moved on completely. And it wasn't until this moment that I realize I have too. Talia lied to me, but it must have come from some sort of shame. I know school is everything to her. Who knows why she got wrapped up with Jet in the first place? It's so out of character for her. Maybe she felt like she had no choice at the time.

I look more closely at Daisy, her diamond bracelets lining her wrist and tight pants showing off her round ass. Daisy is not ashamed. Her goal was always money and money alone.

The lies aren't the same.

Dren walks in, pushing the door open so hard that it slams

against the wall. His hulking form has Daisy, Albi, and my mother shutting up from fear. He pulls out his gun, and my mother shrieks.

"What do you want to do?" he asks me casually.

I walk over to Albi. But the truth is, the weight has already been removed from my shoulders. Albi can have this life because I don't want it. Still, he deserves to suffer.

"For years, I have dreamed of ruining your life. Killing you slowly. I've imagined all the ways I could end you. Seeing you now, there is one element of your planned demise that I will gladly continue. I want you to watch everything you thought you had crumble. I want you to see what it's like to feel destroyed. And alone. I'm going to burn every single building of yours to the ground. I'm going to make sure you can never make a dime in Kosovo again. And when you leave the country, I'm going to know where you are. I might find you. I might even kill you."

The fear in his eyes is palpable.

My eyes move to Daisy and my mother. They're pathetic and scared. "The two of you can fend for yourselves. You are both dead to me. But him"—I point to Albi—"I will ruin."

"You don't mind if I hold this gun up to your head now, do you?" He presses the nozzle to Albi's temple. "Just want to make sure you listen to your big brother and sit still." Dren smiles maniacally as I walk around the kitchen, dropping explosives in the corner.

Daisy jumps up, teetering in her heels before begging us to wait. "I have to get the children's things. Please, give me time to gather!" She bolts upstairs, crying loudly as she goes.

My mother tries to appeal to me. "Leo, you've always been hotheaded. Maybe now, in your older age, you can understand reasonableness. We've all moved on, and it seems that you have too." Her eyes glance from my feet up to my eyes. "You really have always been so handsome. You're even bigger now. Much, much bigger. You should—"

I grab her arm so hard that she screams. I wish it were her throat, but I can't take it that far. Once upon a time, this woman carried me in her womb. She fed me when I was born and took care of me. And while I wish I could shoot her dead, my conscience won't allow it. Still, my anger is a raging fire.

"You are the scum of the earth. And I don't want you worrying about me, okay, Mother? Because now, when I'm sleeping in my beautiful penthouse in New York, I will think about you suffering. And that will bring me more pleasure than you can ever imagine." I let go of her roughly, wanting her out of my sight.

"Don't take our money away! Ruin Albi, if you must, but take care of me. I am your mother after all," she begs.

"I wish I could put her out of her misery, brother." Dren chuckles. "Can't believe this is her. She looks real small, huh?"

"I have one thing I'd like to do." I open up my wallet and take out an envelope, filled with five hundred US dollars. I punch Albi, and he drops onto the floor. *Weak.* "This is how much you gave me before you sent me out. I'm a fair man, so I'll do the same for you."

I throw the envelope at his face as Daisy comes back downstairs with two suitcases in her hands.

"Open them. Any diamonds or jewelry or cash, give it to me."

"Please, take pity—"

"Open them!" I shout, my voice vibrating against the walls.

I glance out the kitchen window, relieved to see the kids still playing.

She unzips the luggage, and I rummage through their things, leaving all the clothing but removing any pouches, presumably holding jewelry. There is another small bag inside, and I unzip it. It's filled with cash. I take it all and walk to the car, unceremoniously dumping it into the trunk. I don't need the cash, but it does feel good to take it away from him.

I go back into the house, ignoring the sounds of the children laughing outside.

"You can close the bags," I tell her.

She does, her hands shaking, diamond bracelets jingling as they clang together.

"You like wearing his ring on your finger?" A memory assaults me

—when I gave her a promise ring. It was silver with a small diamond in the center. It wasn't fancy, but I'd saved up for it.

"This is just for now, right? Later on, you'll give me something bigger?"
"Of course," I replied. "When I finally work full-time, I'm going to buy you a ring that looks more like a rock than a pebble."
She whispered, "Okay then. I'll wear this ... for now."

I clear my throat and spit at her feet. I was so young and so fucking stupid.

"All right, Dren, let's do it." I nod.

"Time to get the fuck out!" he yells.

The women run out of the house, and Albi follows behind them.

Before he walks outside, he turns to me. "Fuck you." He clutches the envelope in his hand.

I walk toward him, pushing him against the wall and lifting him up higher so that we're face-to-face. And with all my might, I crash my fist into his stomach.

"You know where you drove me, don't you? Into the hands of the most powerful Mafia in the world. I'm a member of the Mafia Shqiptare now, and I've built my own construction company that could eat yours alive. I did all of this despite your attempt at crushing me. And I did it all by myself."

He's doubled over in pain as I take my time, lighting the explosives on fire.

"You know, Albi, today was a good day. I burned down many of your buildings."

He coughs.

"Oh, yes. I wanted to do them all, but I love my motherland. Didn't want to destroy the city. But remember this. Anything you try to create, I will ruin."

Because I'm a decent man, I drag him out of the house, leaving him on the corner of the green lawn. After all, I do want him alive. When he's lying on the grass, I smile. Who knows if I'll actually follow him and ruin him? The truth is, I never want to think of him again. Still, I don't mind letting him think that I'm planning on following through with my threats. A little fear never hurt anyone, did it?

Dren and I drive off, leaving the happy family to their own devices. I'm sure Daisy and my mother will leave Albi as soon as they realize that he won't be able to care for them anymore. Daisy will move on to another husband—I would bet money on that. And her kids will be okay. As far as my mother is concerned? Who knows what her fate will be?

The buzz from our tirade seeps through my veins. I'm feeling the exhaustion from the day. I close my eyes, leaning my head against the warm, sun-drenched window. I think about Talia playing music, and it calms me. Yes, I'm mad at her. But, God, do I love her.

A song from The Doors enters into my head. Talia loves the band, and she often had one of their albums on repeat. A line in the song "Break On Through" resonated with me. *I found an island in your arms, country in your eyes.* It's Talia. She's my home now.

We arrive at the hotel, and two men run over to open our doors. Dren asks for the bellboy, but he immediately moves to the trunk, organizing the goods we took and putting them into our duffels. The trolley arrives, and Dren puts our things on it.

"Straight to room 305," he adds, handing the kid some cash.

"Yes, sir!" He runs off, pushing the cart away.

Dren slams the trunk closed. "Let's wash up, eat, get drunk, and sleep like the dead."

"Sounds like a good plan." I rub my eyes, exhausted.

We walk into the hotel, and Dren walks directly to the elevator, heading up to his room. I walk a little more slowly, realizing that while I'm exhausted, I do feel lighter. My revenge is truly complete. I can't wait to get home.

Walking through the lobby, I pause. I must be imagining things. A woman is at the front desk, tiny and curvy. Curly, dark hair down to her waist. Luggage beside her and a huge cello.

I check my watch. Talia must have finished her last exam yesterday. It must be a coincidence. *This has happened to me before*—when I thought I saw Daisy at the liquor store in the city.

I walk off, refusing to give my mind any more control over the truth.

"Leo!" I hear.

I turn. It's ... her. I'm frozen. She doesn't move either. She has lost weight. Dark circles rim her eyes.

I run to her. Lifting her in my arms, I inhale her neck. "What are you doing here?" Kiss. "You're supposed to be taking your exam!" Kiss.

"I'm your second, remember? I couldn't just leave you here. What if you needed me?"

I can't help it, but I laugh out loud. "Well, that depends. Are you still scared of a gun?"

"No." She shakes her head. "Well, I can take one, if you need. I can be behind you when you see them."

"And what about Daisy? Do you think you can take her, if it comes to that?" My heart is filling up, almost spilling over with each moment that I realize she's here. For me.

The fact that she's ready to crack heads on my behalf? Unbelievable.

"Of course I can!" she insists. "I will do whatever it takes. Anything."

"Well, you won't have to."

"No?"

"No. Because it's already over."

"Wait." Her face drops. "I missed it?"

"It's done."

"So, now what?"

"Now, you come up to my room. And you let me feed you and love you."

Without processing my words, she says, "But I have so much I need to say—"

"You'll say it all. But first, privacy."

I take her hand, and we walk straight down the marble hallway to the elevator. We're silent as it takes us up. I walk us to the room. Entering, I pull open the shades before picking up the phone and asking room service to deliver a steak and seafood dinner in one hour. As I'm talking, I hear the shower turn on. I know she needs to clean up after her trip, but there are few things I like more than cleaning Talia head to toe.

I can't help myself. I undress quickly and walk into the bathroom, pushing aside the heavy shower curtain. Her hair is swept up and filled with shampoo, perfect breasts covered in soapy suds.

Turning to the side, she sasses, "Do you mind? I just took a zillion-hour flight all the way to Kosovo for you. The least you can do is give me a few minutes of peace to clean up and shave. And I have so much I need to tell you first before—"

"No." I lean against the wall.

She throws up her hands. "No?" She's exasperated.

"You came all the way here, yes. But before we talk, I'm going to have every single inch of you."

I want to add that I've been through some craziness today, and I want to find solace within her. I stare into her eyes, and they're a little different than usual. Darker with a spray of amber around the pupil. My words won't come. I guess I'll have to show her then. I'll show her my anger and my disappointment but also that I don't care about her past. I love her regardless.

Voice raspy, she tells me, "Come in."

She steps back, and I'm dizzy from her. The steam blurs her nudity, but not her eyes. I know for a fact that I want her more than I want my brother's doom.

I step inside the shower. Sliding my tongue between her lips, I decide that I don't give a shit about anything, except her mouth. At first, we're slow. Kissing, tongues dragging against each other, my hands roaming over her perfect hips and small waist. It doesn't take long for me to remember that we have time for lovemaking. Right now, I want to claim every single inch of her. When we leave this room, I want every single man to know that she belongs to me and only me. Slow is not an option.

I shut off the shower and lift her into my arms.

"I didn't even get to conditioner yet!" she yells, laughing.

I walk back into the room, the water from our bodies soaking the carpet beneath us.

I sit on the edge of the bed. "Get on my lap."

She lets out a full-body shiver, pebbles rising on her arms and stomach. She sits down, facing me, and puts her small hands around my neck. She strokes my shoulders and back, and I let her feel me. I pull her closer, so our stomachs touch, and I feel her heavy breasts, massaging and sucking on her nipples.

In her ear, I whisper, "I'm going to fuck you so good, Talia."

I knead her breasts a little rougher, letting her get comfortable with my physical dominance. She braces her hand on my shoulder as I suction my mouth over her nipple, sucking harder.

"Ahhhh!" she calls out.

"Say my name."

"Leo."

My cock swells, looking for more friction as she grinds down.

"I want to see you," she begs.

I pull my head away from her breast, and she grips my hair, staring into my face.

"You're so handsome. Leo, from the moment I saw you—"

Before she can get another word out, I lift her up and seat her directly onto my cock. Her eyelids flutter, face burning.

"Good girl. Take it." I flick my tongue over her, savoring her lips.

I lift her ass up and down on me. I know she wants me to move her more quickly, but I just need to *feel* her. I'm so much bigger than her, and yet she surrounds me. All I can see, smell, and taste is Talia. I can feel it in my heart.

I groan, the sound bouncing off the walls. She moans, stroking my hair and my back, squeezing her pussy so hard around my cock that I'm the one seeing stars. And when she finally comes, it sends my own orgasm spiraling forward. I pull out, my semen lashing against her stomach and thighs.

We breathe heavy together, coming down. I move her so that I can stand up.

Walking to the bathroom, I wet a warm towel but change my mind. "Come into the shower with me. Let me clean you up."

I turn on the water, and she walks sleepily to me.

I take my time cleaning her, getting down to my knees and soaping her from her stomach down to her feet. Never in my life have I wanted to get on my knees for a woman, and yet here I am. If anyone has been tamed, it's me.

When we're finished, I wrap her in a towel before putting one around my waist.

We get back into the bed, where she flips to her stomach. "Leo, I have to explain myself."

"You don't need to."

"But I do. Now, sit up so that I know you hear me."

I do as she said, lifting the pillow so that it's behind me. I don't want to hear the explanation. The truth is, I wish what happened at the club would just disappear. But I can't. I have to let her have this.

"I never told you about Jet." She swallows hard and looks up at the ceiling before facing me straight on. "Along with an enormous student loan, I had to work like crazy to pay for college. It was a pace I couldn't sustain. Not with my practice schedule and classes.

"One night at the club, I met Jet. At first, I had no idea who he was. He was a nice guy, and he was obviously very well connected. He asked me out, and we had some great dinners. Our dates continued to get more exciting. It was clear he had a lot of money, but I liked it. It felt good, having someone take care of me between all the work I was doing, trying to stay afloat. And when I was with him, I wasn't eating ramen.

"One night, before he dropped me off in my shitty walk-up ... he handed me an envelope. There was six thousand dollars inside. He drove off, and I had it in my hand. I wanted to give it back. At first, I was outraged. But then I realized how much it would help me. The next semester had started, and I now had money for my books."

I wish she'd stop.

Her voice trembles. "The cash kept coming. Once a week, he'd hand me that envelope. And I would take it." She drops her head. "And after a few months, he told me he wanted to pay for my school. And after that, he told me he didn't feel comfortable with me staying in that crappy apartment with my weird roommate, and he wanted to make sure I was more comfortable. I took those things. I was so ashamed—and I still am. But because of his financial help, I finally got to study. My quiet apartment helped too. My grades went up. I'm embarrassed to say it, but it relieved me.

"Yes, I knew he was married. He told me about his family. But I blocked that out."

She's shuddering. I want to touch her and tell her it's okay—that I don't need this. But she won't stop until she finishes her piece.

"And when I met you, I was freaking out. Nico had hired me, but he'd also threatened me. But I want you to know that I'm not a whore. I never meant to keep it from you. But the lie became bigger as we became closer. I never thought this would happen between us. I thought I would help you become a citizen, and then I'd be free. But then I fell in love with you, Leo. But the lie was still there. I know I fucked up."

She's crying in earnest now. "I was taking my last exam and left in the middle. I had to come to you, and I couldn't wait. I did everything for school, but in the end, you were more important. More important than anything else."

"Talia." I take her hands in mine.

"I failed my last exam." She puts her head on my shoulder, and I can feel the wetness from her tears on my skin. "But I would fail again and again if it meant having you in my life."

I hug her tight because I happen to know for a fact that she will not be failing. If I have to show up with a gun and force her professor to administer this test to her, I will do it. "I hear you. And I want us to put it away now. Can we?"

"Can you ever forgive me?"

"Yes. When I saw you downstairs in the lobby, I forgot everything.

Because, Talia, I love you too." She wants to reply, but the doorbell chimes. "It's our food." I kiss her nose.

I stand up, sliding on a pair of shorts, and get the door. I tip the guy and tell him to leave. I bring the foot cart into the room myself. There's no way I'm going to let someone see my woman so vulnerable. I open the silver domes, and it smells amazing. Oysters, lobster, and a rib eye. The bottle of red wine, closed, with a bottle opener beside it.

"Leo?"

"Yes?" I set out the plates.

She wraps her arms around me. "I love you. I'm sorry."

I drop back onto the bed and drag her into me. "Let me feed you. Let's move past this now, okay?"

She nods, and I can sense the relief from her. It's like a weight has been lifted from us.

~

"How did you do it?" Talia glances at me in that way of hers, like she might murder me or kiss me but hasn't decided yet.

I lean against the windowsill, the view of the Angelika Film Center in the distance. "I told you. I went to visit Professor Hirsch. I let her know that she needed to give you another chance at your exam."

She taps her foot. "And she just said, *Sure, honey, anytime that's good for Talia is good for me?*"

The sarcasm isn't lost on me. "Do you really want to know the details? How about a simple, *Thank you, Leo! I can't wait to take my exam so that I can walk at graduation next week!*"

She pours fresh coffee into a mug and hands it to me. I go to take it, but she steps back so that it's just out of reach. "I want every single detail, dirty or otherwise."

"Remind me why you need to know."

"Because we promised each other to never lie or withhold again. Because I refuse to have any more secrets between us. I don't want to be ashamed of my past anymore, and I don't want you hiding your reality from me. Plus, this has to do with my school. And when it comes to that, I can't turn my face away. It's not club business. It's my business."

I look down at her, knowing that if she needs the truth in this, I have to give it to her. "I went to meet her at her office. Hours were posted on the website."

"Mmhmm."

"I went inside and kindly let her know that I was there on behalf of my wife. I explained the situation—"

"Leo, cut the shit. She's tough as nails. Makes me look like sunshine."

"You're right. But I didn't want to put a gun to her head. Well, at least, not at first. So, I started rationally and with the truth. I explained that I had gone to Kosovo and you were worried about my safety and chose that over school. And that no one had ever worked as hard as you. I told her how much you love the music."

"Keep going," she says, a small smile playing on her lips.

"She turned it around and asked me where I went to school. And I let her know that through some unfortunate circumstances, I wasn't able to study at NYU, like I had originally planned. My classes at Baruch were touch and go. One thing led to the next, and she told me that she would let you retake your exam and graduate so long as I promised to meet with the head of architecture at NYU."

"What?!" she screams, jumping into my arms. "So, you're finally going to matriculate at NYU?"

"We'll have to see. I still have to work, you know. I have a wife I want to spoil."

19

Talia

Five Months Later

I open up my mailbox in our condo's lobby and pause when I see the envelope from the New York Philharmonic. After graduating—yes, I took my last exam and passed with flying colors—I immediately asked three of my professors for recommendations to add to my applications to various orchestras. I auditioned for my top choices, but I have been crossing my fingers to get the coveted fourth seat cello for the New York Philharmonic. I've been checking the mail nonstop for weeks, and here it is.

I say a quick, "Please, God, tell me I got the seat," before moving my fingers to the corner of the letter, ready to tear it open.

I blink a few times, trying to focus my vision. That's when I realize it's blurry because I'm crying. I want to open it, but I want Leo next to me when I do. I never thought it would be possible, but my dream is no longer simply playing for the orchestra. It's playing for the orchestra *with* Leo by my side. And it's not weakness. It's love.

I walk to the elevator, and it opens immediately. Up to the eighteenth floor I go, clutching the envelope like a lifeline. Leo surprised me with a two-bedroom condo on the Upper West Side of New York City for my graduation gift—with an elevator in the building. Yes, it's excessive. But the man makes a ton of money, and he was living way below his means for too long. He works his ass off, and he deserves this. I wish he were here right now, so I could show him the envelope, but I'll just have to wait for tonight.

I pull out my mini orange suitcase from the back of my closet and pack a beautiful negligee for after the party tonight and a pair of skinny jeans and a white tank top for tomorrow. My toiletries go in next, all organized in their own small bag. I place my cello beside my suitcase and slide the envelope into the small zipper pocket on the cello's case. My gown and shoes have already been delivered, and there's nothing more to do but go.

The Uber drops me off at The Plaza Hotel, and I spot Rachel and Vesa waiting for me by the concierge desk, beneath an enormous crystal chandelier. I walk in, my smile almost breaking my face. I want to call for them, but I also want to take it all in.

When Leo asked me where we should host everyone for the party, we went back and forth about a small ceremony in Central Park or a lavish affair at a five-star hotel. He insisted on spoiling me for the special day, and I caved—but only because his logic was sound. We've got the money, so we might as well enjoy it. For so long, I was struggling, and for even longer, he refused to spend a dime. But we're over all that now, and it's time to live life. And if that makes us *nouveau riche*, well, *c'est la vie*!

I look down at my five-carat emerald-cut diamond and try not to scream. It's just so beautiful. Arguably ridiculously so but it does look amazing. Especially when I play my cello.

The girls spot me before I let them know I'm here, and they run over, screaming.

"Today's your day!" Rachel hugs me. "And it's finally real!"

We laugh, and Vesa grabs my mini suitcase. "We got the key to your suite. And hair and makeup should be here soon."

A bellboy comes beside us. "Let me take this from you, miss. I'll gladly show you ladies to your suite."

We walk through the hotel, oohing and aahing at the antique lighting and furniture. It almost feels like we're in Paris. Well, at least what I imagine Paris would be like. *Glamorous, elegant,* and *perfect* are a few adjectives that come to mind. A large restaurant sits in the lobby, and it's filled with people eating small tea sandwiches and drinking coffee out of ornate-looking cups.

"So fancy," Rachel whispers as a pair of women wearing large Birkin bags sashay past us.

We follow him to the elevator and go to the tenth floor. Walking down a red-carpeted corridor, he stops at room 1008. He scans the key, and the light turns green. We enter the room, and all of us gasp. A beautiful white living room is on one side and a bedroom on the other. All the windows face Fifth Avenue.

"Welcome to The Plaza Hotel, ladies." He steps inside and turns on the lamps, illuminating the room.

I know he wants to give us more information about the hotel's amenities, but we're too excited to listen.

I pull a ten-dollar bill from my wallet and hand it to him. "Thank you!"

The moment he leaves, we jump onto the queen-size bed with a large white canopy above it. "I can't believe this is finally happening."

The bell rings, and Vesa moves to open the door. It's the hair and makeup crew. Behind them is room service.

We spend the next four hours primping and getting beautiful. It's my wedding day after all.

My gown is long and white. I chose a silk, slightly A-line silhouette with small cap sleeves, a deep V-neck, and a nice slit up the back that will let me spread my legs—for the cello. I have a beautiful piece to play for Leo tonight, after the party is over. I want it to be for him and him alone.

I spin around a few times before checking my phone. My mom texted me that she's relaxing in her room and that I should let her know when to come into mine.

On my way to Kosovo, I called my parents and told them about my debacle. Well, not the whole truth, obviously, but the important parts. *I married a friend of a friend for citizenship, and in return, he paid my tuition. We fell in love in the process but got into a massive fight, and now, he's back in Kosovo.* They urged me to go get him and not let him go.

"You'll find a way to finish school," my mother said.

My dad grunted, "And when you bring him back, we expect to meet him!"

After Leo and I returned to America, the four of us had dinner.

I was nervous before our dinner. Maybe more nervous than I had been in a long time. Not because I was worried they wouldn't like him because I was sure that they would. But I wanted them to welcome him with open arms. After everything he had been through, I wanted Leo to be as close to my parents as possible. My mother could smother if I didn't draw lines, but my father was a tougher sell.

Leo had wanted to take them to a fancy restaurant, but I'd insisted we do something just as delicious but more casual. My parents were decent, hard-working people, and Michelin stars meant very little to them. On Gini's advice, we were meeting them at Persepolis, a Persian restaurant on the Upper East Side of New York City. Apparently, she'd spent some time in Iran before coming to America, so she had told us exactly where we should go and what we should order.

When we pulled up to the restaurant, Leo asked, "Any last-minute tips for me? I've never really met anyone's parents before. And the one time I did, let's just say, it went really, really badly." He stepped out of the Escalade, gave a thanks to our driver, and helped me out of the car.

I exhaled, feeling more stressed out than he was, but trying to hide it. "Just be genuine. And talk about the houses you're building. That you're taking classes at NYU now. Things like that."

"Houses I'm building," he repeats. "NYU. Got it."

He adjusted the collar of his blue—not black—button-down shirt as I tucked the left side of my hair behind my ear.

We said our hellos at the hostess stand but sat right away at a table for four by the window, facing Second Avenue. Luckily, the waiter put spreads and fresh pita bread on the table before we even got our menus, giving us a reprieve from potential awkwardness.

I took a piece of the bread and put some yogurt dip onto my plate. "I hear the food here is delicious!"

We engaged in some small talk and discussed my options for different seats in various orchestras.

When Leo broke the news about our love, our revelation was met with excitement and shock but also major relief—for me. No more lying. No more omissions. My parents had always been so good to me. Keeping facts about my life private had never been easy, but that time was over now. And when Leo finally told them that not only were we in love, but he wanted us to have a proper wedding to solidify what already was—our marriage, my father stood up and hugged him, and my mother was a blubbering but happy mess.

And today, I want to enjoy having everyone I love together in celebration. But also in truth.

I step outside the bedroom to find my friends already drinking in the living room, Vesa relaxing on the white couch with a champagne glass in her hand. She is wearing a soft silver gown with a plunging V neckline, and Rachel is wearing a pink Grecian gown that pools at her ankles. I wasn't going to be that bride who forced a color or particular style on her friends. They should wear what they look and feel great in. My photos will look gorgeous because everyone is happy.

"*L'chaim!*" Rachel squeals, raising her drink to me. "You're a vision, Tal. The most stunning bride I have ever seen."

"One second." I blush, feeling strangely happy about her sentimentality. "Let me tell my mom to come upstairs."

I shoot out a quick text before Rachel pours me a glass of champagne.

A few minutes later, my mom is beside us. We hug, and she cries, telling me how happy she is for me to have found love and how beautiful I look.

The four of us laugh and drink until we get the text from my dad that it's time to go downstairs. I take a private moment in the bedroom before we leave the room.

Arriving to the lobby and walking to Plaza's Oak Room, we find my father in a black tuxedo, waiting for me in a corner by a stained glass window. He looks polished, but he feels just as he always does as he brings me into his arms for a giant hug.

Taking a long look at me, he says, "Talia, you are so stunning. I can't even believe it's possible I made you."

I laugh, but he is serious.

"I know it hasn't been easy on you. When you told us that you married Leo for his citizenship in return for your tuition, our hearts broke. I wish I could have made it easier on you. I wish there had been a way for me to pay for everything. You worked so hard between practice and school and jobs. And you always had. All those years at the ice cream shop and then at the music studio. You are, simply put—"

I shake my head. "Dad, it's—"

"No, listen to me. I know you're tough, but at the risk of sounding mushy, you should know, I'm proud of you. The woman you are, the woman you're becoming. The man you chose. Over the last five months, Leo and I have grown to be good friends. You picked a strong man. He is smart and competent. Most of all, he loves you, and I know he'll take care of you."

"Thank you, Dad." I blink quickly, holding myself together.

"Those friends of his can get pretty rowdy though, huh?" He quirks a brow.

He *knows*, but he doesn't really *know*. And that's one secret I don't mind keeping a lid on.

I laugh, picturing all the men in the shqipe. "You could say that …"

The violinists playing the ceremony tonight, who are none other than Ronna and Leora, begin to play "Light My Fire" by The Doors.

My dad introduced me to the band when I was just a kid, and I still love their music. My father rushes out of the room to make sure Leo has left the corridor and entered the Terrace Room.

Leo and I haven't seen each other this entire week. My parents insisted we keep ourselves apart before the wedding.

"It's tradition," my father made sure to add for good measure, but I wasn't going to tell him no.

I know Leo is walking down the aisle because the entire shqipe is not only in attendance, but also cheering, clapping, and hollering. Leo told me to expect a loud ceremony. Funny enough, it's the same group that was there for our "three-year anniversary" party.

My father and I walk quietly to the entry of the Terrace Room, meeting my mother by the door. They flank my sides, and my father lowers the veil over my face. The traditional "Wedding March" plays as we walk. All around me are members of the shqipe, and the women who love them (or love to hang around them). I guess you can say that I stand corrected and have come to love them, too.

Elira is beside Nico, her pregnant belly protruding. She claps. "You look gorgeous!"

"Congratulations!" I hear from both sides.

From my left, I catch a head nod from Darius. I smile widely, unable to stop the happiness flowing through me. He and Gini are holding hands, looking so at peace with each other. He is always watching her, but I've come to learn that their relationship suits them perfectly.

Both Elira and Gini are incredible women, who are hardworking and genuine. Still, it takes time for me to trust other girls because, let's face it, most of them are bitches. But I think, one day, we might actually become close. They are good people.

In the front row, I spot my grandmother and great Uncle. They are so happy, I can feel it.

I raise my head to see Leo standing beneath the white floral canopy, filled with roses, baby's breath, and orchids. It is called a chuppah, and symbolizes that our home should always be filled with hospitality and openness. It's a Jewish tradition my grandmother insisted we have, and neither Leo nor I minded in the least.

His blue eyes blaze, and my heart stops. Black tuxedo, crisp white shirt, and a gorgeous black bow tie. His dark hair is slicked back, and his smile is showstopping. He moves to straighten his jacket, and I can see black satin suspenders over his shirt.

The three of us stop walking, and Leo strides to where I stand, hugging and kissing my mother and father. They walk away tearfully, and he lifts my veil.

"You're mine now to care for and love." He kisses my palms, first the right and then the left, before we walk up to the canopy together, where Veton stands.

Despite the fact that Veton is not a member of the shqipe, he and Leo have maintained their friendship for years. In honor of our wedding, he became a justice of the peace.

Veton begins the ceremony by welcoming everyone to our wedding. After straightening his tie, he hands Leo's ring to me.

"Leo," I start, blinking quickly, "with this ring, you are made holy to me, for I love you as my soul. You are now my husband." I slide the solid gold ring on his left ring finger.

Veton hands my ring to Leo.

"With this ring"—Leo smiles, lifting the gold band in front of him —"you are made holy to me, for I love you as my soul. You are now my wife." He places it on my index finger so that it's more easily seen. It's another Jewish tradition I promised my Grandmother to keep. I will move it to my ring finger after the ceremony.

Veton clears his throat and hands Leo a champagne glass. Before I can ask what on earth is happening, Leo sets it down by his feet and stomps on it. I hear the crack and turn my head to see my family screaming their cheers—even my grandmother has stood up! And I'm in such shock and utter happiness that he surprised me with this tradition, I laugh out loud.

Veton clears his throat. "By the power vested in me, you are now husband and wife!"

Leo takes me in his arms, and we kiss. The room erupts in noise and cheer, and the men rush up to where we stand. They grab Leo and jump up and down in a circle with their arms wrapped around each other, singing in Albanian. Into the party they go, like a traveling mosh pit, and I trail behind with all the wives and girlfriends, including Rachel, Vesa, and my mother.

I enter the Grand Ballroom, blowing out a breath, so full of joy and happiness. The round tables surround the dance floor, filled with low vases of white roses and golden candles. It's stunning. The men are at the bar, drinking and getting rowdy. I can easily spot Leo among them.

I smile as I pick up another glass of champagne from our table, feeling happier than I ever have.

The physical letter from the New York Philharmonic is still upstairs, but right before I came down for the ceremony, I took a private moment in the bedroom. I unzipped the small compartment in the front of my cello case and tore the letter open. I figured, if I didn't get the seat, the wedding would erase the pain. And if I did get it, I could walk down the aisle with all the pride in the world.

Don't judge me! I might be in love, but I haven't gotten a lobotomy. I'd been waiting all my life, and the suspense was literally killing me.

Leo finally breaks away from his friends as our song comes on —"Hallelujah" by Leonard Cohen.

In his arms, I sway. And into his ear, I whisper, "What if I didn't get a cello seat?"

He holds me closer, and I can feel the tension in his arms. "Then, you will re audition. Another opportunity will come up."

"Hmm."

"Hmm?" He squints his eyes, trying to see what I am getting at. "Talia, you deserve that seat. You're the best cellist in America! If they don't accept you, then fuck them. I'll make them regret it."

I laugh. "Well, this best cellist in America is officially seat four of the New York Philharmonic."

He twirls me around and runs up to the stage, grabbing the

microphone from the band's singer. "My wife is the new cellist for the New York Philharmonic!"

All of our friends whoop, and I straighten with pride. I give the biggest smile my face can manage to Leo, my real husband, in law *and* reality.

READY FOR MORE MAFIA KINGDOM?

Hi Readers!

Did you know there are two other books in my Mafia Kingdom Series, which can be ready in any order? Get to know Nico and Elira in **Light My Fire**, and Darius and Gini in **Love Her Madly.** Both books are available now and FREE with a subscription to Kindle Unlimited!

Light My Fire (A Mafia Kingdom Novel)

He saved me from war.
Fed me when I was in too much pain to eat.
Smuggled me and my family into America when it became too dangerous to stay.
But, Nico didn't flee with us.

While I began elementary school in the United States, he was building the greatest and toughest Mafia of the century.

The Mafia Shqiptare.

Nico is now King of all underground trades.
Sexy. Aggressive. Brilliant.

After years of nothing but silence, he's back in my life,
Ready to do whatever it takes to bring me into his universe.
He isn't leaving until he takes me with him.

Available on Amazon: Light My Fire

Love Her Madly

Darius is a man with power and control.
As a child in the Mumbai slums, living among lethal street gangs, all
he cared about was his safety and where he would find his next meal.
That is, until the Madam of the most famed brothel in India finds
him, offering him a life he can't refuse.

As an intelligent, beautiful woman raised in a small mountain village,
Gini never would have imagined a place like The Mansion exists.
Stolen by Darius into a dark underworld where the famed Mullah
Omar arranges pleasure marriages to the highest bidder, Gini fights
for survival.
At first frightened by the dangerous man who keeps her prisoner,
Darius slowly becomes the one light in her dark world.

The Madam. The Mullah. The Protector. The Beauty.
Who will win when money reigns supreme and power is everything?

Available on Amazon:Love Her Madly

KEEP IN TOUCH!

I love hearing from readers and staying connected! Feel free to e-mail me at: JessicaRubenAuthor@gmai.com

Subscribe to my Newsletter to get all the information about sales, new releases, and bonus content: JessicaRubenAuthor.com/newsletter/

Want to see all of my books? Take a look at my Official Amazon author Page: https://amzn.to/3aQ7SPy

Check out my Website and blog: JessicaRubenAuthor.com

Want to connect with me on my writing journey? Join my Facebook Reading Group: https://www.facebook.com/groups/jessicasjetsetters

Instagram: @AuthorJessicaRuben

BookBub: https://www.bookbub.com/authors/jessica-ruben

Goodreads: https://bit.ly/3vmp9cu

BLURB: RISING (VINCENT AND EVE BOOK 1)

My entire international bestselling series, **Vincent and Eve,** is complete! Get ready to binge + Read FREE with a subscription to Kindle Unlimited.

As the bus approaches my stop on the Lower East Side, I raise the hood of my black sweatshirt. Anonymity is key in my neighborhood—particularly as a lone female walking at night.

All I want is to leave my crime-ridden shadow of a home in New York City. I've done everything I can to keep my head down and focus on my studies. College is my only goal; love has never been on the map... That is, until my sister brings me to an underground fight, where I meet a gorgeous and mysterious man: Vincent.

He is the ghost in my shadows, showing up to feed me pieces of his upper-crust life, then evaporating into darkness until his next visit. I'm falling hard and fast. How can I trust him amidst the depth of his secrets?

Vincent may be even more dangerous than the dark world I'm trying to escape.

Read on for an excerpt!

VINCENT &EVE
BOOK ONE

Distraction is the last thing I need—
especially one who is dark and dangerous

RISING

JESSICA RUBEN

EXCERPT: RISING (VINCENT AND EVE BOOK 1)

Oak desks, scuffed from years of abuse and handy knife work, stand single file in the back of the dingy public library. Curled up in a dark wooden chair, with elbows resting on the etched wood, I read the newest novel recommended by my teacher, Ms. Levine. I lift my head for a moment when my gaze lands on the nearly opaque second-story window, grimy from New York City pollution.

My eyes widen. "Oh shit," I say out loud, my voice ringing through the empty room. Eyes registering the darkness outside, my stomach liquefies with dread. I check my cell to confirm the time—it's ten fifteen.

Grabbing my ratty backpack off the floor, I slide the book inside and zip it closed as quickly as my shaking hands allow. Throwing it over my shoulder, I rush out the front door and make it to the dimly lit bus stop, just as the M-6 pulls in. I walk up the steps and swipe my metro card at the kiosk by the driver.

Noticing an empty seat by the window in the second row, I walk over, squeezing my small five-foot-one frame past the woman sitting in the aisle seat. She sighs as if annoyed, leaning back in an attempt to maintain distance. Wearing green scrubs, she has exhaustion written all over her drawn face. I take my seat and lick my dry lips, turning my gaze to the window.

As the bus approaches my stop on the Lower East Side, I raise the hood of my black sweatshirt. Anonymity is key in my neighborhood —particularly as a lone female walking at night. I live in the Blue Houses, a New York City housing project recently dubbed by the *Post* as "the hellhole houses." The nickname came as no surprise, as the complex is dilapidated and crime-ridden. It's common knowledge that cops always enter the building with their guns drawn, assuming that all tenants are packing weapons. To make matters worse, two gangs, the Snakes and the Cartel, are in a turf war for rights to push crack, the preferred pastime for many Blue House residents. The gutters run blood daily. Although I'm born and raised here, my time spent with my head inside the books has left me with street smarts that are at best decent, and at worst delinquent. My older sister Janelle reminds me of this constantly, and in this moment, I'm proving her right.

I'm so close to the building now, only about nine hundred feet away from the front yard. My eyes scan the eerily empty streets that, during daylight hours, are full of commotion. I force myself to stay calm by focusing on this morning when my sister's friends chatted about who's banging who, while old-school Tupac blasted on someone's iPhone speakers. I pull the hoodie closer to my head as my mind revists to the scene.

∾

"Jem got pregnant—"

"Ohhhhh shit! No way! No fuckin' way! That poor mama of hers—"

"—I heard that Mark is gonna kick Sean's ass. He owes him money, but who's gonna pay that debt? Everyone knows he spends all his money on his—"

I shift my focus from the gossip mill to the girls jumping rope in front of me, crisscrossing and jumping with ease.

"Yo Eve, you listenin'?" I turn my head to Vania, one perfectly plucked eyebrow raised in frustration.

I plaster a smile on my face. "Sorry, what?"

She rolls her dark brown eyes. "Girl, you've got to get your head outta la-la land!" I flush with embarrassment; this isn't the first time I've been accused of spacing out. "I asked you if you saw Jason. He told Jennifer that he thinks you're: Hot. As. Fuck."

I shrug my shoulders. "Nah. I'm not really interested." She looks at me like I've got a screw loose in my head, and I immediately wish I said something other than the truth. Jason is tall with jet-black hair, blue eyes, and totally tatted from his head to his ankles. Most girls would give almost anything to be with a man like that. And while my eyes recognize his relative attractiveness, he doesn't affect me the way he does everyone else.

"I love your shade of lipstick!" My voice is full of forced enthusiasm, but I'm hoping to divert the conversation.

"It's called Honey Love. It's MAC." She purses her lips together, showing off the creamy nude shade.

I nod my head, relieved that the conversation of Jason is now behind us. "That's cool. I gotta tell Janelle to try it on me sometime."

Warmth fills her face. "Yeah, baby girl. And with your tan skin, pouty lips, and huge brown eyes...shiiiit. You'll have guys lining up." I blush, uncomfortable with the praise.

I turn to my sister, who is all long blond hair and legs for miles. While I share her small nose and bow-shaped lips, our physical similarities are minimal. Janelle is five-foot-seven and statuesque, whereas I'm short and curvy.

Vania clears her throat, rummaging through her purse. "Here. Let me put some on you." She takes out a lipstick and lipliner from her huge black tote bag that looks more like a suitcase than a purse, and gets to work on my lips. When she's finished, she leans back, seemingly pleased.

"Yo, Janelle. Take a look at baby sister over here." Janelle turns her head, smiling as she takes me in.

"You're smokin'. Je-sus!" She winks at me before turning back to Vania. "What color is that? Honey Love?"

"Of course, you know, you bitch!" They laugh together, Vania turning her attention back to Janelle. "I read that Mario uses this new color mix on Kim Kardashian—"

I slide up closer to them, trying to listen to their conversation, but everything they say goes in one ear and out the other. I'm the listener. The dreamer. The girl with her head in a book at all times. But even I know that in order to survive here, I've got to belong. Loners get picked on and picked off. But Janelle? She's the social butterfly. The girl everyone loves. And if not for her, I'd probably be floating in the Hudson by now. I move my body closer to the group, doing my best to fit in.

I stumble on a hard piece of trash on the sidewalk, bringing my focus back to the present. The unnaturally silent air has alarm bells ringing in my head. I wonder if the gangs are roaming hard tonight. I look to the park adjacent to the Blue Houses, trying to find the regular late-night junkies. It's the most secure place for people to do drugs, as the cops never make regular patrols; apparently, they're too busy answering 911 calls. I take a sharp breath; the entire park is seemingly abandoned.

I tighten my hold on the straps of my backpack and quicken my pace, focusing on making it to the front door of my building. My heart rate increases as my imagination spirals. Maybe someone was shot earlier, and now everyone is home scared? Did someone die? Someone must have died. Is there blood on the sidewalk? There's blood. I know it. Fear takes hold, choking me. For all the laughter and friendly neighborhood vibes during the day, the reality is the Blue Houses are a deadly place to live.

When I hear the telltale *hiss* of the Snakes, the blood in my veins turns cold. I run as fast as I can, but the *hissing* only increases in volume. Risking a glance over my shoulder, I see a group close behind me. Janelle's voice enters my mind, *"If you run, you'll look scared. And looking scared makes you more vulnerable."* Even though my heart is pounding like a steel drum into my rib cage, I force myself to slow down. My legs beg to sprint forward, but showing fear isn't an option.

I make it a few more feet when they circle me, blocking any path of escape. My mouth opens, poised to scream, but my throat locks shut. It's so dark, but the shadows of the streetlamps bring their red and black colors into focus. My body quakes from my fingertips down into my toes. Dropping my head, I stare at the ground as the lieutenant of the Snakes moves in front of me. Focusing on his black steel-toe boots, a cold sweat breaks out on my forehead.

It's Carlos. As a kid, he used to torture and kill mice in the stairwell and leave them as threats for people by their front doors. He's been in and out of prison more times than I can count. In my mind's eye, I can see the blue teardrops tatted under his left eye down to the corner of his thin lips, each oval bead signifying a kill.

"Take that hood off. I wanna get a good look at you." His voice is low and menacing. I move to lift my head, pausing at his muscular bare chest. I shudder, making eye contact with his black-and-red snake tattoo. It peeks over his right shoulder, tongue hissing between two pointy white fangs like a beast from hell.

When Carlos sees I'm not doing as he demanded, he throws off my hood, roughly grabbing my chin and forcing my head straight. I can smell his rancid breath as he fists my hair in his hand. Staring at my face, he nods with what looks like appreciation.

"We found something good tonight, boys," he chuckles as if he's found a new toy he can't wait to play with. Bile rises up my throat as his smile widens.

My eyes dart from side to side as my breathing turns erratic. I'm fresh meat, and these animals are in it for the kill. Screaming won't make a difference. How many times have I heard yelling outside my bedroom window, but never thought to help the victim? Countless. Maybe it's karma. Maybe I deserve this for all the times I dropped my head and tried not to get involved. If I only listened to Janelle and made sure not to be alone on the streets at night—

Carlos steps back, pulling a cigarette from behind his ear and placing it between his lips. Taking a black lighter from his front pocket, he flicks it on and off, letting the fire burn at his will. Bringing the flame to the end of his cigarette, he takes a hard pull, turning the tip into a shining ember. With an exhale, smoke wafts around his face and blends into the night. He stands silently, assessing every detail of my trembling body.

"Looks like we're gonna have some fun," he laughs as his boys cackle in delight. My jaw slackens as my mind searches for an escape. If I can't physically get out of this, maybe I can force my mind to move elsewhere.

He grabs my upper arm. I can feel the bruising take shape as he turns me around forcefully, dragging me like a rag doll toward the Blue Houses. The others trail behind us, reminding me with every step that I have nowhere to go. Nowhere to hide. Nowhere to run.

Pushing through the front door of the building, we stop in front of what I always thought was a storage room. Carlos stuffs his hand in his pocket, removing a key. Shoving it inside the keyhole, he throws the door open, using his free hand to push me into the room. I trip over my own feet, the cement greeting me as I fall to my hands and knees. He flips a switch and the light casts a shadow below me. I lift my head and see a tiny barred window above a small bed. I look to my right, only to see a kitchenette with a round table surrounded by plastic chairs. Carlos bends down, grabbing me by the neck and pulling me up to face him. I want to scream, but my throat is closed. I see the exhilaration in his eyes and briefly wonder if death isn't the better option.

He loosens his hold on my neck, and I take deep, but shaky, inhales. The moment I catch my breath, he slaps me hard across the face. My body gets the message—he's the one in control. I open and close my mouth, shutting my eyes and willing my brain to tune out and turn off.

He grabs my chin. "I've been seeing you around. And get this?

You're just the one we need for tonight. You see, we've got lots of energy we need to burn off after where we've been." He licks his lips and I can see the dull yellow of his teeth. "I know you like to hide in those baggy clothes with those books in your hands, but I think it's about time you show us what you've got goin' on underneath all that shit." He laughs, pulling out a fresh cigarette and lighting it up. "Take your clothes off for us, and do it niiiice and slow. I think we're all in the mood for a little live show tonight."

A chair is pulled out and I lift my head to the sound. I make eye contact with one of the guys and his head snaps back in recognition. "Oh shit, Carlos, that's Janelle's little sister." It's Jason. His hair is styled in an undercut, buzzed on the sides and long on top. I'm shaking so badly it takes me a second to realize he's staring right at me, waiting for a reply.

"Y-Yeah," I stammer. "I'm J-J-Janelle's sister."

He shrugs casually at the guys. "Let's get rid of her. She's harmless. You know Janelle; she's the one who does all the old ladies' hair for free, and—"

Carlos throws a hand up in the air, silencing him. "Rid of her? Like, shoot her in the head?" He cocks his head to the side in question and the blood drains from my face. "Nah. I don't think I want to kill her just yet. Fuck her virgin brains out, yeah. Let all you guys take a turn when I'm done, hell yeah. Afterwards, you can kill her if you still want." He smiles and grabs my hand, lifting it above my head. I shut my eyes as he twirls me in a slow circle, showing me off to his crew. I hear wolf whistles and try to turn my thoughts into white noise.

A scratchy voice from the side of the room starts up. "Don't rough her up too much at first. I want her to have some fight left when I get my turn."

Tears drip from my eyes, burning as they fall down the sides of my face. "I'll d-d-do anything. Just let me go. Please..." I beg, dropping down to my knees and lifting my hands in prayer. "I'll do anything you want, but I don't want to die."

"Anything, huh? Get up," he commands. I stand on wobbly feet as

Carlos grins maliciously. "Ah, you take directions. That's good. Very good." He lifts his steel toe boot, kicking me in the stomach. I double over.

Carlos bends low, grabbing my hair to lift my head and bringing his lips to my ear, his voice a dark growl. "Let me give you a piece of advice. Shut the FUCK up and take what we're all about to give you. You may even enjoy it after the first few times." He puts his nose to my neck, smelling me deeply as he presses a sharp object against my side. My eyes widen; I feel the cold sharp edge of a blade drifting from my ribs up to my chest.

"Listen to what I tell you. Don't want to mess up that gorgeous face. But..." My breathing stops. "I will, IF you don't do as I say. You want to live? Shut up and take it." He moves his knife back to his pocket. "Strip."

He chuckles.

I oblige.

I remove every layer of clothing and stand crumpled. My shoulders are curled down and my arms cover my bare breasts. He thrusts my arms away.

His dirty fingertips grope my intimate parts as if he owns them. The body I thought belonged to me is now on loan. Finally, my mind separates from my body and floats away. But Carlos, unwilling to let me go in body or mind, pulls the cigarette out of his mouth and presses it against my shoulder.

I let out a scream from the burn.

He laughs.

Carlos turns to his boys, rubbing his hands together in eagerness. "I'm gonna make sure she's good enough for you all, first." They all chuckle at the joke, while one of them stares at me with rapt attention and a look of utter excitement.

"Poker—"

A cabinet opens and shuts.

The smell of old and wet laundry.

I close my eyes.

"Open your eyes and look at me!" Yelling, he grabs my neck to face him, forcing me to watch his ministrations.

My eyes connect with his, nothing but evil lurks in his depths.

I'm thrust forward, face down on the bed. I hear pants unzipping and falling to the floor. I hold my breath. If I hold it long enough, will I die?

"Yo, snake charmers! Cartel is In. The. Houssssse!" Voices and laughter radiate straight through the barred window and into the room. Carlos pauses, turning toward the glass and screaming, "We're coming MOTHERFUCKERS!"

My body shakes uncontrollably. I can hear him pull his pants back up, heaving. "The FUCK? If the Cartel is looking for a fight tonight, we'll give em' one!"

I dare to crack my eyes open, watching as they nod to each other. The rivalry between the Snakes and the Cartel is vicious. While the Cartel has fewer members, they make up for less manpower with intense and frequent bloodshed.

I'm in a state of shock, watching them pull weapons from their pants. Am I going to die? I shut my eyes again, moaning.

"Yo!" Carlos slaps my ass so hard I bite my lip, tasting copper. "Don't think you're off the hook, bitch. I got a glimpse, and now I want in. I'm coming back for you." He raises his gun and thrusts it into my mouth. I choke as he pushes it deeper down. Tearing it out, he nods—his version of a guarantee.

Seconds later, I feel warm hands on my naked back. "Open your eyes and get up." The voice is soft but urgent. Jason is on his knees by the bed, my clothes in his hands. "Put your clothes on, and get out of here!" he whispers loudly.

Somehow, I stand. I'm a machine, clothing myself like I've done millions of times before. He has the decency to turn his head as I put one foot and then the other into my underwear. As I slide my T-shirt and sweatshirt over my head, I realize I am no longer the priority to these criminals. If there is a time to run, it's now.

I take my bag and run out of the room with a speed I didn't know I was capable of. Opening the heavy stairwell door and running up the steps, I take two at a time as sweat pours down my temples. Are they after me? Are they coming? I want to turn my head back to see if they're behind me, but my fear won't let me turn around.

I hear cursing and some screams, but all the sounds are muffled by the whooshing sound in my ears. The stairs seem to vibrate with the sound of gunshots. Have I been shot? Adrenalin mixed with confusion pumps through my veins as I jet up the darkened stairwell; the lights are all out on the third floor, and it feels like I'm running through a black hole. My heart pounds into my throat.

In a blink, I'm back inside my empty apartment, staring in a trance at my gray threadbare living-room couch. I look at my feet and realize I'm barefoot. Oh shit, I'm going to need to buy a new pair of sneakers. I wonder if there's any in my size at the thrift store.

Turning toward my bedroom door, my mind registers the crack down the center. I briefly remember one of my mom's old boyfriends throwing a vase against it, splitting the wood. I walk into my room like a zombie and complete my nightly routine of brushing my teeth, washing my face with soap and scalding hot water, and changing into a clean pair of pajamas. In the recesses of my mind, I know what just happened to me is horrifying, but I keep telling myself if I just act normal, maybe it'll all just go away.

Before getting into my bed, I kneel on the floor, fisting my worn-out navy comforter in my hands. Prayers tumble out of my mouth to God, begging him to get me out of here before Carlos finds me. All at once, I feel punched in the gut. I run to the toilet, dropping my head into the bowl and emptying all the contents of my stomach.

Are they going to come for me tonight? Should I hide? I shut the bathroom door and curl up in the fetal position by the toilet, too afraid to go back into my bedroom where there's a window.

What feels like seconds later, I hear the front door open and close. As footfalls get closer to the bathroom door, my chest constricts, my mouth gaping open and poised to scream.

"Eve, are you in the bathroom? Get out, I need to wash up!" Janelle throws the door open and looks down at me on the floor, momentarily confused.

She gives me a once over. "You look like shit, girl." Her voice is quiet and laced with concern. "What are you doing in the bathroom? Are you sick?" I hear her, but can't manage a reply. She squats down, placing the back of her hand on my forehead.

"Holy shit, Eve, you're burning up! And your face is pale as hell. You think it's food poisoning or something? Let me get you some meds." She helps me up off the floor and walks me to my bed, letting me lean on her as we walk. A few minutes later, she drops two pills into my hand. I put them on my tongue when she hands me a glass of water. I swallow the medicine and a few minutes later, I'm plunged into sleep.

KEEP READING!
Vincent and Eve's story begins in Rising, Vincent and Eve Book 1.
Check it out on Amazon: Rising (Vincent and Eve Book 1)

ACKNOWLEDGMENTS

Writing has been in my blood for as long as I can remember, but turning my words into books takes a village.

Firstly, I want to thank the readers for taking a chance on me. You guys have made my dreams come true. If you have the time, consider leaving a brief review of this book on Amazon, Goodreads, or Bookbub. Better yet, tell a friend!

Hugest thanks to my beta readers: Jana, Candice, Leigh and Autumn. When I think I can't go on, you guys propel me forward. Your excitement for my words and belief in me as an author means more to me than any of you can imagine.

To my editors, Nicole Bailey and Jovana Shirley: You turn my work into something I never dreamed it could be. Your comments, edits, and absolute attention to detail make all the difference.

To Sarah Hansen at Okay Creations: I can officially say that nothing about your work is simply okay. You're amazing and have created the most spectacular cover!

To my publicist, friend and soul sister, Autumn at Wordsmith Publicity: Thank you for all of your input, love, and faith. If any aspiring authors are reading this, understand that without Autumn, my author world would never turn.

To my reading group on Facebook, Jessica's Jet Setters: Thank you all for supporting me and coming with me on my book journeys throughout the world!

I can't even begin to list the book bloggers and bookstagrammers who make teasers, shout my books from your platforms, and post incredible reviews. You guys are unbelievable and without you, my books would never be on any map. I am SO thankful!

Most importantly, to my husband and my children: Between work and the writing, I know things can get crazy. But because of the four of you, I can say with all that I am that I know what love is. Love is you.

With all my love,
Jessica

ALSO BY JESSICA RUBEN

Vincent and Eve series: Must be read in order

Rising (Vincent and Eve Book 1)

Reckoning (Vincent and Eve Book 3)

Redemption (Vincent and Eve Book 3)

Vincent and Eve, The Complete Series

Mafia Kingdom series: Standalone books

Light My Fire: A Dark Mafia Romance (a Mafia Kingdom novel)

Love Her Madly: A Dark Mafia Romance (a Mafia Kingdom novel)

Standalone

Warrior Undone

Holiday Springs series, co-written with MJ Fields

The Irresistible Irishman: For St. Patricks Day (A Holiday Springs novel)

The Broody Brit: A Hot Single Father Second Chance Romance (A Holiday Springs novel)

www.ingramcontent.com/pod-product-compliance
Lightning Source LLC
Chambersburg PA
CBHW060916250626
47159CB00008B/3028